Madame's Deception

RENEE BERNARD

POCKET BOOKS

New York London Toronto Sydney

Pocket Books
A Division of Simon & Schuster, Inc.
1230 Avenue of the Americas
New York, NY 10020

This book is a work of fiction. Names, characters, places, and incidents either are products of the author's imagination or are used fictitiously. Any resemblance to actual events or locales or persons, living or dead, is entirely coincidental.

First Pocket Books paperback edition September 2007

POCKET and colophon are registered trademarks of Simon & Schuster, Inc.

For information about special discounts for bulk purchases, please contact Simon & Schuster Special Sales at 1-800-456-6798 or business@simonandschuster.com.

Cover illustration by Alan Ayers

Manufactured in the United States of America

10   9   8   7   6   5   4   3   2   1

ISBN-13: 978-1-4165-2421-2
ISBN-10:   1-4165-2421-5

"I am not here for lessons, Madame."

Lord Colwick took a sip of port. "I have always put duty and responsibility first, and it occurs to me that I haven't made much time for pleasure. I've decided to remedy that mistake."

"And how is it exactly that I can assist you?" Jocelyn asked.

"I want you."

She held still for a moment before replying. "I'm flattered, sir, but I'm sure I've made it clear that—"

"You do not take appointments, yes, it was made clear, Madame. I'm not asking for an appointment. You are the object of my desire and I wish to spend time with you while I'm in London."

"How much time?"

"Time enough to discover why you have haunted my thoughts these past few months. Naturally, I will expect to pay for the privilege."

She stood as well, her hands at her hips, her eyes bright with anger. "And do you *naturally* just expect me to agree to this?"

She took a ragged breath and he knew she was about to vent pure fire to ward off his bold request. But before she could speak, frustration and desire pushed him into action. He pulled her against his chest and kissed her hungrily.

To my mother, who taught me to love books and never complained when as a teenager, I snuck romance novels to the dinner table when I didn't want to set a good story down. She is the most beautiful woman I know, and no matter where the journey takes me, I know a part of her will always follow and keep me safe. Thank you, Mom. I love you.

Your presence draws me out from vanity
and imagination and opinion.
Awe is the salve that will heal our eyes.

—Rumi

Madame's Deception

Prologue

1861

The carriage lurched on the uneven cobble-stone streets, and Jocelyn shivered at the dreary night's chill that seeped into her bones. Fear, inspired by her own daring, hadn't lessened during her journey from the Wheaton School for Young Ladies. But terror wasn't the undercurrent that kept her moving.

Her mother was dying.

When the usual correspondence from her mother had ceased, anxiety had made her frantic. The headmistress, Mrs. Wellings, had tried to deflect her worries, but Jocelyn's instincts wouldn't quiet. Unable to sleep, she had slipped from her bed to seek out Mrs. Wellings for more assurances. Walking down the stairs in her robe and slippers, she'd hoped she wouldn't be punished for roaming the school's halls without permission. That concern made her hesitate outside the headmistress's door and it was then—when she'd overheard Mrs. Wellings talking with her sister, Mrs. Foster—that she'd learned the truth.

"Apparently she is very ill," Mrs. Wellings said. "But doesn't wish Jocelyn to become alarmed."

"Oh, dear," the querulous voice of the younger Mrs. Foster replied. "Is there cause for alarm?"

"I should think so," Mrs. Wellings answered sadly. "For the note mentions that Mrs. Tolliver's will provides for her daughter's care, and that we'll receive further instructions when the time comes."

"Oh, dear," Mrs. Foster repeated uselessly.

"I cannot think why a mother wouldn't want her only child's comforting presence in her last moments . . . but it is not our place to dispute Mrs. Tolliver's wishes. She has been a generous patron and we—"

Jocelyn had heard nothing more, fleeing with her hand clamped over her mouth to hold back her sobs. Her mother was dying. And hadn't sent for her. It was too cruel and too impossible to fathom. Even with their unique family arrangements . . . Jocelyn had accepted that the mysterious separation of their lives wasn't normal. For as long as she could remember, she had lived at boarding schools. Her mother's letters and visits were the highlights of her childhood. When other girls went home for the holidays, Mrs. Tolliver arrived to take her abroad, or on an excursion to the country, or to rented rooms at a seaside resort. It was always someplace new. The only destination never selected for their rare adventures was London. It was to further her education, her mother would say, and Jocelyn could only accept her at her word. After all, she loved her beautiful mother, with her quick wit and lively airs.

"Dull birds fly home like sad pigeons, dearest," Mrs. Tolliver had said once when Jocelyn had pressed her for more of an explanation. "I want you to fly free." Looking at her mother, Jocelyn had wanted nothing more in the world than to please her and she'd decided simply to savor their brief times together. After all, Jocelyn had learned from an early age that expressing loneliness or asking too many questions gained her nothing and only guaranteed longer intervals between her mother's glorious visits.

Her mother was a famous dress designer and couturier to London's elite, and with her busy schedule, she could hardly be blamed for relegating Jocelyn's education and upbringing to others. Of her father she knew less, but had been told that after his death, her mother had vowed never to marry again. Instead, her mother had determined to make her own way in the world as a widow and provide a better life for her only daughter. She had told Jocelyn repeatedly, "You will be a grand lady someday, my love. So clever and beautiful, with a husband and servants and a house of your own, you will live like a princess and no one will ever look down on you."

No one will ever look down on you.

It was the refrain that made her determined to make her mother proud. She'd buried herself in her studies and tried to become the grand lady that her mother desired. She'd learned Latin, French, Russian, and Italian. She'd voraciously read every book that came into her hands and attempted the feminine arts of watercolors and flower arranging. She'd practiced embroidery and learned the dances that all the other girls were sure would be the ultimate test of their grace. She'd done everything she could to prove that the daughter of a dressmaker could hold her own amidst her more blue-blooded schoolmates.

Now none of it mattered.

She wanted her mother, and none of her mother's admonishments about staying away from the foul, unhealthy air of London meant anything. She'd raced to her room, dressed, and packed a few of her things. Then with the house completely still and dark, she'd crept back downstairs and into Mrs. Wellings's empty office. In the correspondence files, she'd finally found what she was seeking, the records for her mother and her mother's London address.

She'd felt like a thief, but the guilt paled next to her need to reach her mother. She would be forgiven for breaking the rules once her mother saw how much Jocelyn loved her. Perhaps she wasn't too ill. Perhaps there was time yet for a miracle.

It was a slim hope, but it kept fear from overwhelming her.

Streetlights glowed in the murky gloom and Jocelyn risked a look through the carriage's curtains at the city she had previously only imagined. Her mother's determination to keep her from its "unhealthy vapors" seemed ominously merited as she pulled her coat closer. The smells and the closeness of the buildings unsettled her, and Jocelyn hoped her mother's shop and house wasn't a pinched, confining space.

Stupid to think of such things, she chided herself. Her mother was all that mattered now. She'd be arriving in the early hours of the morning at a house she had never seen. But her mother needed her.

As the carriage slowed, she squared her shoulders, trying to draw on all that her schooling had given her. A lady was equal to any situation and would bring a quiet calm to any crisis. She would show her mother that she had taken her lessons to heart.

There seemed to be more trees than she'd anticipated and it was a nicer street than many she'd passed through, but in the dark it was difficult to take in too many details.

Except that one house up ahead wasn't dark at all.

And when the carriage came to a halt in front of it, Jocelyn wasn't sure what to think or do. The driver called down, "Here it is, miss!"

The door was opened, and she felt like a downy chick being pushed from her nest onto the hard pavement. "You're sure this is the correct address?"

He gave her an odd wink, his look like a man enjoying a private and unseemly jest. "No mistaking this house, miss. 'Tis the Belle without a doubt."

He turned before she could ask him why bells would apply. Were her mother's dresses so well known that the location of her home would be common knowledge? She glanced at the windows ablaze with light and heard laughter within. Had Mrs. Wellings's records provided the wrong address? How could her mother be dying and yet there seemed to be an ongoing party at her residence?

A footman in a braided coat came down the steps. His look was less than welcoming, sizing her up like a potential opponent. "It's late in the evening for applications, miss. You'll need to clear the steps."

"I beg your pardon!" Her chin came up defensively. She couldn't believe her mother would hire such a rude and scornful servant. "I am Jocelyn Tolliver. This is my mother's residence and I have come to be with her!"

"Your mother's residence? I think you're lost or into your cups. There's no Tolliver here and unless you're off these steps with your baggage I'll fetch a whip to—"

"Enough!" A tall figure filled the door frame and ended the servant's threats. "Take her things inside." Without another word, the footman picked up her satchel and retreated into the house as if a bucket of cold water had been thrown over his head.

Jocelyn forced herself to hold her ground as the man approached, his skin as dark as coal. He seemed ageless to her, a striking, ebony giant whose skin was barely marked by time but whose eyes were careworn and sad as if from centuries of worry. If pressed she would have guessed he was in his late thirties, but she wouldn't have risked a farthing on a wager of his true age. "I-I'm Jocelyn Tolliver and I—"

"I knew you would come." His voice was soft this time, much gentler. The cadence of his speech was vaguely exotic but nothing she could place. "I am Ramis, her manservant. She swore to keep you from this, but I knew you would come to her side."

"Then I'm not lost?" Her relief was overtaken by anxiety that this one small truth meant the worst of it was also true. "Then my mother is . . ."

His eyes confirmed it. "It is good that you have come. Please"—he offered his arm—"I'll take you to her."

Instead of leading her directly up the steps and into the house, he guided Jocelyn around to the back of the building. Before she could ask why, they'd crossed into the kitchens. The people working there looked at her oddly but didn't utter a word as Ramis led her up a back staircase toward the first floor. The sounds of a merry party were muffled but unmistakable. It was unreal, and all she could do was simply to take in her surroundings. Through a door, they entered a beautifully appointed hallway with paintings and lavish oriental decorations.

"I'm not sure I—" Jocelyn stopped midsentence at the shocking sight of a woman exiting one of the rooms wearing nothing more than a corset and pantalets.

The woman simply smiled as if it were common to meet strangers in her underclothes. "Evening." Without waiting for a reply, the woman sauntered down the hall toward what appeared to be a more public staircase.

"Sh-she forgot her clothes!" Jocelyn sputtered.

Ramis nodded his head before propelling Jocelyn gently forward. "It is this door." He stopped at the threshold of an ornate mahogany door at the hall's end. "I can go in with you, if you wish."

Jocelyn hesitated. It seemed cowardly to ask a stranger to accompany her. She glanced back down the hall to where the half-naked woman had gone. It was madness to hear music and laughter and shrieks of some sort of giddy celebration and to be hovering outside her dying mother's doorway. She'd imagined her arrival at her mother's home in London countless times—but never like this.

There was a logical explanation, of course, and her mother would set everything to rights. Jocelyn's chin came up at the thought. Her mother's illness would pass and the world would be put back on its axis.

"No, I'll see her alone." Without waiting for his response, she squared her shoulders, braced for the worst, and reached for the handle to open the door. It gave easily, and Jocelyn stepped inside, ignoring the terrible pounding of her heart.

She held her breath only for one moment before rushing toward the bed. Alone in the vast bedchamber, her mother looked so much smaller than she remembered. It had been nine long months since they'd taken a brief trip to Scotland together. Her mother had always been so vibrant and beautiful, so that everything around her would suddenly pale in comparison. But now the gray wash of illness had drained even her hair of color. Dirty white streaks had overtaken auburn, and her face was waxen and gaunt. It was as if her mother had been replaced by a different creature, one diminished by unseen forces.

But the shadow of familiarity was there.

This was no stranger. This was the woman she loved most in the world.

There was no physician present, no one in attendance. Her mother's eyes were closed and Jocelyn's throat shut at the terrifying possibility that she'd come too late. Trembling, she knelt gently by the bedside and took her mother's hand. It was chilled, but the soft fingers fluttered against hers to confirm that there was still time.

"Mother," Jocelyn whispered as she stroked her mother's face. "I've come to you."

Her mother opened her eyes, their sapphire hue clouded and dulled by fever. "Jocelyn."

Jocelyn let out a sigh of relief. "You can lecture me later about disobeying and I'll accept every punishment you devise as soon as you're well again."

"I shouldn't be pleased that you are here . . . but I am." Her voice was tired and hollow, and Jocelyn leaned in to kiss her on her forehead.

"Rest now."

"No." Her mother shook her head, then swallowed hard before continuing. "It's better now. I thought . . . I wanted you to have a better life."

"And I will." Jocelyn glanced around to see if there were medicines on the sideboard, or a bell pull to request more coal for the fire. "Please don't trouble yourself, Mother. I'm here and it's my turn to take care of you."

She went to the door and opened it, not entirely surprised to find Ramis still standing guard. "Perhaps some broth and—"

"Come in, Ramis! I want . . . you must witness . . ." The imperious command trailed off to a moan.

Jocelyn hurried back to the bed, now with the manservant in tow. "Mother, please don't tire yourself. Whatever you need, we shall see to it. Your hands are so cold. Why don't you let me tend the fire and make you more comfortable?"

Her mother's expression changed, her eyes locking onto Jocelyn's face with a new intensity and energy, and she gripped her daughter's hand to ensure that she had her complete attention.

Jocelyn gasped. "Mother!"

"I wanted more for you but there's no time.

You'll have to do it alone." The effort to speak took its toll, but it was as if her mother were possessed. "The Belle will be yours. The girls fall to your care. If you abandon them now, they will fall to other hands, Jocelyn."

"The girls?" It was incomprehensible. Jocelyn shook her head. "What bell?"

"Swear to me that you'll keep them safe! That you won't destroy everything I've built and the girls with it."

Her mother's grip became almost painful, and it was hard to see past the tears in her eyes. "I'll swear whatever you want, but you cannot talk like this. You cannot mean to go . . ." Jocelyn choked on the plea. "Mother, please."

"Swear it, Jocelyn."

"I-I swear." She tried to pull away, but her mother's icy hands were unrelenting.

"I should have told you, but I never could. I wasn't brave, but *you* will be. For them, you can't show any fear. The house is yours. You must keep them together and guard them as best you can. Ramis will help you. I was Mistress of the Belle but now it falls to you."

"B-but—"

"As you will, Madame." Ramis touched his forehead and bowed.

Jocelyn began to feel a new sense of panic. "What falls to me?"

"Everything I have, and everything in my keeping including the women of the Belle. You are responsible for them all." Her mother gave her a sad smile. "Grieve quietly, my love. Don't let them see it beyond this room. Ramis will show you . . . the account books are all there. Say you're unwell and stay hidden for a few weeks until you're ready. Then, take your place."

"My place," she echoed, lost and bewildered.

"Take my name, Jocelyn. It has a certain weight. No one . . . will question it after a time."

Jocelyn looked at Ramis for clarification, but it was as if he were carved of pure ebony. "Don't I already have your name, Mother?"

Her mother's voice dropped to a whisper, her grip lessening on Jocelyn's trembling fingers. "Now you are Madame DeBourcier, Mistress of the renowned and wicked Crimson Belle."

"The Crimson Belle is . . ." Jocelyn felt the heat drain from her face and wondered if all good nightmares included a good fainting spell. "N-not a dress shop?"

Mrs. Tolliver shook her head. "Don't . . . think less of me, my love."

"No! Never!" Jocelyn's spirit returned in a flash of instinct to protect and shield her dear mother. "You're the most beautiful and accomplished woman I know! I don't care about the Belle and what it is or is not."

"You must! You must care!" Her mother's distress was unmistakable. "The Belle is . . . an odd sanctuary, Jocelyn. Sin is relative in such a world . . . please . . . you promised . . ."

Jocelyn's heart tripped and she forced herself to swallow the lump in her throat. "A lady always keeps her word, Mother. I promise . . . I'll keep them safe."

"And . . . I," her mother prompted, tears flowing freely down her cheeks.

Jocelyn's mind raced to recall the words that would ease her mother's fears. "And I . . . won't abandon them or allow them to be destroyed. I-I'll take the name . . . and do whatever I must to protect the . . ."

"The Crimson Belle," her mother supplied with a sigh, her expression taking on a new calm.

"I swear it," Jocelyn whispered, praying that the promise would be enough to save her mother. "I love you, Mama. Please, don't go."

"Ramis will look after you . . ." Her eyes began to lose their focus. "Always loved you . . . my sweet girl . . . such a lady . . . be . . . brave . . ."

Jocelyn felt it instantly. That in one moment, her mother was whispering words of encouragement and the next, she simply was gone. Anguish overwhelmed her and she collapsed across her mother's body, sobbing. It was useless to beg her mother to return, useless to deny that her mother's spirit had fled. But she couldn't stop herself. And then warm hands pulled her away from her mother's body, and her head was resting against Ramis's shoulder as he tried to comfort her.

"There, there, Mistress," he said soothingly, though his voice betrayed his own grief. "Let her go now."

She clung to his shoulder and cried until no more tears would come. At last, she was able to push away from him, modesty and reason returning to her. Her breath hitched in jagged bursts, but she was determined not to crumble again. She glanced back at the door and then slowly took in the details of the room for the first time. It was an opulent room, with expensive furnishings and antique oriental decorations.

"Mistress?" Ramis asked gently.

"Th-the girls," she countered softly. "How many?"

"Almost a dozen are now in your care."

She met his gaze and realized that some fates are inescapable. Her mother had deceived her, and the reasons for her lies were all too clear. Her mother hadn't been a dressmaker. Her mother was a fallen woman—one of those ladies that others whispered about and pointed at when carriages passed. All the money that had financed her education and schooling, all the talk of "a better life" were now put into a broader context.

Almost a dozen women were now in her care. She didn't need to be told what future awaited them if she turned them out and burned down the house. Even in her sheltered upbringing, she knew the dire consequences for a woman living on the streets. At least, she understood the general threat, if not the exact details of the world's dangers. An unprotected woman's survival was unlikely.

And what of my survival?

A lady always keeps her word, another part of her echoed in response.

Jocelyn was two weeks away from her eighteenth birthday.

She'd never been to a dance or even had her hand kissed.

And she was now the sole owner and Madame of an infamous London brothel known as the Crimson Belle.

One

1870

"Will you attend?"

Alex Randall realized his sister must have repeated the question. Her tone had that edge of exasperation. He set aside the newspaper with a firm hand. "I hadn't given it any thought."

"I do not see that you shall ever manage a wife, sir, if you do not bother to enter into good company," Eloise reprimanded him, rearranging her skirts in a huff as she sat next to him.

"The Season hasn't even really started yet, Eloise." Alex tried to keep his voice level to conceal his frustration. His tolerance for his older sister's lectures had long worn thin. "I'm sure I'll have opportunity enough for company, good and otherwise."

"You are too old to play the rake."

Lord Colwick rewarded her with a wry smile. At thirty-two, he was hardly ready for a cane and ear horn. And while he enjoyed his freedom, he also was hardly a candidate for notoriety. Even his close friendship with other more scandal-ridden members of the Ton hadn't clouded his reputation. And if he envied his friend the Duke of Sussex for his recent shocking love match with a beautiful widow, he wasn't prepared to confess it.

As it stood, the life of a bachelor wasn't devoid of entertainments, and since his sister had moved in several weeks ago with an eye to managing his household, he saw no need to rush to misery and regret. "Eloise," he continued, deciding on a new strategy to give himself a moment of peace. "You have spoiled me for a wife. There is no better hostess, and who else would put up with my nonsense?"

She made an attempt to give him a disapproving look, but failed as his flattery hit its mark. "True, but if I've ruined you, should I abandon you to the worst so that you'd see the necessity of a good match?"

Instead of composing a reply, he simply waited.

"N-not that I would abandon you . . ." Her color changed and he knew she was envisioning her own dear prize of a husband and how much less trouble a bachelor brother was proving to be. Alex had surmised that her marriage must have fallen into difficult straits, but his sister was far too proud to openly admit that anything might be strange in her husband's prolonged absence. Which meant that Eloise wasn't going to push so hard that she found herself out of a comfortable place under his roof.

But neither did he foolishly believe she would drop the matter for long.

"Of course not, Eloise. If you'll excuse me, I really need to finish my work."

She took the unsubtle hint and rose from her seat to leave him to his papers. "I'll send the marquess your acceptance, then, for his party." She retreated before he could think of a way to avert her victory.

Damn. He raked a hand through his brown hair. A man needed to breathe! It wasn't like him to admit to feeling restless, but Alex was aware that for some time now, he'd hardly felt like himself.

After all, his friend Drake's match and Alex's inclusion in the new duchess's introduction to society should have been a welcome change. He should have been generously wishing his friend all the happiness in the world. But instead, he felt the grudging sting of envy at Sotherton's luck.

And that wasn't like Alex at all.

Drake had once dubbed him "the Saint" for his steadfast adherence to the rules of good society, and Alex had laughed.

The nickname didn't seem as amusing now.

Following the rules meant yielding to the inevitable marriage of convenience that his peers would applaud. He was no fool to hope that he might have the same good fortune as his friend. The Duke of Sussex's love match was an exception to the rule and had been achieved through seemingly miraculous methods. Even now, he wasn't sure how Drake had turned wicked scandal to sweetest union, but he was fairly sure it was a feat no one else could duplicate.

Scandal was not an option for the fourth Lord Colwick, he silently intoned. Thanks to his father, Alex's sensitivity to any public missteps was firmly ingrained. The third Lord Colwick had been a notorious wastrel and cad, leaving behind a legacy of debt and lost honor. Worst of all, he had died a miserable, humiliating death after his body gave out from the excesses of his lifestyle. He had been unrecognizable at the end, and unrepentant to his last breath. So, it had fallen to Alex at the tender age of fifteen to take on the title and to make what reparations he could. Alex had never shirked his responsibilities and duties. It hadn't been easy, but he'd slowly pulled the family out of debt and restored their credibility.

Now he was honor-bound to continue the family line and, if possible, improve and strengthen its financial health for future generations. As a titled Peer of the Realm, his options for acquiring wealth were limited. Careful investments and the management of his land and rents were the balanced foundation that maintained all. But it could be a precarious existence if commerce soured or his tenants had a poor harvest. A good marriage was the only sure means of survival.

Other men ignored the structure that supported them and played aimlessly at gaming tables, enjoying the distractions of London's entertainments. As for Alex, he enjoyed his freedoms, such as they were, but had never given in to reckless play. His conscience plagued him with bitter memories of his father's follies and he had no taste for games of chance.

Whereas other men sought seductive conquests, Alex was saddled with the perception that empty dalliances had led many men into ill-favored matches or worse. He was hardly a rake.

Alex shook his head to clear away the tangle of his thoughts. He wondered what Drake would make of all this self-inflicted torment and pictured his reaction. Drake would arch an eyebrow with friendly cynicism, dismissing the entire debate with a gesture. It was one of the reasons Alex had always admired him so much.

Saint or no, the staunchest man exercising self-control can still appreciate another man's total lack of fear in the face of wagging tongues and social disgrace.

But discipline was not much of a consolation when it came to cooling a man's hot blood, and he wasn't oblivious to the opportunities that London afforded him. It occurred to him now that he may have stumbled onto the crux of his current restlessness. Alex glared past the columns of text and calculated that he hadn't sought intimate company for many weeks.

No wonder I'm out of sorts, he assured himself. *A man needed to—*

"Word has it you're moping like a lost sorrel horse, Lex."

Declan's brogue pulled Alex around, and he smiled at the welcome intrusion. Mr. Declan Forrester was a good friend, and if Eloise disapproved of his easy manners and quick wit, all the better.

"Nonsense," Alex scoffed, but straightened his spine to counter the image of some sad, droopy equine. "A man can be deep in thought without being melancholy, Declan."

"Never! And I should know. I make it a point never to think too much and I am the most jovial man I know." He laughed at his own expense, demonstrating his good nature.

Alex stood and clapped him on the back. "You're a fool."

"A *jovial* fool," Declan amended. "Better that than a pinch-faced philosopher, wouldn't you agree?"

Alex shrugged, playing along. "I don't aspire to either role."

"Come out tonight, then. I'll pretend I've not been to London before and you can forget your troubles by giving me the grand tour."

"I haven't admitted to any troubles, Declan."

His friend was unfazed. "As you wish. A distraction by London's finest is still the remedy." He didn't bother to recount that he'd heard from various sources that Lord Colwick had lost his good humor and that if they found Alex at home midday in the dark interior of his library, he'd have trouble denying the truth of the rumors. "At least come for a ride and blow some of this dust off, old man."

"I'll meet you in the stables." Alex closed the leather binder on the desk.

Declan laughed. "That's the spirit!"

After quickly changing into riding clothes, Alex's spirits lifted as they rode their horses down the fashionable thoroughfares of Park Lane. It was not the brisk exercise he usually sought, but his muscles felt good as they stretched and worked with his mount. Their conversation was minimal.

No words were really necessary between the men. Though Declan could be as loquacious as any, he respected Alex's quiet mood and Alex was grateful for the reprieve.

At the entrance to Hyde Park, Alex accepted that his avenue of escape may not have been the most prudent choice. Despite the late hour, the day's lovely weather had brought out many riders still determined to see and be seen. Declan managed one apologetic look before the inevitable.

"Lord Colwick!" a woman's voice hailed, and Alex dutifully reined in his mount.

"Mrs. Preston, a delight to run into you again."

The woman beamed from her perch, her carriage parked to afford her the best view of the parade of riders along the park's lanes. "It has been ages, sir, and I'd begun to fear you weren't yet in town."

"I do enjoy the quiet of the country, but I could hardly neglect my obligations here." He gestured back to Declan. "May I introduce you to my good friend, Mr. Declan Forrester?"

Mrs. Preston nodded, openly assessing the Irishman. "Good day, sir. Are you also in town for the Season?"

"Always." He touched his hat in polite deference. "Lord Colwick is too generous a friend to send me packing and I'm too wretched a friend to offer to leave."

Alex rolled his eyes, then did his best to steer the conversation back onto polite ground. "Well, we shall see you again, then, Mrs. Preston."

"Yes." The feathers in Mrs. Preston's bonnet wobbled merrily in accord. "And you shall have to meet my lovely daughter, Winifred. She will be present and accepting dance offers at the Marquess of Threxton's ball. Will you attend?"

Damn. If Eloise hadn't just wrangled his agreement . . . "Yes, I believe I am committed to doing so."

"Wonderful! We shall be sure to see you there, then." She gave Declan little more than a passing wave of farewell, apparently more pleased to think of introducing her progeny to a titled lord than to his less polished friend.

When they'd barely ridden beyond earshot, Declan jested, "Hmmm. Looks like Miss Winifred Preston has won herself a miserable dance or two, eh, Alex?"

"By all means, just try not to make her cry, will you, Declan?"

"Very funny, Mr. Randall. Oh, come now. It's not so bad, is it?"

Alex gave him a piercing look meant to squelch the discussion.

Instead Declan looked positively encouraged. "Can a man complain about having young women thrown into his path? Hell, just step over them if you prefer! Now, myself . . . it's a different game altogether. I'll just have to troll in your wake and see what lovelies I can catch."

"There's a plan," Alex intoned sarcastically. "I'm not taking you 'trolling' anywhere."

"Are you sure? I might prove a distraction while you escape out the windows."

"Thank you, Declan. I knew I could count on you."

"Ah, hell. Always so serious, you are. I've known you since short pants and you've never been one to see the game for what it is."

"And that is?"

"A chance to play!" Declan shook his head. "It's not as if they have the power to tie you to any bird they choose."

"That's not entirely true, and avoiding the nets can be exhausting." Alex adjusted his coat, the grip on his riding crop tightening. *Damn it! A man wants to hunt, not be hunted!*

"Why not enjoy the rounds, and see if something doesn't catch your eye?"

Alex was just about to tell him how horrifying a flock of greedy, gossiping birds could be—when something *did* catch his eye.

A flash of copper curls beneath a riding bonnet made his breath catch in his throat. Without answering Declan, he spurred his horse forward to get a better look. He hadn't seen that color in months. It was almost impossible that he would see *her* here, that a woman in her position would be as bold as to ride along the Ladies Mile and draw attention to herself. Logic dictated that he was about to embarrass himself for no good reason. But logic wasn't keeping up with the memories that flooded back to him at the sight of a certain hue of red hair.

He'd only met her once, the mistress of the Crimson Belle. One meeting, in which he'd managed to become completely captivated by Madame DeBourcier and just as quickly to completely alienate her in his quest for information to help Drake. His "help" had almost ruined everything, and resulted in an oath to abstain from interfering in any more of his friend's domestic affairs.

But as for Madame DeBourcier, not even the humiliating sting of being dismissed from her house had kept her from his dreams. She hadn't been at all what he'd expected the mistress of a house of ill repute to be. Alex still couldn't reconcile the beautiful young woman who'd perched like a cat with her feet tucked under her skirts, taking umbrage at his questions, and the business she ran. Surely women in her profession couldn't afford to be so sensitive? Yet she'd bristled in defense of her honor, and he could swear he'd actually hurt her feelings somehow.

She was a mystery.

"Madame!"

The rider turned, her brow furrowed at the abrupt greeting, and Alex's stomach lurched in disappointment. Hawk-thin features and an icy glare were proof that he'd let his imagination run riot.

"Excuse me, sir?" The young woman's voice dripped with contempt.

"I apologize for the mistake." He touched his hat and bowed in contrition. "I mistook your profile for another's."

Declan caught up, adding a confused bow to the social muddle. "I told you that wasn't my sister! Pardon my friend, miss, his eyesight's not what it used to be."

She rode off in a huff, and Alex shook his head. If he was lucky, Declan was the only witness to the debacle. Then again, when had his luck ever held?

"Something you care to explain?"

"No." Alex turned his mount around and headed back. "I would not."

"I don't think I've ever seen you run after a woman before."

"And you haven't now."

Declan laughed. "I hope so! If that one exemplifies your tastes, I fear for your future."

Alex didn't bother responding. They rode back

and Alex mulled over the strange turn of the day. He wasn't the kind of man to obsess over a woman he barely knew and certainly not over a woman like Madame DeBourcier. But then again . . .

There was no getting around it. A man needed to get out every once in a while and instead of fighting it, he would go that very night to the one place that had haunted his thoughts for months. He would go to the one place where he could put this simple mystery behind him—the Crimson Belle.

Two

Enticing smells of freshly baked bread and sugary sweets filled the large kitchen, and along the length of a simple wooden table, laughter rang out. It was a lively table filled with women in various stages of dress and undress. There was no mistaking the celebration at hand, as each girl tossed bright ribbons at the guest of honor.

"Happy birthday, Moira!"

Moira stood to curtsy, an awkward gesture softened by her shy smile. "Such a fuss, but thank you." She gathered the brightly colored silk ribbons, enjoying the traditional tokens offered by the women of the Crimson Belle. Their birthday breakfasts were a world away from the formal floors and luxurious bedrooms upstairs. Here in the cozy sanctuary of the kitchen, they could relax and savor the liberties of their life.

Jocelyn sat at the head of the table, resplendent in a green silk morning dress decidedly more modest than the others. She surveyed the scene with pride. They were her family. As unorthodox as it might appear to an outsider, all the girls and women of the Belle shared a bond and their young Madame was as protective as any mother tiger. As they threw ribbons and sampled sweet cakes and mead, Jocelyn was sure that but for the lack of decorum and the generous show of bare skin and curves, they could have been mistaken for a room full of schoolgirls.

Not innocent schoolgirls: Jocelyn watched with a smile as a sultry favorite named Jez planted a less than maidenly kiss on the birthday girl's bare shoulder.

"For luck," Jez purred, deliberately making Moira blush.

Giggles broke out around the table, followed by playful pleas for more lucky kisses. "I want luck!"

"Me too!" A petite blond beauty named Amelia pouted.

"I know a bit of tasty that could use a kiss!" Suzanne flipped the lace of her lilac petticoats to flash her shapely bottom. "One for luck, Jez?"

Ribbons flew at Suzanne and then they all squealed with mirth when Jocelyn's manservant,

Ramis, inadvertently chose that moment to enter the room with a tray of trinkets. The tall, handsome black man didn't even blink, which only added to their fun. Jocelyn shook her head in wonder at the way the ladies fluttered and fidgeted at his entrance, and Suzanne actually managed a rare blush of her own.

Ramis set down the tray at the center of the table. "Compliments of Madame DeBourcier to celebrate your birthday, Miss Moira."

Moira clapped her hands together in delight. "Thank you! Thank you, Madame!"

"You are welcome." Jocelyn leaned back against her chair's back, wishing these simple moments of pleasure could be more plentiful. Her role as Madame of the Crimson Belle left little time and it was a rare treat to sit with her household in unguarded company. "You may share the gifts as you wish. No squabbles, as there are enough for all of you."

Like eager children, the decorated little boxes and silk pouches from the tray made quick rounds, and Ramis crossed his arms, overseeing the merry carnage with the barest hint of a smile.

"The Mistress is generous." He intoned without looking in Jocelyn's direction.

"The Mistress is grateful for her ladies and their talents." Jocelyn responded with as much starch as she could muster.

"When's *your* birthday, Mistress?" Gilly, her newest girl, asked innocently.

Ramis answered first. "She does not age. Decades and decades have passed, but immortal is my Mistress's beauty."

"Fie, Ramis." Jocelyn threw a small piece of bread at him. "I age well enough. Stop spreading tales or you'll have them asking me for potions and secret spells."

"H-how old are you?" Gilly asked.

"She is three hundred and eight," Ramis supplied, his ebony gaze never wavering at the unbelievable lie.

"I will not waste another sugared roll on that one!" Jocelyn stood up from the table, withdrawing from the game of conjecture. "I'm old enough to know when no one is going to listen to me."

One of the parlor maids came to her elbow, delaying her exit. "Madame, there is a gentleman to see you."

"Did he give his name?"

The maid leaned over, whispering, "It's that devil, ma'am." The girls quieted, exchanging knowing glances but doing their best to keep up a festive front.

Jocelyn grasped the identity of the devil at once, but gave the women a cavalier smile. "Not to worry, ladies. Enjoy the rest of your party and your morning off." She turned and Ramis followed silently. Once safely in the hall beyond the hearing of the ladies, she gave the maid her instructions. "Ruthie, ask Mr. Marsh to wait in the gold salon. Ramis will fetch him shortly."

She headed toward her rooms, with Ramis still in tow. "Fergus Marsh! Today of all days."

"You could send him away and enjoy the morning with the others."

She shook her head. "No, better to deal with him quickly. Bring him to the green drawing room when I'm ready and then stay close. If he's come alone, then I'm sure this is no more than another one of his explorations."

Ramis shadowed her as they reached the narrow landing outside her rooms. "I pray he chooses to explore hell soon."

"Ramis!" Her shocked objection was hollow to her own ears. The very thought of Fergus dipping his toes into a river of lava and brimstone was too wonderful to ignore. He'd been a plague to her since she'd inherited the Belle. It was tempting to voice her own thoughts on just how much of hell would be familiar to a man like Marsh. "Just stay close."

"As you desire." He bowed, touching his forehead as a sign of respect, and withdrew to follow her instructions.

She trusted Ramis with her life on a daily basis and marveled at the gift of his loyalty. No matter how much she paid him, or tried to thank him, Ramis was immovable in an odd attitude of humility, as if he were the one indebted. He had served her mother before her, and during Jocelyn's nightmarish arrival, it had been Ramis who had shielded her from the worst of it. It had been Ramis who had possessed the clarity of mind to send word to the school that she was safe and "with her family," to avoid an inquiry. It had been Ramis who had made sure that no one questioned her authority in the early weeks while she mourned and recovered enough to fulfill her promises to her dying mother.

Whatever bond existed between him and her mother, he had refused to speak of it. Jocelyn had wondered if they had been lovers at one time, but had never dared ask him about it. Jocelyn needed him too much to risk offending him. So instead, she chose to honor his wish for privacy by never pressing the matter. Not once in nine years. It was a feat her old schoolmistress would have bet against for her most inquisitive and feisty student. It was quite an accomplishment for a girl who had never previously mastered the art of holding her tongue.

She'd learned to do so at the Belle.

But then, she'd learned many things at the Belle.

She reached the sanctuary of her rooms and

immediately headed for her wardrobe. There wouldn't be time to really change, but the addition of a darker green silk robe embroidered with purple flowers would give her the exotic touch she sought. Jocelyn drew the wrap across her shoulders and then stopped at her vanity table to retrieve an amethyst-encrusted hair comb. Tucking it into the long red curls piled on her head would have to do for artful accents. Marsh was hardly someone she wished to entice with her beauty, but she would rather die than look unkempt or flustered during his unexpected visit.

She hurried downstairs to the green drawing room and settled in to await the worst. By the time she heard Ramis's footsteps in the hallway, along with the clodding rhythm of Marsh's, she was prepared for any attack. At Ramis's knock, she allowed herself one slow release of breath and wondered if warriors did the same before battle.

"Come in." She rose from the couch, setting aside a small book on Eastern fashions. "Why, Mr. Marsh, what an unexpected pleasure! And so early in the day! You are truly a man of enterprise."

"Bah! It's too early in the day for compliments and lies." Marsh gripped his hat, the tension in his fingers matching the tight expression on his face. He was a large man, with a pinched face that revealed his cruel nature. Dressed in black like an undertaker, he was rarely identified as a man who traded in London's notorious pleasure markets. The true owner of the Crescent House, he hired hostesses to provide his establishment with a gentler atmosphere that disguised his iron control of the women in his keeping.

Jocelyn was grateful he'd left his usual companions—thugs and bodyguards—behind this morning. Their presence always made the confrontations between herself and Marsh a bit more ominous and, were it not for Ramis, she was sure, more dangerous.

"Well." Jocelyn settled back down on her cushions, tucking her feet beneath her. "If you didn't come to lie or pay compliments, then I'm not sure why you're here, sir."

"Cheeky creature." Marsh took a seat on a padded chair, an uncomfortable raven in Jocelyn's silk-lined lair. "It's business, as well you know it."

Jocelyn simply waited.

He cleared his throat, then turned his dark eyes in her direction. The stare was intimidating, and he knew it. That Madame DeBourcier seemed impervious to the technique that caused countless gels to cry was a mystery to him. Women were all stupid creatures, in his opinion, and easy to control. All but this one. She'd vexed him from the start. First, by simply existing when he'd been sure Marie had no heirs. And second, by never doing anything he expected her to do.

"Because of my esteem for your dear dead mother, I'm going to share this complaint personally, Madame. Consider it a favor."

"I ask no favors, sir." She sat up, alert and attentive but unconcerned. "As you know, Mr. Marsh, I prefer not to ever be in your debt. For anything."

"Your preferences mean nothing to me. I'm not the only owner who's looking to the Belle and wishing you'd leave it to more professional hands."

She sighed, her feet reappearing beneath her skirts as she shifted into a more conventional position. "And the complaint?"

"You're too liberal with your girls." He ground it out, restraining himself with difficulty. "I can't see that you make much profit. My offer to buy the Belle stands."

"The complaint is that I don't make much profit?"

"The complaint"—he took a deep breath before continuing—"is that you're soft with your girls and the others are hearing word of it. The girls talk and I've had more than one at the Crescent take a beating from me for cheekily demanding the same pay as you provide here at the Belle. They're whores and I pay as I pay. But you . . ."

It was familiar territory, but Jocelyn knew she balanced on a knife's point. Marsh wasn't the worst of the other owners. Just the most vocal. And the most open about his desire to take the Belle away from her.

"I am . . . sorry for your troubles."

"I'd not have troubles if you'd fall in line, Jocelyn. After all, it was—"

"I did not give you leave to use my Christian name, Mr. Marsh. You will address me as Madame DeBourcier, or Madame, or not at all." It was a foolish point to make, but the sound of her name on his lips made her feel nauseated. Of what little in life she could control, she was determined to have charge of this at least.

"Forgive the misstep, Madame. I'd forgotten your penchant for etiquette—though you seem oblivious to my efforts to teach you the manners of the profession you've chosen."

"Your advice has always interested me, Mr. Marsh, and I strive to keep it in mind even when I choose to follow my own inclinations. I regret you seem to take the matter of that choice personally."

"It's business, Madame. It's never personal."

"Good." She nodded her head. "Was there another complaint or have we finally reached the more entertaining lies and compliments?"

"Damn it, woman. One of my pigeons is flown.

Becky Sweet is her name, and if I find you've sheltered her—"

"I've taken in none of your pigeons, Mr. Marsh. We have a different breed of bird here, no offense intended, and even so, I know better than to poach without your express permission."

"So you say! But my property's missing all the same and it's your house that's making them think of cheating me out of hard-earned coin!" A vein on his forehead throbbed the warning that his patience was close to its end.

"I'm hardly responsible—"

"If you're paying your whores as rumored, and padding their heads full of education and nonsense, it will be your own fault when the Belle crumbles around you! And since it *is* business, that's your right." He stood, fury finally moving him to action. "But you are angering people you don't want to anger and I came to tell you that I'll not stand in their way."

She stood as well, crossing her arms defiantly and wishing she were taller so she wouldn't have to tip her head backward to meet the man's gaze. She felt like a child trying to stare down a tree. "I have never engaged you for protection, Mr. Marsh. And since you've made it clear from the first that you wished me gone, I can hardly think why I would look to you to stand in the way of anything or anyone that will achieve your foul ends."

"You'll wish you had! You'll wish you'd paid me what was my due! And if you solicit my girls or harbor any of their worthless hides, well then, your business and mine will meet in a most unpleasant way. I'll not hesitate to teach you just how rough and bloody this business can be."

She held still, the creak of the door opening assuring her that Ramis had just filled the door frame and was now a witness. "Good day, Mr. Marsh. My manservant will show you out."

Marsh took a step toward her and lowered his voice. "I'll buy the Belle for a song after you're ruined, and you can beg pennies on my doorstep, Madame."

"Always a pleasure, Mr. Marsh. I will count the days and hours until you come again," Jocelyn replied with an extra dose of cheer to willfully grate on his nerves. Ramis's hand on Marsh's shoulder ended the exchange.

"Another time, then," Marsh spat, looking frustrated and angry. He gripped his hat and turned, shrugging off Ramis's guiding hand as he left the room.

At Ramis's signal, one of the footmen followed to ensure his safe departure while Ramis remained with his Mistress. "He means you harm."

Jocelyn crossed her arms defensively. "He is more bluster than anything else."

"He spoke of blood." Ramis crossed his arms, mirroring her gesture. "This is more than empty threats."

"He said nothing unexpected. He comes every few months, sputters and fusses, and then we go on with our lives."

"A good sign?"

She relaxed her arms, unwilling to dwell on Marsh, and sat back down on the divan. "It is as good a sign as any." She sighed. "You should check on the ladies and remind them they're at liberty for the afternoon, but that we've guests expected early this evening. Jez has been specifically requested by an admirer to wear blue. You should remind her maid."

Ramis didn't move.

Jocelyn arched her eyebrows. "Was there something else?"

"You cannot ignore Marsh."

"I've never ignored him." She smoothed out her skirts. "Don't worry, Ramis."

"You have a plan, then?"

"Of course I do." She raised her chin, as if daring him to voice any doubts about her ability to outmaneuver her enemies. "We've stayed one step ahead of them all so far, haven't we?"

He nodded. "So far."

Jocelyn smiled, deciding to treat the matter

as happily settled and ignore Ramis's stony look of displeasure. "Well, then. I'll be in my rooms." She breezed past him and headed for the hidden passageway to her rooms on the top floor, aware that the issue was far from settled. Still, she was not willing to forgo a rare afternoon of peace and quiet. As far as she was concerned, she'd earned a few hours to herself—besides, if she was going to come up with a plan, it wouldn't happen with Ramis glaring at her.

The plain staircase and undecorated wood panels heralded the separation of her private world and the public decadence of the rest of the house. She'd converted some of the servants' quarters into a comfortable master suite and deliberately created a sanctuary away from the business of the Belle.

Jocelyn reached her rooms and strode purposefully to her tiny "study." She loved her miniature library, which was little more than a closet hidden by a hanging tapestry, and would curl up on the oversize chair and cushions that dominated the space to steal a few minutes to read Greek history or sigh over poetry. For now, she entered the small private space to catch her breath and consider Marsh's latest threats.

He was her most vocal enemy and in an odd way, she was grateful for his lack of subtlety. His rants gave her valuable insight into the other houses and their methods. She had long been aware that the Belle treated its women more gently and generously, and that her insistence that certain liberties and privileges be given in return for their services was not in keeping with her competitors' approach. No one else hired the finest tutors or rewarded the women with higher wages when they'd mastered a new subject or genteel, ladylike skill. But the girls of the Belle were her beloved charges, and the life of a prostitute was hard enough even with the environment she labored to create for them. She wasn't about to alter her rules to please men like Marsh.

It was hard not to wonder about the young woman who had escaped from Marsh's establishment, the Crescent House. *If this Becky Sweet had sought my protection, would I have turned her away?* The unspoken answer sat in the pit of her stomach like a hot stone, and she pushed away from the seat to escape her study and avoid the unpleasant truth.

Mercy is a luxury I cannot always afford.

A sigh escaped her. She wished that her life held more room for mercy—and a dozen other sentiments that she dearly valued and missed.

"Enough!" Jocelyn smoothed out her skirts and stretched out her legs. It had long been her belief that melancholy could only take hold if one lingered in its company too often. Dwelling on things she couldn't change was a useless exercise and she refused to waste any more of her time.

If Fergus Marsh chose not to believe her denials about his gel, he might try to cause further trouble by—

"Mistress." Ramis interrupted her thoughts, his serious expression explaining his intrusion without his customary knock.

She stood, a curl of cold dread whispering down her spine. "Tell me."

"There is word of the missing woman."

"Ramis, tell me."

"She was found dead a few streets from the Crescent. Murdered." His gaze never faltered, though concern softened his tone.

"How?" She regretted the morbid question as soon as she voiced it.

"Strangled. The details will come soon enough. Marsh will have heard by now."

"How did you hear of it so quickly?"

He gave her an apologetic shrug. "A friend within the Crescent sent a runner, perhaps in an attempt to find Marsh here. At the least, his accusations against you are irrevocably proven wrong."

Murdered. Not by Marsh or any of his minions at the Crescent, or he would never have drawn attention to her disappearance. No, Marsh would be equally surprised at the news. "The authorities?"

"Will make note of it, I'm sure, but . . ."

But it will not be a priority. Few would make much of the murder of a whore. Jocelyn shivered and sat down slowly. "Who else in the Belle knows of this?"

"Cook overheard, I am certain, Mistress."

"Then the house knows," she sighed. "Just as well. Though I'm sorry that the women's day of leisure has been spoiled by it."

Ramis nodded in agreement. "Better they are cautious."

"Yes, and in the meantime, make sure the footmen keep a close watch on our guests. I want no trouble under this roof." Jocelyn watched Ramis's bow and graceful retreat, leaving her once again to her thoughts. Women who worked on the streets were often assaulted and even murdered with sad regularity, but the more fashionable houses and their lovely occupants had little cause to fear violence. The bordellos provided a measure of protection for their working women, but if Miss Sweet had run . . .

There was no telling what random mischief had taken her life. A jealous lover? A rough thug mistaking her for an easy mark? Or even hired muscle from another house striking against the Crescent for some reason . . .

Jocelyn shook her head. The afternoon was slipping by quickly and soon the evening's guests would start arriving. Appointments would be kept, services rendered, and payments made. There was nothing to be done now but to wait.

And pray.

Three

W elcome, sir." The butler opened the carved doors to the fashionably situated house on the edge of an upper-class neighborhood in London. The discreet appearance of the Crimson Belle contributed to its success, and the tolerance of her neighbors was a credit to the Belle's management and craft. He knew of a few similar houses, but none had the Belle's reputation for elegance.

The last time he had crossed the threshold, the hour had been unfashionably early. Alex had never seen the house lit and fully occupied. At the time, he'd been at leisure to note the artwork and admire the owner's tastes. Now there was a great deal more to catch a man's eye.

Brightly lit candelabras added to the ambience, though only to augment the beautiful gaslit fixtures throughout the rooms. The foyer was warm and welcoming, and a uniformed attendant was instantly at his elbow to take his coat and hat. "Is the gentleman expected, or shall I make arrangements?"

"I have come impulsively without an appointment." He heard music and muffled male laughter coming from one of the adjoining rooms, and questioned the wisdom of his decision. "And would prefer to avoid . . ."

"Of course, sir." The man instantly ushered him into a smaller salon off the foyer, unoccupied and separated from the livelier part of the house. "This room is entirely private, m'lord. You wish to make an arrangement for the evening?"

"I wish to see Madame DeBourcier."

The man's expression became more guarded. "Madame DeBourcier does not receive guests this evening. Is there something else we can do for you? Several of the ladies are available, if you care to—"

"No," Alex cut him off, unwilling to hear him recite some kind of illicit menu. "If she isn't available this evening, then I will make arrangements to come another time."

"If you'll excuse me, sir." The man made a brief bow and exited the room, leaving Alex to wonder if he'd just met with success or failure.

The answer wasn't long in coming. He recognized Madame DeBourcier's manservant in the doorway and ignored the surge of resentment at the sight of him. In all his privileged life, Ramis was the only one who had ever "shown him the back door."

Ramis bowed respectfully before greeting him. "You have returned, sir."

"Yes. I wish to speak directly to Madame DeBourcier."

"Madame DeBourcier is not receiving guests this evening."

Alex took one deep breath to try to calm his fury. "She would prefer another evening?"

"No offense is meant, but I think not, sir. The house is not closed to you, but Madame DeBourcier is not receiving guests. It is rare for her to do so and I have my instructions." If the man's tone was apologetic, his expression was implacable.

He has his intructions? What the hell does that mean?

"No offense is taken." He reached inside his waistcoat pocket for his card. "If you will be so kind as to give her my card. Ask her again if she'll make an exception. I will wait."

Ramis eyed the card before accepting it reluctantly. "As you wish."

He nodded, confidently waiting until the man

bowed and left to deliver the card as ordered. *At least I'll exit through the front door this time if the woman sends me packing.*

He certainly had no intention of allowing history to repeat itself, but he accepted that if he pointed out to her manservant that there were any number of respectable establishments that would be glad of his card, his coin, and his company, his chance at an interview with the elusive mistress of the house would undoubtedly evaporate.

No woman is worth this aggravation.

Begging for a damn conversation with a reclusive Madame wasn't a likely method for satisfaction, he told himself.

Of course, if a man was honest with himself, Alex conceded, it would take more than a conversation to relieve the heat that coursed through his body. Since that morning when he'd chased her ghost, he'd composed a hundred speeches to reintroduce himself to the beautiful vixen of the Belle. The hours of waiting had put his nerves on edge and fueled an unmistakable desire for more than Madame DeBourcier's witty repartee. There was no logic to it, and for a man of reason, the irrational pull of memory was difficult to accept.

He pulled back the heavy drapes from one of the windows and looked down the street from the Belle. Beyond the wrought-iron gate, he could see how the bordello blended into the fashionable street. The building's stones faintly glowed from the street lamplight, stately grays and browns of unpainted carved bricks a contrast to some of her whitewashed neighbors. It was not the largest of houses, but situated on the corner, it boasted a greater footprint than most. His two visits to its interior had given him a glimpse of the labyrinth within, but not many clues about the woman who owned it.

He turned away, the wait grinding against his nerves.

Declan had accused him of running after a woman. Alex squared his shoulders and began to pace. *So be it,* he told himself. *The hunt is on.*

"He sends his card," Ramis noted as he extended the object in question toward her. "And insists on waiting below for your response."

"I see." Jocelyn accepted the thick ivory card and carefully considered the elegant script. "And I honestly thought never to see him again."

Lord Colwick, the Hon. Alex Randall.

She hadn't known his name until this moment. It had been months and somehow she'd never forgotten him. Her first thought when she'd seen him had been that she'd somehow magically conjured up the man from her schoolroom daydreams of romance and first dances and heady courtship. He'd stood in her house, a striking man in elegant clothes, tall with broad shoulders and an impossibly handsome face and figure—lithe and athletic but not menacing. She'd guessed at his good breeding, but was more impressed by his lack of arrogance—at least at first. His hair had been unfashionably wild with dusky caramel curls and she remembered how warm his brown eyes had looked, blazing with sincere concern and curiosity. He'd come seeking information, no doubt with a bribe tucked into one of his well-tailored pockets, and Jocelyn remembered the telling moment when her handsome visitor had hesitated to give his name. She'd refused to help him and had angered him beyond measure after she'd signaled Ramis to show him the back door. Since then, he had featured in countless daydreams of opportunities lost and sensuous interludes found.

And now he'd left his card and was insisting on an appointment.

Why? Perhaps he has another question I won't be able to answer.

Ramis cleared his throat. "He will be turned away."

"No." Jocelyn tucked the card into a deep pocket in her skirts. "I'll see him."

"But..." His protest trailed away. "As you wish."

An odd flutter of nerves made her smile. "I wish it. Now stop worrying and please make sure that the Sauterne is chilled properly for Mr. Everton and remind Moira to keep her feet bare. The gentleman wishes to see her toes."

"I will do so and then return to ensure that this man does not—"

"No!" Jocelyn cut him off, surprising them both. "I do not need a chaperone, Ramis. Not tonight."

He touched his forehead briefly and bowed before leaving to carry out her orders.

She retrieved the card to study it again. Ramis was being protective in his role as the head of security and her trusted adviser. Her sudden decision to alter her own habits was hard to explain. After all, she'd been reclusive originally to hide her age and inexperience. Then, in an attempt to scare away clientele, Marsh had spread rumors of her being a diseased and disfigured hag, and in doing so he inadvertently gave her a great gift. Jocelyn had decided to play along, turning the tales to her advantage. Few guests had ever seen her face, though they enjoyed the rare conversation with a masked, elegant hostess. The mystery served its own purposes. It added to the allure of the Belle and gave her an interesting vantage point from which to manage her business. Rather than getting tangled in petty politics, she gave her edicts from the shadows—that way they carried more weight and met with little resistance.

Besides, the Belle's wealthy clients respected a desire for anonymity.

But months ago she'd met with Lord Colwick face-to-face on a whim. She'd been in another odd mood to break her own rules that day.

Like the mood I'm in now.

The ghost of an idea coalesced, and her fingers trembled as she made her way to her desk. Marsh's threats and news of murder had unsettled her, but somehow a simple vellum card offered calm.

This is foolish. It's just a calling card and he is just a man.

Jocelyn sat carefully at her vanity to ensure she'd not wilted entirely from the long day. She smoothed a long red curl that had escaped the loose twist atop her head. She quickly selected a carved ebony hair comb to secure what she could and to accent the riot of gleaming copper tendrils. Jocelyn added a small touch of rouge to her lips, a defiant and mischievous light coming into her eyes. She'd had a taste in their last meeting of his sensibilities. With a flourish, she pinched her cheeks and decided she'd better change her clothes and head downstairs before she changed her mind and the impulse evaporated. "Let us see what you're up to this time, my lord."

* * *

Alex refused to look at his pocket watch to count the minutes he'd been left to cool his heels. He'd studied every object and evaluated the art, and his mood had hardly improved. Alex began to consider that the only thing worse than being refused an appointment with the elusive Madame DeBourcier was having to wait for that refusal.

"To hell with this!" he muttered, only to hear the door open. He turned, expecting Ramis to haunt him like a dark demon, but instead an angel in peacock hues breezed in to steal his composure.

She was just as he remembered, but even more impossibly lovely. Patrician features were softened by a mischievous smile, and her jade-green eyes sparkled as if she were receiving an old friend or welcome acquaintance. His anger evaporated and his heartbeat increased as he took in more of her appearance. Over an iris-colored dress, she'd draped an Oriental embroidered shawl with green beads that shimmered in the lamplight across her ivory shoulders. Petite in stature, her figure was lush and balanced, the sight of her narrow waist making his hands itch to span it and draw her close. Her hair was an artful tangle of curls secured by an ornate comb of black lacquer, and he marveled again at the color of molten copper that beckoned a man's touch. There was simply nothing understated or muted about Madame DeBourcier.

"I'm sorry to have kept you waiting, Lord Colwick," she said, offering her hand.

He bent over her fingers, his breath alone grazing her warm fingertips to savor the connection between them. "I understood it was a woman's prerogative to make a man wait." He straightened, unconsciously keeping a soft hold on her hand.

"Nonsense!" She laughed. "It's rude no matter what a person's gender, and judging from your expression when I came in, you had quite a lecture composed and ready, sir."

"Perhaps just a line or two," he conceded. Her humor made it impossible for a man to keep his balance, and Alex began to experience the same delicious sense of play that he recalled from his last encounter with her and that had kept her so fresh in his mind.

"Lord Colwick?"

"Yes."

"As a hostess, I would normally offer you a drink"—she lowered her voice as if they were friendly conspirators—"but I'm afraid I'll need my hand back."

"Of course." He released her fingers, wondering at his own lapse.

"Come, sit!" She gestured toward the settee

he'd been circling earlier, taking a place near a side tray. "Something to drink, then?"

He took the seat she'd offered, nodding. "Whatever you are having."

With graceful hands, she poured them each a small glass of tawny port before settling in. She tucked her feet up into her skirts and faced him like an exotic house cat content on silk cushions. "I rarely meet visitors, sir. But for some unknown reason, here we are again."

"I'm glad you've made an exception for me, Madame."

"Did you wish me to guess again why you've come to the Belle?"

"You've a talent for it, Madame DeBourcier." God's truth, he recalled she had an uncanny talent for it.

She straightened, alert for the game. She took a moment to study him, an open assessment that did nothing to slow his heart rate. Alex couldn't recall the last time he'd volunteered for a woman's scrutiny, but with the lovely young Madame it was an experience he had no desire to forgo. She completely bemused him as she even went so far as to lean over to carefully note his shoes before sitting back to begin her queries. "Well, if you've come to do battle again, it's clear you're trying a new strategy. You've certainly come at a different hour this time, though Ramis advises me that you discreetly used a hired coach, so you aren't entirely comfortable with your own coachman knowing your destination."

He nodded, conceding the point reluctantly.

"It seems you haven't come for a simple evening's entertainment," she continued. "Or you'd have accepted any number of the ladies' company when offered. I assume it was offered?"

"It was." He took a sip of the port, beginning to enjoy the game.

"Instead you asked for me." She shifted slightly, pausing to enjoy a taste of the amber liquid before going on. "And gave your card, probably to make up for being so difficult on your last visit."

"I wasn't difficult. I was unprepared."

"There's a difference?" she asked him playfully.

"Absolutely."

She shrugged, merrily dismissing the past. "You asked for me, and since you are not a client and have not accepted an offer to become a guest of one of the ladies . . ."

He held his breath.

"It's a puzzle, my lord." She set her glass down, then smoothed out her skirts to retuck them around her feet. "Perhaps you wished to speak to me before making a request for the Belle's services because you have a unique need that you aren't sure we can satisfy. Something you feel is forbidden or unspeakable?"

He sat up abruptly, unable to hide his dismay at this unanticipated turn in her thoughts. "No! I can assure you that my needs are not unique."

She smiled apologetically. "I meant no offense. I admit there are tastes we do not serve. Younger girls, for example. Or boys, for that matter. I would have to direct you elsewhere."

"Damn it, I didn't come here to ask for—"

"Of course not." She waved away the notion, apparently unruffled at the prospect. "And since you're not here for the business of this house, I'm left with only one conclusion."

"And that would be?"

"You're on another mission."

He let her guess linger, beginning to question his own sanity. How does a man come to this place without any logical cause and expect to apply reason? She sat there, an irresistibly pert siren challenging him with each glance, and Alex considered that no man should fight every temptation placed in his path. "In a way, yes."

"You'll simply have to confess then, sir."

"I wanted to see you again." Alex took a deep breath, determined to navigate the next few moments without losing any ground.

Her expression conveyed surprise. "To see me again? Your mission was to see me again?"

"Why does that shock you?"

She recovered her glass from the tray and he

recognized it for the defensive gesture it was. His curiosity was aroused as he realized the lovely young Madame DeBourcier was actually nervous in his presence.

"It seems an odd mission . . . after all this time."

He nodded. "Perhaps. But time did nothing to diminish your memory and I could wait no longer."

"I wasn't aware that I'd made an impression on you, Lord Colwick." The color on her cheeks heightened by another delicate shade. "At least, not a favorable one that you'd wish to sample again."

"Not at all," he countered. "I fear I was the one who made an unfavorable impression, remember?"

"Did you come to apologize?" She shook her head. "You needn't have troubled yourself. I understood you were under a good deal of stress and worried about your friend. I've harbored no ill will."

"Your manservant has a different view, I suspect."

"Ramis is protective and slower to forgive." She smiled, and Alex's breath caught in his throat at the sweet beauty of it and the small jolt of jealousy he felt as she spoke fondly of another man.

"Madame," he began again. "I have no gift for

intrigue and, as my friends are fond of telling me, no talent at all for deception. Not that the art of flirtation necessarily involves either one—"

"Not always!" she chimed in merrily. "Pardon the interruption, Lord Colwick. Do go on."

"So," he continued calmly. "I thought you would respect a more direct approach."

"A direct approach to . . . ?" The question trailed off, and one slippered foot peeked out from beneath her skirts as she shifted forward.

"I want my own decadent Season."

"P-pardon?" It was a breathless whisper, and Alex suddenly didn't care how much aggravation or how many challenges this woman presented. He would have her. She was everything he shouldn't desire, but there was nothing he wanted more.

"You helped a particular friend of mine to enjoy a single decadent Season. And I don't see why you couldn't help me as well."

"You . . . came for lessons?" Her confusion was transparent, and both feet now emerged as she moved to find her footing. "I generally only counsel women on the art of seduction. Perhaps another tutor would suit you better."

"I am not here for lessons, Madame." He took another sip of the port, savoring the flavor before he went on. "I am normally not a man who . . . looks beyond his circle and I don't have a reputation for reckless indulgences. In fact, I have a decidedly stern reputation for following the rules of polite society. But since I met you, I can't seem to stop wishing that things were otherwise."

She held her place and Alex decided it was all the encouragement he could expect at this point.

"I have always put duty and responsibility first, and it occurs to me that there hasn't been much time for pleasure. Or more precisely, that I haven't made much time. I've decided to remedy that mistake."

She shook her head slowly. "There is nothing to stop you, Lord Colwick."

"I'm glad you think so." He let out one slow breath, savoring the moment before he continued. "And that brings us back to the matter at hand."

She smoothed her skirts. "And how is it exactly that I can assist you?"

"I want you."

"Oh, my!" She held still for a moment before replying. "I'm flattered, sir, but I'm sure I've made it clear that—"

"You do not take appointments, yes, it was made clear, Madame." Alex studied her over the rim of his glass, appreciating each curve and line that comprised her beauty. "I'm not asking for an appointment."

"As you say, but . . ." Her argument seemed to

falter and fade before she gave voice to it as her eyes met his. "What are you asking?"

"You are the object of my desire and I wish to spend time with you while I'm in London."

"How much time?"

"Time enough to discover why you have haunted my thoughts these past few months." He stood, determined to end the negotiation. "I will naturally expect to pay for the privilege."

She stood as well, her hands at her hips, her eyes bright with anger. "And do you *naturally* just expect me to agree to this?"

She took a ragged breath and he knew she was about to vent pure fire to ward off his bold request. But this was no wide-eyed innocent debutante, and Alex's temper flared to match hers. Before she could speak, frustration and desire pushed him into action.

He pulled her against his chest, enveloping her smaller frame with his, shock tilting her head back and a gasp of surprise parting her lips for his kiss. He lowered his lips to capture hers, struck by the sweet heat of her soft flesh against his. She began to push against him, but Alex compelled her surrender in a relentless campaign, sampling the textures of her mouth and the taste of her. His hands splayed against her back, caressing her spine and tracing her trembling curves through the silk of her dress. Her response was a tentative flutter at first as her tongue met his, setting off a cascade of electric sensations through his frame, before she leaned against him with a sigh, eagerly matching his kisses with her own.

A surge of pure triumph overtook him. Her hands whispered over the linen of his shirt and caressed his chest as he tasted her and teased her lower lip with his teeth, suckling on the plump, wet flesh before moving on to gently explore the shell of her ear. She shivered and sighed, gasping when he caught her earlobe between his lips to suckle and draw out her responses. His breath was hot against the delicate skin behind her ear, and he abandoned the perfect labyrinth and curves he traced with his tongue to follow the wild pulse of her heartbeat down the soft column of her neck, deliberately slowing at the sensitive juncture at her shoulder.

She moaned and he felt her weight shift as her knees folded beneath her. He caught and held her up easily, his thoughts careening out of control to keep up with the fire in his blood. He'd intended a kiss and nothing more. But his body cared nothing for plans and intentions. It had been far too long since he'd felt the silk of a woman's skin against his or experienced release in a woman's embrace. Alex cupped her bottom to fit her to him, his thigh finding a harbor between her thighs as the hard length of his cock throbbed at the friction of layers of fabric separating him from the damp core between her legs.

Her legs tightened around his, as she arched against the intrusion and rode his thigh as if to heighten the sensation, exposing more of her throat and shoulder to his attentions. Her skin was so hot against his mouth, Alex gripped her more tightly and began to seek the sweeter curves of her body to taste and sample. She was a feast of firm, yielding flesh and his hunger grew with each heartbeat that pounded through him.

The modest cut of her bodice only encouraged his quest, and his right hand tugged impatiently at the corded tie that held her décolletage together. An odd squeak caught in her throat as the fabric gave way, but her slender fingers tangled in his hair and guided him toward the hardened peaks of her breasts. The pert curves were lush and firm, ripe and bountiful as their weight filled his hands. His fingers worked across them, the gentle friction causing the porcelain orbs to color and blush, her nipples puckering in anticipation of his attentions. At last, his tongue teased each strawberry-tinted crest in turn with the lightest dance, flickering and lathing to elicit her soft cries of pleasure. Then he deliberately exhaled against her to cool the skin he'd moistened, making her writhe and buck against him.

Gentle seduction gave way to a primal need to possess, and Alex suckled her as if her body alone sustained him. Her hair had somehow come undone and brushed his face, the scent of jasmine and the caress of her silken curls against his skin pushing him over the edge. A wave of desire so strong it stole his breath pulled at him, and Alex lifted his head for the briefest second only to ascertain where they would land if he carried her to the carpeted floor.

"W-wait . . . ," she gasped, pushing against him weakly but with a tenacious rhythm that caught his attention.

It was all he could do not to growl in frustration, but Alex held still—albeit after another second or two of sampling the ripe curve of her breast. "I am waiting, Madame."

She continued to struggle, and within moments was freed of his embrace as he reluctantly released her. Her hands shook as she tried to reconstruct her décolletage for modesty's sake. The flush on her face bewitched him, and it was all he could do not to drag her back into his arms.

"What are you doing?" he asked.

"I am . . . considering your proposal." She stood back and moved beyond his grasp. "I realize it may seem a deliberate tease on my part, but"—she steadied herself against the back of one of the chairs while she continued to hold together

her bodice and shield her breasts from his eyes— "I never make decisions with my eyes closed."

"Pardon?"

"When you kiss me, I find that my eyes close . . . and I lose track of my senses." She gathered the ties and made faster work of the repair as her humor appeared to return. "Not an uncommon occurrence when being kissed, but I owe you an answer."

"Keep them open if you wish." He extended his hand. "And I thought your answer was understood."

Temper flashed in her eyes again, but her expression remained calm as she made no move toward him. Alex marveled at the quicksilver changes in this lovely woman. One moment she was a sensual goddess in his arms and the next as prim and remote as a dowager. *Is she going to reject me after all? After what has just passed between us? Damn it, my cock is so hard I'm light-headed . . . this is not good.*

"No, Lord Colwick," she replied, keeping the chair between them, ignoring his proffered hand.

"No?" He did his best to ignore the ache of his engorged cock. His mood darkened at the unexpected twist in the encounter. "You mean to dismiss me out of hand?"

"No, Lord Colwick," she repeated, gently this time. The shadow of a smile hovered over her lips and Alex was sure that no man kept his equilibrium for long during an encounter with Madame DeBourcier.

"Let's have it, then." He crossed his arms, bracing himself.

"I am considering your proposal." She touched her hair, repositioning the comb to recapture a few of the curls that had escaped, though most of the tendrils eluded her efforts. "It is no small thing to commit to just one man for the Season."

"I can imagine." He clenched his jaw to bite back any additional comments regarding the sacrifice of limiting herself to just one lover.

She gave him an arched look, as if she were a teacher displeased with a precocious student. "I don't think it's too much to ask to be given a few days to consider what this agreement might entail. You yourself might be grateful for the time."

"To what end?"

"To change your mind," she offered airily. "You may reconsider and decide that a more conventional and less expensive arrangement with another lady will suit, or perhaps this visit was enough to satisfy your curiosity and set me from your mind."

He shook his head. "I don't think so. I don't require any time. Name your price. Send word to me when you're ready, Madame." He managed a polite bow, ignoring the protests of his body at the delay in possessing her. Without another word, he made his way from the Belle.

Name your price.

For Jocelyn, it was as if someone had stolen all the air from the room. Once the door was shut behind him, she sank down onto the settee in amazement. Of all the turns in the long and unusual day, she never would have predicted that Alex Randall would land on her doorstep—and that she would land so dizzyingly in his arms.

Her thoughts danced and she leaned back against the cushions to catch her breath. "Why did I ask for time?" she whispered to the empty room. The safest choice was to refuse him politely and instantly. She had never before risked forgetting herself in a man's arms, always wary of being exposed as a fraud and losing ground to the gossip that might give her enemies the edge they had always sought against her. "Have I lost my wits?"

She hadn't been defenseless. Freeing Ramis to attend the working floors didn't mean one of the muscular footmen wasn't a cry away. They'd have come if she'd summoned them, but she'd never even considered it. There'd been no fear, not even when Lord Colwick had seized her. Not even when she'd forgotten who she was—where she was.

Always trust your first instinct.

It was an old adage but one that gave her a small measure of calm now. Jocelyn deliberately took a slow, deep breath to focus, then stood to make her own way back to the sanctuary of her rooms, but every sensitive inch of her skin clamored for attention. It was as if his kisses had stripped away an invisible cocoon that had kept her apart from the physical world around her. Now the silk of her dress against her thighs, the weight and caress of her curls against the back of her neck—even the cool air of the stairwell moving across her face and shoulders—distracted and taunted her.

It was a dangerously delicious feeling, and Jocelyn acknowledged that if nothing else came of him, she had gained an intoxicating memory. But if she believed him . . .

Alex Randall was a man who was hard to dismiss, with his steady mahogany-colored gaze that set off smoldering waves of heat down her spine. He was impressively tall and athletic. He was nothing like most of the soft, pale aristocrats who dominated the house's client lists. Handsome didn't seem an adequate description for the regal lines and masculine power of him. He was straight-backed and impossibly polite and controlled, and she marveled at the forces he seemed to master. When he'd dropped the façade of reserve and taken her into his arms, she'd been swept up in the storm of need he'd unleashed. His touch had tapped into her own hidden reservoir of wanton desires, and now there was no denying her response.

To refuse his offer would be all too simple and a hundred ready excuses sprang to mind, but Jocelyn realized that accepting his offer had an appeal and logic all its own. The business of the Belle, all the pressure and worries associated with the world she'd created, weighed heavily on her. To accept his offer was to take a bit of pleasure for herself. She would be carving out her own path and taking a great risk.

Is it a good time to be so selfish? With Marsh barking and a potential threat out there to my girls? But then, perhaps this is the perfect time. A titled lover might give me more cachet when I need it most—and a chance to earn a substantial nest egg of my very own. Or would I be forfeiting everything I've done here? After all, there is the chance of exposure to Marsh and the others . . . but haven't I come too far now? So many years had passed and she'd accomplished so much to create her mysterious persona. *Would it make a difference? If I accept Lord Colwick's proposal and gave up my secrets . . .*

Jocelyn reached her door and hesitated with her hand on the brass knob. She'd always told the girls that every experience and every choice shapes a woman, and that only they had the power to direct their own paths. And now it seemed her own path might take a remarkable turn. If she wanted it to . . .

Timing was everything, and she'd begun to fear that she'd already waited too long to experience a grand affair of her own. The longer she'd avoided it, the more daunting the decision had become. None of the men frequenting the Belle had ever interested her, and Jocelyn had shied away from competing with the women of the house. But with Alex, she found herself unwilling to direct him into the arms of anyone else—especially after a small, sweet taste of what could be hers for the Season.

"With great risks come great rewards," she reminded herself as she turned the handle.

And this will be the greatest risk of all.

Name your price, he'd demanded. *But what if I am the one who ends up paying?*

Four

❧

"A brutal crime, by all accounts," Declan went on as he refilled his coffee cup. "One of the girls said her throat looked like it had been ringed with pitch from the bruises left by the strangler's hands. And not two hundred paces from their back door . . ."

Alex grimaced. "This is not a topic for the breakfast table, Forrester."

Declan shrugged. "I can see your point, but admittedly it's far more interesting than recounting how much I lost at cards last night."

"For a man who never wins, I'd think you'd find a more suitable amusement."

"There's nothing more amusing than an evening playing cards with a beautiful woman perched in your lap whispering gory tales and ghost stories." Declan laughed, then lowered his voice. "It's not as if they aren't willing to comfort a poor man after a bruising hour or two at the gaming tables. You should come back with me to the Crescent tonight."

"No, thank you," Alex answered firmly. A fleeting image of Jocelyn perched on his lap, with her sweet bottom nestled against him, gave his tone a sharper edge than he'd intended.

"Another place, then. What about the Jade?" Declan went on cheerfully. "Get out for a real bit of sport, Alex. It would definitely beat chasing hawkish spinsters down in the park."

"No." Alex shifted in his chair, wishing he could rein in his thoughts when it came to sport these days. Madame DeBourcier had sent him off in a state of total frustration—and he wasn't sure he could face another session of working his own flesh to climax with his hands, sweating and conjuring her in a myriad of fantasies. No man would blame him for enjoying a convenient bit of solace and relief in another pretty doxy's arms, but Alex knew that no other woman would satisfy his desires. It rankled him that she'd sent him off to "think" last night. Hell, he'd been able to do nothing else. He'd spent a sleepless night thinking—of her, in his arms, spread across his bed, wrapped around him while he—

"And where were you last night?" Declan interrupted the torrid flood of his thoughts.

Alex wasn't in the mood to share. "Out."

"Out?" Declan scoffed. "Out sitting in a room full of dusty cronies at your club, no doubt. You'll dry out before your time at this rate, old friend. And you're being a wretched host, Lex."

Alex made a show of stretching his long legs under the table and settling back to his breakfast plate. "What happened to 'Leave me to my own devices' and 'I don't want a chaperone'? I could have sworn that was you just two weeks ago . . ."

Declan tried again to coax him out. "I'm not asking you to hold the reins. Just come along for the ride. Go with me to the racetrack and watch me lose money I don't have."

Alex reluctantly begged off. "Another time. I promised to meet a business associate this afternoon." Declan's entertaining banter would have been far more distracting than Sir Lenton's monotonous speeches, but there was nothing to be done for it. "You could come along and enjoy a discussion regarding the deteriorating state of the textile markets."

Declan shook his head sadly. "Tell me again why we're such good friends?"

"You love my sense of humor," Alex supplied with a wry grin. "I believe you once said I was the most cheerful company you'd ever kept."

"Was I drunk at the time?"

"Very funny!" Alex laughed at Declan's barb. "You probably were, but then—"

"When isn't he?" Eloise finished, sweeping into the dining room and cutting them both with a disapproving glance. "Good morning, gentlemen."

Declan stood abruptly, rattling the tableware and earning another glare from Eloise as she took her place opposite her brother. "Good morning, Mrs. Wadley." He regained his seat with equal grace before adding, "And don't you look lovely this morning!"

Eloise colored immediately and abandoned her campaign to civilize him with matronly stares. "Oh, please!"

"Have you plans for today, Eloise?" Alex attempted to break the tension.

She sighed. "A few social calls to make. Lady Andrews has invited me to see her new litter of pug puppies this afternoon."

"If she threatens to give you one of the little dragons, what will you do?" Declan asked.

"Why? Are you not fond of dogs, Mr. Forrester?" she replied brightly.

Declan's brow furrowed. "Love 'em! But I'm not sure those black-faced creatures count. Besides, you're too young to take up toting around some foul-smelling little animal to keep you company."

Eloise's eyes narrowed. "I'll keep your advice in mind when the critical moment arrives."

Alex quickly took another bite of toast to keep from smiling at the routine exchange. Their bickering was never mean-spirited and he knew that Declan went out of his way to tease her. It had gone on for as long as he could remember and truthfully, Alex thought it was good for his serious-minded sister to spar with a man who took nothing seriously.

The butler interrupted, coming to Alex's side with a small silver tray. "This came for you, my lord."

"Thank you, Adams." Alex retrieved the sealed envelope, noting immediately the insignia CB embossed in a bloodred seal on the fold and the smell of jasmine wafting toward him. He'd expected a response, but the speed of word arriving from Madame DeBourcier didn't bode well. He tucked the envelope into his jacket pocket and made a point of returning to his meal.

A moment of silence lingered and grew into an awkward void of conversation, and Alex finally looked up to find them both staring. "What?"

"Is that perfume I smell?" Eloise asked archly.

"Is it?" Alex asked innocently.

Declan grinned. "If it's a note from a business associate, I'd say he's a bit partial to you, Lex."

Alex decided retreat was the wisest course.

He stood to leave them to their conjectures. "My apologies, but I'll be in my study for a while."

Before either one could protest or come up with another rally of comments, he slipped from the room and headed to his study on the second floor. Once he was alone, he retrieved the envelope and fingered the old-fashioned wafer seal a second or two before breaking it.

Did women scent letters of refusal? Was she that eccentric and cruel?

The expensive paper yielded an answer quickly enough in an elegant and even hand.

Lord Colwick,

   If you have not yet changed your mind, then I ask you to come again to the Belle. I will look for you tomorrow evening to discuss the proposal you made.

                              M. DeBourcier

Alex scanned the brief note several times, absorbing the polite but curt invitation. It was neither a refusal nor an acceptance. It was a summons to a negotiation.

Well, if the Madame of the Crimson Belle was nothing else, he told himself, she was bold. If he'd expected a simpering note of gratitude or a flowery bid for his return, he would have been disappointed. But Alex knew better. If he expected anything, it was to be surprised at every turn.

He lifted the parchment to his lips, inhaling the fragrance and remembering the sensation of her mouth beneath his. She'd trembled in his arms, and the power of his hunger for her had sweetened every taste of her skin. The memory mastered him, overtaking any effort to keep her effects on him at bay. She was a siren song of feminine beauty, of flesh and heat, and he had no wish to avoid the danger of drowning.

Tomorrow night. It would feel like a century passing before then, but at least he would have his answer.

"It is not my place, mistress, but—"

"No, it is not your place, Ramis." She closed the account book on the desk in front of her with a forceful sweep of her hand. "I sent him a note earlier today. I've made my choice."

"I will, of course, respect your decision, if it is truly, as you say, 'for the best.' "

Jocelyn held her breath, unable to admit that she wasn't sure whose best interests she'd had in mind when it came to accepting Lord Colwick's proposal. "If he comes tomorrow night, then he is to be shown directly to my private quarters. If . . . we come to an arrangement, he will come and go as he wishes, and the staff will be hospitable when he does."

For long seconds, Ramis stood without moving. Jocelyn held still, counting on the years of trust and understanding between them. He had been her right hand and confidant, overseen the security of the house, and helped her keep a close eye on the women of the house. But now she needed him to stand aside and allow her the freedom to take this step.

Finally, his eyes dropped. "As you wish."

"Thank you, Ramis."

He bowed, touching his forehead respectfully, and withdrew in a single fluid motion, leaving her alone with her thoughts.

Jocelyn restlessly began to file away the leather volumes on her desk and carried them back to tidy the tiny nook of her study. Shielded behind the woven tapestry, she put the accounts and business journals in order, then eyed the more colorful books that lined one corner. Volume after volume of well-worn tomes stood on several narrow shelves, covering a variety of scholarly topics from classic literature and science to ancient history and philosophy. On the two lowest shelves, within easiest reach, were exotic texts worth their weight in gold to her—from erotic illustrations and an expensive book of artistic photographs of women in every guise of naked play, to translations of foreign texts on the extensive arts of love and pleasure.

After years of study, she knew them all intimately. She ran her fingers gracefully along their spines, the informal inventory of touch calming her nerves. Each book memorized and revisited repeatedly, guiding and steadying her hand at the helm of the house. Only one or two had belonged to her mother; the rest she had painstakingly acquired from rare-book dealers and through quiet channels of trade. She'd secretly taken pride in her ability to gather what she deemed valuable facts and information from the more prurient content available. Taken alongside the simple observations of a woman in her position, Jocelyn had always felt supremely confident on the subject of men and the methods used to seduce them.

She'd trained the newer girls who'd come to the Belle and even a few women of wealth and status beyond their walls who wished to sample the delights of a "good education." It was one of those pupils who had inadvertently led Lord Colwick to her door, and Jocelyn marveled at the events she'd set in motion when she'd agreed to help Mrs. Merriam Everett to achieve her goal of bringing a rake to heel.

She'd tutored and advised, sympathized and supported. She'd coached and strategized in a game she'd never actually played, but Jocelyn had never considered her lack of personal experience important. She was sure that it was simply a technicality. After all, one could understand the nature of explosives without ever building a bomb, or be an expert on geography and cultures of the world without traveling, couldn't one? In nine years, she'd never once been tempted to cross the line that would take her beyond redemption or rescue. At least, not until Alex Randall.

Not until Alex Randall had abruptly appeared months ago and reminded her that she had once only aspired to be everything that was refined and proper—the perfect lady. Not until she'd seen him and wished that there was nothing in the world to keep her from abandoning the duties and responsibilities that made her life a charade. Not until Alex Randall had announced his intentions and then set her on fire with his blazing kisses and incinerating touch.

Temptation had given way to impulsive acceptance and now she would be truly just like the other women in the house. Any differences she had clung to, any illusions of separation would forever be destroyed.

I'm selling myself to a stranger.

Internal lectures on the sound reasoning behind her decision, about the money or the advantages of becoming the mistress of a titled lord even for a Season, seemed feeble and jarred her nerves. *It is a simple transaction for the good of the Belle during these uncertain times,* she reminded herself. The business of it was like a shield against the truth.

I'm doing this because I want to.

There it was, the truth, unvarnished and shameless. She curled up on the sofa, tucking her feet up underneath her, and retrieved a small leather volume she had overlooked. It was a collection of erotic poetry and prints. She held it to her chest and let out one long, slow exhale.

I've made my choice. Now I just have to decide to relax and enjoy myself while it lasts, because only a fool would waste this chance. She'd spent years envying others their grand love affairs, all the while counseling courage or caution whenever it was warranted. Now it would be her turn at last.

She was no timid soul to second-guess her instincts.

I'm doing this because . . . I want him.

Ramis retreated, wondering if his young Mistress's loneliness had driven her to this rash course of action. Still, it was true that it was not his place to judge or intervene—especially after so many years of service. He would simply support her as he always had and pray for a good outcome. Ramis put thoughts of his Mistress's unexpected announcement aside and went about his usual routine. He surveyed the dark, quiet hall, his ears attuned to the sounds of the house. It was close to noon. The last of the previous night's guests had left, and the women slept now. But as he rounded the corner, he noted that one room's light had yet to be extinguished.

His brow furrowed with concern. Gilly was the newest addition to the working floors and reminded him of a young sparrow, with her bright eyes and sweet spirit. While the others had learned to shield their natures, he could detect no hardened edge to her smiles, no prevarication.

At least, not yet.

He accepted that this change would be inevitable, but he dreaded it. His steps were whisper-quiet on the thick rug. He lingered outside her door for a moment, studying the pale sliver against the woven carpet. Had she suffered a difficult evening, or was she simply having trouble sleeping? An illness? The last possibility drove his hand to gently strike the door.

"Miss Gilliam? Are you unwell?" He kept his voice low, respectful of the hard-earned peace of the others.

After a few seconds, the door opened and Ramis felt an odd rush of relief. Her cheeks were free of tears and her complexion's color reminded him of peaches laid against soft, warm linens. A sparrow's bright and inquisitive eyes looked at him without a shadow of fear, and when she smiled he almost forgot himself and returned a rare one of his own. "I am well, thank you, Ramis."

He scanned her again for any telltale signs of distress, then clasped his hands behind his back. "I apologize for disturbing you. I saw the light and wanted to make sure—"

"Would you like to come in? I was going to have a bit to eat, but things always taste better when they're shared." She stepped back, opening the door a little wider to give him entrance. "Please?"

The invitation came as a surprise, and Ramis stiffened as he held his ground. He did not dally with the women. He did not flirt or tease. Long years, he'd guarded himself carefully against any hint of favoritism. He'd treated them all with respect and great care. He was their guard and protector, but the nature of the house always made that role difficult. How did one protect such women in what was sometimes a dangerous trade? He had long ago resigned to love only the house, and not the beautiful flowers in its gardens. They came and went too quickly, and a man would lose sight of his purpose.

"I should not. It is not proper, Miss Gilliam."

She tilted her head to one side, her curiosity apparent. "Ramis?"

"Yes." *Now she will ask why it is not proper, and I will explain it and she will nod and pretend disappointment and she will not speak of it again.*

"How old are you? Are you as old as the Mistress?"

Again, he almost lost the battle not to smile. She referred to his jest in the kitchens on Moira's birthday, and now for the world, he could not take back the lie—not if it meant this sparrow might frown. "I am far older than the Mistress. I have almost forgotten to count the centuries."

"Oh, my!" Her eyes widened in open wonder and admiration. "You must have so many stories to tell!"

"More stories than a girl can hear on such a night." He bowed. "I will leave you to your dinner and your rest."

"Another night, then. You cannot keep so many stories to yourself, Ramis."

"Can't I?"

She shook her head, soft brown curls bouncing against her bare shoulders. "It isn't proper." She curtsied, gifted him with one last sweet smile, and retreated behind the door, closing it gently.

He continued down the hall and was halfway up the steps to his attic quarters when he realized that he was smiling after all.

Five

"This way." Ramis gestured and led Alex down one of the beautifully appointed hallways toward a decidedly less glamorous door, which opened on a plain, unvarnished staircase. Alex hesitated briefly before he placed a foot on the first step.

"I could be wrong, Ramis, but it seems your Mistress is determined never to meet me in the same room."

The giant didn't even blink at the attempted jest.

Alex took a deep breath and simply waited for the man to continue leading him to his appointment with the Madame of the house. After long moments, the servant at last turned to head up the narrow stairs with Alex in tow.

Alex thought he'd seen the private side of the house previously, but this was clearly a servant's passage, with its poor whitewashed woodwork. When they reached the top floor of the house, the décor didn't improve, but Alex wasn't about to make another comment and start another staring match with a man who openly would have preferred escorting him to the back door.

At the end of a short, uncarpeted hallway, Ramis stopped at a single door on the left. "She is expecting you, sir." He bowed and brushed past Alex to return the way they'd come.

Alex shook his head. In hours of fantasizing the moment, he hadn't come up with being dropped off in a drafty attic hallway in front of a garret room door. As the sound of Ramis's footsteps faded, Alex held his place and for a fleeting moment considered that Madame DeBourcier might be amusing herself at his expense. Perhaps she intended to test his resolve or see if he would throw a fit at the climb to the third floor and the rough setting.

If that is the case, he intoned silently, *she has only succeeded in adding to my curiosity.*

Alex knocked, realizing the door was a bit more solid than it appeared. "Madame?"

"Come in, my lord."

He opened the door and stepped into another

world. A cocoon of warmth and comfort awaited him, from thick Oriental carpets to silk-draped panels on the walls; the overstuffed furniture boasting inviting cushions and soothing colors of autumn made him want to sigh. The ceiling was crossed with exposed wooden beams, giving the room the feeling of a cottage. It was a sitting room out of a fanciful daydream where one might drink hot chocolate and read before retiring for the night. Uncluttered, it appealed to his senses and increased his admiration for its primary occupant. His eyes lighted on a large four-poster bed partially concealed by opaque curtains, and Alex smiled. Set on a low pedestal, it was the sumptuous bed of a sultana, with delicate floral carvings along the posts and headboard. But there was something touching and far less regal about her bed when he saw the hand-stitched quilts that covered it. Madame DeBourcier had eclectic tastes and if this room reflected nothing else, he suspected it betrayed her love of the simpler pleasures in life.

"A drink, Lord Colwick?" She stepped away from one of the curtained alcoves, in a modest dress of sapphire blue with silver threads in the trim. Her hair was pulled back in an elegant chignon, and as she came toward him, it occurred to him he'd never seen a more beautiful woman.

"No, thank you." He was going to keep a clear head about him, at least until she'd agreed to his proposal.

"Please, come and have a seat, then." She indicated the sitting area that centered around a small unlit fire grate in the corner. "I realize it's not as refined a room as one of the salons on the first floor, but I thought we would be more comfortable here in my quarters . . . discussing the terms of our arrangement."

"Then you've decided in favor of my idea?" He wasn't going to relax until she stated her intentions in plain terms.

She sat down amidst the cushions at one end of the sofa and smiled. "I have."

Alex felt everything fall into place with those two delicious words. "I'm glad you came to your senses and—"

"For a price," she added. "Naturally."

"Naturally." Alex chose the chair across from her, hoping to keep his wits for the negotiation but indulging in an appreciation of her beauty. "Name it."

"Ten thousand pounds," she stated without preamble and without even a hint of embarrassment.

"That's no small fortune." Alex did his best to keep his voice level. *Ten thousand pounds—by God, there's a living wage!* But there she sat, clear-eyed and lovely, as calm as if she'd asked him for a handkerchief.

"I am no small thing." She shrugged, then shifted to lift what he realized were bare feet from the floor, to tuck them into her skirts. The glimpse of her slender ankles and naked toes was remarkably distracting, and Alex was sure she knew it.

"Ten thousand pounds." He repeated it, as if saying it magically made it less than an amount that could have financed a dozen indulgent seasons.

"You'll understand if I'm not willing to haggle, Lord Colwick." She leaned back, extending an arm along the back of the settee. "It is, after all, extremely personal, this matter. I am not in the habit of meeting clients, much less sleeping with them. But you intrigue me and so I'm hoping you'll agree to my terms."

"And in exchange for my substantial investment?"

"You can come and go as you wish. For the London social season, or until you retreat to the country for the hunt, whichever comes first. You will be free to access my rooms, my hospitality, and my company—without limits within this house."

"Perhaps I can arrange for you to have a town home and carriage of your own for the duration of the Season. We could meet more privately without—"

"Without limits *within* this house, Lord Colwick. My presence is required here. I do not leave the Crimson Belle."

Alex took a deep breath. It was such a civilized conversation and she was so genteel and lovely, quietly outlining the arrangement his money would buy him. But there was so little of civility in the nature of his thoughts when it came to her. His lust for her cared nothing about agreements or the costs involved. *She would be his without limits.* He wanted her in a dozen ways—raw, wild images of her beneath him, wrapped around his waist as he took her against a wall or pressed against the cushions of the sofa or sprawled on the Oriental rug beneath his feet—and Alex knew the negotiation was an illusion. He would pay any price to have her.

"Agreed." Shame and exhilaration raced through him as he spoke the word.

"The arrangement begins when you wish, then. I'll inform the staff to—"

"Now." He leaned forward, the last vestiges of pretended indifference falling away. His brown eyes blazed with an open desire that left no room for prevarication.

"Pardon me?" she asked a bit more breathlessly than she wanted. She'd thought there was a slight chance he'd be impatient to begin, but somehow now that the moment was at hand— she felt an electrifying jolt of fear and anticipation.

"I'll have the money delivered to you tomorrow, but I don't see why we should wait." He held his place, not moving from the chair, but Jocelyn could have sworn that some shift had taken place and that his relaxed stance resembled a cat ready to spring at the slightest provocation. His eyes never wavered and her heart began to race in response.

It would be now.

He continued, apparently misreading her hesitation. "I am a man of my word, Madame De-Bourcier. But I can sign anything you wish to secure your promise of payment."

She shook her head, wondering for one fleeting moment how one would word such a document. "I trust you, Lord Colwick. There's no reason to wait."

Jocelyn didn't want to wait, but the reality of her decision made her tremble with a sudden case of nerves. This was not the time to play the innocent, and for ten thousand pounds, the man no doubt expected to be in expert hands. Jocelyn stood, deciding that a bold plan of action was the only solution to her dilemma. It was business and nothing more. But even as she stood, Jocelyn realized—looking into his caramel-brown eyes and feeling the strength of his desire telegraph across the empty space between them—that business transactions were, oddly, the last thing on her mind.

Instead, it was as if her body began to extend delicious tendrils of warmth skimming over her skin, preparing for his touch and demanding his attention. Every wicked image and forbidden game danced in a fleeting parade in her mind's eye, and she smiled at the possibilities.

She held out her hand, the barest tremor betraying her anxiety, but once his hand engulfed hers, a new feeling of calm drowned out all her fears. He stood easily, and without speaking, she began to lead him toward her bed.

She felt invincible and complete, basking in his open look of appreciation. Stepping up onto the dais, she drew him toward the bed and gently pushed him back up against one of the ornately carved bedposts.

He raised his brows, but he didn't protest.

Jocelyn smoothed her hands over the warm planes of his chest, enjoying his height and strength, before reaching up to trace her fingers along the back of his neck, tangling them in his hair to guide his face down to hers. The man needed very little coaxing, responding to her unspoken request to let her kiss him. His mouth claimed her, possessing her, and Jocelyn felt the room spin as he feasted on her lips and tongue like a starving man given a banquet. He teased, tasted, and consumed until she lost track of where he ended and she began. She moaned at the bruising heady exchange and leaned against him—eager to take in all the new sensations and experiences he could provide.

Her hands moved under his coat and up his back to cling to him for balance, but also to revel in the sensation of his warm, firm flesh separated from her bare fingertips by the soft linen of his shirt. Lord Colwick was athletic and muscular, and she loved that there was more to him than might initially meet the eye. The broad span of his back narrowed at his waist and intrigued her as her fingers encountered his trousers. A new flutter of anticipation sprang to life inside her as she skimmed her hands along the curve of his backside and the firm lines of his thighs.

He lifted his head, his breath hissing through his teeth in reaction to her bold explorations, and caught her hand to press it against his arousal. Jocelyn gasped at the size of it beneath her fingertips. It was so firm and warm, and even through the cloth it seemed to throb and shift at her touch, as if protesting its confinement. With the heel of her hand she pressed against the base of him before tracing the column upward, her eyes fluttering in surprise to realize the swollen tip of him was trapped in the buttoned waist of his pants. She'd seen hundreds of photographs and drawings of the male anatomy, and glimpsed a dozen examples here in the house, but this . . . touching him through a barrier of cloth made her itch for more.

His buttons bulged from the pressure, and she ascertained with a smile that it couldn't possibly be comfortable for a man. "You feel warm," she whispered, her voice betraying a hint of surprise.

"I'm on fire, Madame."

"I need my hand back to remedy that." She accented the request with a trail of kisses across his jawbone, praying he hadn't noticed the way her voice trembled.

He released his hold on her hand and was rewarded instantly. She worked through the buttons of his shirt and pushed back the cloth to kiss his chest, while her fingers moved down to the fastenings on his pants. Once she'd oriented herself to the puzzle of male tailoring, she was able to free his erection, gasping as it pressed against the soft curve of her stomach.

He moaned again, but she knew it wasn't pain. She gently traced the length and girth of him with her fingers, marveling that it was so much heavier than she'd expected—the skin so much silkier, like the thinnest layer of soft velvet in a sheath over a hot stone. The head was almost the color and shape of a plum, jutting out shamelessly atop its thick mast, bobbing with every ragged breath he took. She gripped him and released him, stroking the length and finding each sensitive juncture and texture to make his flesh respond to her touch. It was such a beautiful alien thing, this part of him, and a cascade of new desire shimmered through her as she shamelessly thrilled in the claim of her touch and the power she felt.

"Madame . . ."

Whatever request he'd planned on voicing, she interrupted him simply by ever so gently dragging her nails around the base of him and then drawing upward to the round, swollen tip, where one ivory pearl of crème had appeared.

His breath hitched at the playful assault, and Jocelyn smiled at the sweet victory in knowing that she could arouse and affect him so powerfully. She drew her nails across his lower abdomen, wondering if—

"Enough," he growled softly, capturing her hands to pull her taut against his chest. Jocelyn could feel and hear his heartbeat, sure that he was equally aware of the racing pace of her own. "I don't wish to . . . rush things."

Nor do I.

She pushed him onto the bed, both of them

grinning at the humorous tangle of his half-opened clothes. He helped her remove his clothes, until at last she'd achieved the sight of him, naked and aroused like some rampant Greek god set in the midst of her feather bed. He reached for her, and she melted against him, tumbling into his arms. His hands smoothed over her breasts through the barrier of her dress and corset, and Jocelyn arched against him as sensual fire ignited a warm pool between her thighs, and his every kiss sent arcs of raw need through her petite frame. She groaned at the discovery that while the novelty of a beautiful naked man is titillating, the frustration induced by layers of material separating them was maddening.

"I am—overdressed for the occasion, my lord."

"I agree." He rewarded her with a wicked, bone-melting grin, and Jocelyn shifted back to amend the situation, withdrawing from him completely to stand next to the bed.

As she stepped away for just a moment, her breath came quickly and once again, his gaze sustained her and fueled her desire to please him and be pleased by him.

She reached up and withdrew the jet comb that held the twist at the back of her head. Several smaller carved hairpins followed, and she shook her hair out to let it cascade wildly down her back in a riot of fiery curls. With practiced hands from years of attending to herself, Jocelyn began to undress. But somehow the familiar ritual was anything but easy with her audience of one.

The choices we make change us. I've always said so. And now I'm transforming right in front of him, and he doesn't even realize it.

The thought made her even more bold and Jocelyn kept her eyes on him to absorb the impact of the simple act of unhooking her bodice and stepping from her gown, of unlacing her corset and revealing her body to him one inch at a time. It was a delicious blend of power and vulnerability, to strip away the last layers that would keep him from her. Jocelyn imagined that it was like a sultry dance without music as she deliberately turned and posed for him.

At last, she stood completely naked next to the bed, allowing him to take a slow, sensual inventory of her body's curves and ripening colors. His eyes met hers with approval and he held out his hand to draw her back onto the bed.

She slid into his arms, her limbs immediately entwining like vines around his and marveling at the delicious friction of his skin against hers. She loved that the disadvantages of her height disappeared as his body fit perfectly to hers. His erection pressed against her belly and Jocelyn closed her eyes against a new sharp wave of need and the anxiety of surrender.

Not surrender, she silently amended. *Conquest.*

She shifted with a laugh to gain the higher ground, and spread her legs to sit astride his hips. She surveyed the surprising sight of a beautiful man beneath her thighs, and felt a throbbing twinge between her legs sharpen to a sweet tension that demanded the loss of all rational thought and reason.

In this position, damp curls and the ripe lips of her core grazed his cock and she held her breath as it inadvertently pressed against the taut little button of her clitoris. She reached down to grip him, guiding him against the fiery, slick heat of her body and back over the exquisitely sensitive bud. He gripped her hips as she hovered over him, a slave to the pulse between them, but reveling in the power to take him at whatever speed she desired. Jocelyn's legs parted a tell-tale inch to lower herself onto him, her eyes widening at the tight sensation of his cock notched just inside her, suckled and teased by the tight, wet opening. He gripped her hips harder, but allowed the torture. "Dear God, woman . . . hurry."

"Hurry?" She laughed softly. "I thought you said you didn't wish to rush. And it's Jocelyn."

He groaned again, then whispered, "Jocelyn . . . hurry."

She worked her thighs up and down, taking just the head of him, stretching slowly, finding the rhythm again, dancing over his cock and working her hips in a lazy elipse that made him shudder and buck beneath her, sweat breaking out across his chest as he strained not to lose control. She teased, denying his upward thrusts the access he sought, but in the game, her own hunger and need overtook her. A red-hot coil of tension began to release, faster and faster until the climax outpaced her ability to think. The coil exploded against the frantic touch of his ripe head across her clit. She came in a wave of sensation, screaming with pleasure. Jocelyn tasted faint metal and salt as she bit her tongue at the strength of the spasms that radiated from her clit and pebble-hard nipples throughout her frame.

She cried out again, and he seized her. The world spun and Jocelyn found herself beneath him, the spasms of her climax still lingering and working her inner muscles. He spread her thighs, and she complied eagerly, open to him, desperate to have all of him without limitations. She was so sure that she was ready; the fleeting burning sensation caught her off guard but there was no time to absorb the pain before his intimate presence within her encompassed her entire being. There was no room for thought as he drove himself again and again into her slick core, pounding mercilessly into her until she was dizzy with it. Bright pain shifted into an ache she couldn't name. A new kind of tension at the base of her spine began to mount inside of her—stronger, deeper, and slower to build—and Jocelyn braced herself for the release, aware that an invisible tether was seconds away from being severed.

She dug her heels into his back and he suddenly held still, embedded up to the hilt inside her, and howled in triumph. Jocelyn could feel a flood of hot liquid against her core, and she clung to him as his orgasm magically seemed to demand that her body answer in turn. The tether gave way, and she threw her head back against the bliss that carried her off into a moment of oblivion.

Long quiet seconds ticked away and Jocelyn smiled at the marvelously slow return to reality. *My God. No wonder the ladies of the Belle are so busy . . .*

He raised himself up, his breathing harsh and uneven. "You were a virgin!"

"Was I?"

He pulled his fingers over the telltale trace of blood on her thighs and held them up. "I would say so. Damn it, how is that possible? Is it some trick of the trade to make me feel as if I've had my money's worth?"

"I don't know that trick, Lord Colwick." Jocelyn did her best to stay calm.

"You led me to believe you'd had other lovers!"

"I don't recall saying anything to that effect. But it would have been a natural assumption on your part."

"A natural assumption? You're Madame DeBourcier of the Crimson Belle! You spoke of the sacrifice of limiting yourself to one man," he growled. "What else was I to think?"

She sat up straight in the bed, the linen sheet pooled around her hips, making no effort to cover her bare breasts. "Why are you so angry? I would have thought the surprise a pleasant one. Men are generally so keen on being the first to—"

"How am I the first?"

"I wasn't trying to be clever when I said I didn't make appointments, Lord Colwick." Jocelyn shrugged, ignoring the blush that bloomed on her cheeks. "I never made appointments. I run the house. I never thought it was a good idea to attempt to manage things if I were too . . . close to the business itself."

The anger waned from his expression as he absorbed what she had imparted. "However did you manage to land in this business in the first place?"

Jocelyn shook her head. "I ask myself that same question sometimes. But I don't want to talk about it, Alex." Jocelyn held her ground for a moment, unwilling to share the sad tale of her mother's demise or the painful details of her childhood.

He nodded. "Very well, but you might at least tell me why I'm the first?"

"Why does it matter?" She blushed. "Does it alter our arrangement?"

"I'd have approached you differently, Jocelyn." He took her hand, her smaller, slim fingers lacing with his. "I wouldn't have been so—rough."

She smiled. "It wasn't . . . terrible, Alex."

He groaned at the pronouncement. "I deserved that. Now, allow a man to try to make amends, for God's sake."

She laughed, sweet unguarded peals of laughter that defied him not to smile. "I . . . I was teasing," she confessed breathlessly. "But if you wish to make amends, who am I to say no?"

"All right, where can I find your water closet?"

She pointed to a door a few feet from the bed, rolling over onto her stomach to watch him, openly curious. "Do I get to choose the nature of these amends?"

"No." He headed for the door, turned up the gaslights, and quickly found what he needed in the small but beautifully appointed room. He eyed the oversize claw-foot tub for just a moment, but decided it would wait for another time. For now, he hurried and cleaned himself before gathering the essentials and heading back to the bedroom and the mysterious siren who awaited him.

On the trunk at the foot of the bed, he set out the bowl of hot water and towels, then turned his attention to Jocelyn. "Let us see if we can set you right again."

Ever so gently, using the warm water and soft cloths, Alex removed the light traces of blood from her thighs and her velvet pink folds. There wasn't an overabundance of blood, but it jarred him to think of how thoughtlessly he'd taken her innocence. Not that Jocelyn necessarily fit any notion of innocence he had ever held.

She lay open for him, without any shyness, a wanton creature, but there was something intangibly vulnerable and naïve about her. She'd given herself to him so completely, holding nothing back, and he wondered at the courage it had taken. Still, he winced at the signs of bruises against the soft curves of her inner thighs. Even as a part of him offered the consolation that he probably had matching bruises on his backside where she'd spurred him on with her ankles—he felt like a bit of a brute.

Not enough of a brute to forgo another hard tumble if she wished it, a cynical part of him noted. But he would do his best to attempt civility. He wanted to win her trust by proving that he could be a tender lover as well.

The sight of her ripe ruby folds spurred him on, and once Alex had finished with the wet cloths, he lowered himself to blow a cool breath over her damp, clean skin. A blush of deeper pink rewarded his efforts and Alex decided that there was nothing better than a kiss to soothe her soft flesh. He lowered his mouth, using his tongue to tease and "heal" each beautiful fold, savoring the taste of her arousal and the sounds of her gasps and sighs. He pressed the tip of his tongue in a lazy circle around her glistening opening, purposefully avoiding the sensitive crest that began to swell in miniature protest at the omission. Her clit jutted out and finally Alex performed a dance of flickering movement around and over it, faster and faster, gripping her hips to keep her still.

"I'm . . . ," she began breathlessly, and then apparently lost her train of thought as he suckled her, his kisses deepening and the pace of the dance shifting as he deliberately strove to drive her over the edge. Her fingers gripped his hair, clutched at his shoulders, and he mercilessly doubled his efforts until she shuddered and squealed as she came against his mouth.

He lightened his touch, but kept a gentle pattern of feather-light licks on her skin until the last spasm subsided. Finally he raised his head, enjoying the sight of his new mistress so completely undone. "There. Feel better?"

"What of . . . you?"

"I don't wish to hurt you," he told her softly, climbing back up to hold her against his chest, breathing in the jasmine scent that clung to her long copper tresses.

"Then don't," she whispered, and reached down to caress him until his cock began to harden again. Jocelyn kissed him as she guided his cock ever so slowly back into the slick, molten confines of her body.

Shock and fatigue gave way to her brazen invitation, his body finding a renewed strength and desire he'd just been about to explain to her was unlikely. Alex entered her slowly and reverently, feeling her inner muscles grip and release him with each deep, slow stroke, milking and working his sensitive length until his body shuddered at the sweet, dark agony of it. The sensations hovered on the line between pleasure and pain, his erection feeling so heavy and hot that it took his breath away. He came again quickly, the climax harder, shaking him to the core and pushing him past his limits to lose all sense of the world beyond the bed they shared.

Alex reveled in the sensation of floating blissfully as every muscle in his body relaxed. The sheen of sweat on his skin cooled in the night air from one of the small garret windows. He scanned the languid beauty at his side, then noticed a small brass-framed photograph on the vanity table beside her. The woman in the photograph was laughing, the sparkle in her eyes matched by the necklace she was wearing—the necklace all the more striking since it seemed to be all that she was wearing. The resemblance was vague but unmistakable. "She's beautiful."

"My mother was . . . magnificent in her day." Jocelyn's eyes darkened with emotion as she traced the frame with one fingertip. "She always said that she never wanted anyone to look down on me."

"I'm not sure posing for such photographs set the example she might have wished." Alex's mouth tasted bitter regret before the last word slipped from his tongue. "I meant . . ."

She shook her head and gave him a sad smile. "You really have no talent for guile, do you?"

He shook his head. "Not with you, apparently." After a moment he said, "I could promise to make an effort, but I cannot guarantee success."

She playfully swatted his arm, her humor returning. "I think I prefer you to be honest. Don't worry, Lord Colwick. I am not so fragile that you cannot speak your mind."

He caught her hand and drew her closer. Her lips curved into a smile as he lowered his lips to hers. The first chaste touch slowly melted into a soft, sensual kiss that demanded nothing, giving instead a sweet, gentle pleasure that threatened to reignite his hunger and overtake the quiet peace that had settled between them. He slowly ended the kiss, thinking she was probably feeling a bit too tender for another round. He caressed her face, pushing back a wayward curl that clung to her cheek. "Let us always be as honest as we can with each other . . . in this sanctuary away from the cares of the world . . . and in this bed."

For a moment he thought she would refuse him, but at last she whispered back, "Yes," before closing her eyes and nuzzling against his side, her breathing becoming slow and even as she drifted off to sleep in his arms.

Alex made his way from the house in the damp, gray dawn and pulled his hat down before heading toward the coach he'd hired to wait for him. Leaving the warmth of her bed had been difficult, but he preferred not to have his absence noted at his breakfast table. God only knew what Declan would speculate in Eloise's presence just to rattle her, and he wasn't sure he was ready to expose himself to their casual banter. No, this was his. She was his and he wasn't willing to share her in any way—it was still too new.

And too awkward. Alex shook his head as he climbed into the carriage's confines unassisted. He felt like the worst kind of cad; like a groom abandoning his bride after their wedding night despite all her assurances. Her virginity still shocked him, and she had never really offered an explanation of how such a thing was possible.

What have I gotten myself into?

"My lord?" the coachman inquired.

Alex flinched, aware that he'd let himself drift. "Home."

None of it mattered, he chided himself. They had an honorable agreement between them and he would be ten thousand pounds lighter in his pockets within hours to prove it. Besides, there was an even harder truth to deny.

He could no more stay away from her than he could fly.

Six

J ocelyn finished her bath, lingering in the steamy heat to savor the subtle and tender changes in her body. She felt oddly stretched and sore, but the ache between her legs harbored a desire for further injury—as if the only cure was Alex's return. It had been so much more than she'd expected, and Jocelyn marveled at how strange and wonderful it was to realize that there was so much more yet to experience. She'd awoken alone, which hadn't been a complete surprise. Only realizing that she already missed his heat next to her had been startling.

"I am a wanton woman, after all," she whispered to her reflection, and then laughed. It was more than a little humbling to realize how much she'd guessed incorrectly about the acts of love.

Apparently, living in a bordello, surrounded by sex, hadn't made her any less of a virgin. A part of her had assumed that her innocence was long lost, emboldening her to keep a tight hold on the reins of her authority.

Now it astonished her that she'd held the reins at all, let alone with such total panache. She smiled at the private jest, gingerly stepping from the bathtub and drying herself with the towels she'd set out. "It's a wonder they didn't mutiny those first few months—each and every one of them."

The answer was Ramis. He'd stood behind her, and their respect for him and for her dead mother had carried the day until she'd had the time to prove her leadership. Of course, it hadn't hurt that she'd been even more generous than her beloved predecessor. She'd bought their loyalty until they'd given it to her without question.

She studied her reflection in the full-length mirror in the corner and wondered at what Alex perceived when he saw her like this. Her only criticism was that she was far too short to be fashionable, but otherwise the curves and shapes pleased her. Vanity was a curse she'd never suffered from, but Jocelyn had learned from her years at the Belle that beauty was as varied as the men who sought it. She turned and glanced over her shoulder at the ripe shape of her bottom in the glass. It was a part of her anatomy she'd never paid much attention to, but Alex had made it clear by his caresses that he held a different opinion.

Perhaps I've literally been sitting on my best asset and didn't know it.

She laughed and gave up her inventory. She'd already lost too much of the morning daydreaming, and there was a great deal to be done before the evening's guests arrived. Jocelyn selected a simple green day gown and dressed quickly before ringing the bell to summon one of the maids.

"Take these revisions down to Mrs. Brooks and remind her that the centerpiece cannot have roses. Mr. Darrington prefers lilies." She handed the menu with her notes to Ruthie to carry downstairs. "Remind Suzanne's maid to make sure everything in the room is prearranged so that he can choose her lingerie."

"May I speak with you, Mistress?" Amelia interrupted from the doorway, peering in tentatively.

Jocelyn smiled, waving the maid off on her mission and leaving them alone. "Of course, come in and close the door behind you." She rose and shifted a few cushions to offer Amelia a more comfortable seat. "How was your afternoon with the bishop?"

Amelia giggled as she settled onto the sofa in a flurry of silk petticoats next to Jocelyn. "As delightful and strange as it usually is, but how could I complain? He is always such a polite dear, never so much as brushes one pinky against me—not the entire time I'm serving him high tea and discussing his latest sermon. I mean, there I am as naked as the day I was born, and he's just an absolute gentleman."

Jocelyn shrugged, and then teased her gently, "Perhaps he's working up the courage to hold your hand."

"It's been three years, Madame. I'm fairly sure he just enjoys the conversation and the scenery." Amelia laughed, but then sobered as she approached the reason for her visit. "Speaking of time passing . . ."

"Yes?" Jocelyn waited, her curiosity piqued.

"I have been at the Belle for four years, and I've learned so much . . . you've been so generous. But you always said that if we wanted to go . . ." She took a deep breath, openly struggling for composure.

"You are always free to go." Jocelyn leaned over to touch her hand, hiding her regret at losing such a bright, sweet girl. "Without any hard feelings or difficulties. That was the promise I made, Amelia, and I meant it."

Amelia's posture deflated a degree with relief. "It's not that I'm unhappy here, but it's . . . time for me to try something else while I still can."

"What are your plans?"

"I want to see the wilds of America. And from what I hear, it is still an open country in the West, where fortune and adventure are possible."

Jocelyn swallowed a sigh. Penny novels were the source of all of Amelia's information on the wilds of America, and their accuracy was questionable. But holding anyone back from a sincere desire to follow a dream was unthinkable.

"The American wilds. It sounds . . . dangerous."

"And exciting!" Amelia clapped her hands, unable to contain her enthusiasm. "I could be anything there! With the money I've saved, I can start a little store in a small town in the West, or even become a schoolteacher."

"A schoolteacher?" Jocelyn's astonishment outran her control. "You really want to be a schoolteacher?"

Amelia blushed. "Well, I'd have to get over my fear of children . . ."

Jocelyn recovered and took Amelia's hands into her own. "You have the money to go and do almost anything. I've held it just as I said I would. And it is yours to spend as you wish. I just want to make sure that you're set on this course, but that you also know that there will always be a place for you here."

Amelia nodded, her blue eyes glowing with anticipation. "I'm young still. I want to get away while it still seems possible to have . . . you know . . . a chance to discover a place of my own outside of the Belle."

Penny novels.

"Then you shall have it." Jocelyn released her hands. "Let's see to your savings and we'll deduce the best way to get your money to America. A transfer of funds to a bank on the East Coast, and then you can move the money as you wish."

"I shall write you letters and tell you about the Wild West." Amelia sighed contentedly. "I long to see a real cowboy."

Jocelyn surveyed her charge with a rueful smile. She had heard the same tales of rugged men and the landscape of magnificent beauty that shaped their characters. Though a letter from Amelia would be wonderful, a letter from one of those cowboys conveying their impressions of an English beauty with a penchant for flowers in her hair would be even more entertaining. Rugged or not, the poor creatures wouldn't stand a chance. She only hoped the women of America tolerated Amelia's sweet, playful nature better than their English counterparts ever had. "So much for teaching school!"

"I could start a school for boys . . ."

Jocelyn smiled. "With perfect attendance and never a late lesson from a room full of lovesick boys, I'd warrant. All right, enough of that. When will you go? Shall I rush to the books for your balance or is there time yet?"

"I'll leave in three days. I don't want to linger and no fuss, please."

"A farewell breakfast, at least!"

"No. I don't want the women moping into their kippers. Better to leave on a lark when everyone's so busy, there won't be time to cry."

Jocelyn leaned back, conceding the point. "The bishop will be heartbroken."

"Gilliam will take my place. I'll show her how he prefers his pours and give her a list of his favorite topics. He'll love her, I'm sure of it."

"As you wish," Jocelyn replied.

The women rose to their feet and embraced briefly. She hated farewells and couldn't blame Amelia for wanting to skip a formal send-off. But the women would grieve her departure in either case, and Jocelyn dreaded telling them. They would worry about Amelia's fate—and their own. Whether they stayed or left, the trade marked and scarred them in so many ways that Jocelyn wondered if escape was the ultimate illusion. They could leave the house, but would their pasts at the Crimson Belle always follow?

Melancholy thoughts were pushed aside, as Amelia left the room beaming with smiles at the future ahead of her. Jocelyn sank back into the cushions to give herself a moment to regain her balance. Whenever one of the women left, it was difficult not to feel abandoned somehow.

Not to feel envious. Her spine stiffened, and she returned to her desk to go over her notes and instructions for the evening. There was no time for maudlin self-pity. There was only the reality of another day. Besides, now she had Alex's visits to look forward to. *For now, but for how long?*

She closed her eyes and dismissed the thought. This was business and she was determined to keep her guard up. How could she dread his departure when they'd only shared one night? The women of the Belle saw dozens of lovers come and go, and she'd never heard any of them complain. *This is ridiculous! You can't lose your perspective so easily.*

She opened her eyes and forced herself to focus on the papers in front of her. *It must be different your first time*, she decided. *I'll feel like my old self in no time.*

Until he comes again.

"I don't care what you say, Lex." Declan lifted his glass in a mock toast. "There's not a net in sight, but I've seen several lovely birds you might show some interest in."

The Marquess of Threxton's ball was exactly the pompously suffocating gathering Alex had dreaded, and it was all he could do not to pull a face at his friend's ribbing. Even an escape to the library, where several male colleagues gathered to talk politics and smoke cigars, was impossible so long as Eloise remained on his arm.

And well she knew it! Eloise gave Alex a triumphant smile, actively ignoring Declan while continuing her matchmaking. "Oh, look! It's the Markhams, and I believe that young lady with them is their niece, just graduated from school. She is in line for a nice settlement on her twenty-first birthday from her—"

"I said I'd attend, Eloise," he growled. "I didn't say I'd let you line up unseasoned heiresses all night long."

"Didn't you?" Declan chimed in merrily. "How's a man supposed to comfort the rejected lambs if you won't even pretend interest and break their hearts?"

Eloise shot Declan a look of pure venom before she recovered to focus on more important matters. "A dance or two won't kill you, brother dearest, but I can guarantee that if you embarrass me this evening, I may not be so merciful."

"Mrs. Wadley!" Declan whispered in a comical imitation of shock. "You'd better appease her, old man. I think she means to do you terrible violence."

"Shouldn't you be annoying a wallflower somewhere, Mr. Forrester? Or perhaps another trip to the punch bowl?" Eloise countered with a wicked smile.

Alex looked away from the pair of them, forcing himself to relax and make the best of it. It was a glittering affair and the lively noise of conversation and music should have lifted his spirits. But past the crowd, all he could envision was the quiet of a garret room and the memory of Jocelyn sitting in the middle of her bed with the sheets pooled around her hips—unashamed and beautiful, laughing with bawdy pleasure.

"There you are!" Mrs. Preston's piercing tone shattered his reverie, and Alex managed a polite smile as he prepared to "dodge the net."

Mrs. Preston beamed as she snapped her fan closed. "How delightful to find you are a man of your word, Lord Colwick!"

"Was there any doubt of it?" Eloise cooed, extending her hand. "What a joy to see you again, Mrs. Preston! Is your beautiful daughter not with you this evening?"

For one fleeting moment he thought the gods might have spared him.

"Of course she is!" Mrs. Preston bobbed her head like a mother goose, then glanced back through the throng to summon her little gosling. Declan winked at him and made a point of taking several steps back to prepare to disappear in the direction of the library and leave him to his fate. "Winifred! Come meet dear friends of mine."

The woman's voice cut a path for her offspring, and a lovely young lady in a ghastly pale yellow dress of ruffled layers appeared to reluctantly answer the call. She was tall, with a willowy figure that gave one the impression of watching a racehorse forced to walk when it would have preferred to gallop. Unlike her stout mother, Miss Winifred Preston was a graceful creature and Alex could only pray that Declan didn't choose this moment to comment on the quirks of human ancestry.

"Lord Colwick, may I present my only daughter, Winifred?"

He bowed over her hand. "Charmed."

Eloise gushed over the young lady's horrid gown and Alex began to strategize on the quickest method of getting away. But as Mrs. Preston began to boast in alarming detail about the expense and time involved in outfitting her daughter for her debut, Alex noticed he wasn't the only one casting about miserably for an escape. Miss

Winifred Preston had the look of a woman calculating to see if a faint would help.

It was a strange twist of fate. Miss Preston was exactly the sort of beautiful young woman that he was destined for—and he found her apparent dislike of the game appealing, but something in that predictable path made his heart rebel.

"I chose all her clothes! After all, I have an excellent eye for these things," Mrs. Preston proclaimed.

"Indeed," Eloise marveled, barely managing to keep a straight face.

"Miss Preston." Alex took a deep breath. "Would you care to d—"

"Wait!" Mrs. Preston hissed.

The reprieve caught him completely off guard. "What?" *Damn it. Couldn't a man just go through the motions and make the wretched evening go faster?*

The music had just ceased from the last waltz, and Alex traced Mrs. Preston's icy stare out toward the dance floor. Pairs moved off, but one couple seemed oblivious to the transition, and whispers rustled around the room like leaves in the wind. The Duke of Sussex was in no hurry to release his wife and was causing quite a sensation.

Before Alex could redirect the woman's attention, Drake looked up and noticed him. With a broad smile, he led his wife off the floor directly toward Alex.

"Randall, it's been too long!"

Mrs. Preston made a hasty retreat with a strangled gasp, and practically dragged her precious daughter through the veranda doors to avoid meeting the infamous duke and his new wife.

Some whispers never die.

Drake's previous notoriety hadn't diminished very much in the last year, instead only increasing with his unorthodox courtship and marriage. Alex fought the urge to embrace his friend for the gift of his scandalous presence. "Far too long!" He kissed Merriam's hand. "Your Grace, you are too beautiful."

"Oh, stop it!" The new Duchess of Sussex snatched her hand back and clung to Drake's arm. "I think we frightened away your friends."

Eloise curtsied, her face two shades too red to blame on the overcrowded room. "Not at all, Your Grace. I-I believe Mrs. Preston said she had to . . . get some punch for her daughter."

Drake gave her an arched look of amusement. "My God, Alex. An inability to lie runs rampant in your family."

The Duke was rewarded with an elbow in his side from his wife. Drake cleared his throat in apology. "Why don't we leave the ladies to their small talk? You don't mind, do you, Mrs. Wadley?"

"Not at all," Eloise conceded, forced to free Alex, if only temporarily.

The men stepped away onto a narrow balcony overlooking Threxton's gardens, and Alex sighed with relief to be out of sight of his sister. "God, she's as tenacious as a pit bull, Drake."

"Word has it you'll be married before the Season is out."

Alex gave him a murderous look, and Drake yielded the point. "Come now, Saint Alex." Drake laughed. "When have I ever given a farthing for what people gossip about?"

"I hate that nickname, Sotherton."

Drake shrugged, unfazed. "Only because you misinterpret it, Randall."

"For the last time, I am not a saint."

"You certainly look like a paragon of virtue whenever I'm standing next to you. After all, you do seem to strive for perfection, Alex. I never hear so much as a wisp of gossip telling me otherwise." Drake gave him a wry smile. "It would all be boring, except I'm fairly sure that most saints achieve their status by surviving notoriously prickly situations or suffering disastrous endings."

Alex sighed. "Somehow I don't feel comforted by that."

"You should. Although you may wish to avoid the part about the disastrous ending, I don't think a life is well lived until you've broken a few rules.

Damn the consequences, Alex. Wasn't it Martin Luther who said something about sinning boldly?"

"Such wisdom," Alex commented drily. "I'm sure he meant it in a completely different context than the one you're advocating."

"I'll send the Church of England a donation to make amends." Drake clapped him on the back. "I should rejoin my wife. Merriam loathes crowded rooms almost as much as I despise crowds."

"Agreed. Grant me a favor and see if you can find Declan and ask him to see Eloise home."

"You aren't rejoining the party?"

Alex smiled. "I have a nickname to live up to. Tell your wife it was a pleasure."

"I will." Drake grinned wickedly. "After all, I have a reputation of my own to support." They parted at the doorway, and Alex moved without hesitation toward the foyer to retrieve his coat and hat. *Sin boldly.*

It was the best advice he'd received in years.

Seven

I couldn't stop thinking about you."

Jocelyn smiled at the surly admission, his words pleasing her more than she'd expected. She'd found herself counting the hours since he'd left and discovering that the distractions of the Belle were no match for the memory of his touch. *Though naturally he would think of me,* she chided herself. *For ten thousand pounds, I don't think I would think of anything else either.* "It must be that potion I slipped into your drink."

"I didn't have a drink the last time I was here." He took the chair across from hers, a man at ease with his surroundings. He had pulled his evening clothes loose at the throat, giving him an elegant, disheveled look. "Did I?"

"Ah, you see? I have you completely befuddled." She teased him, marveling at how quickly his presence was familiar to her and at how naturally he became a part of her sanctuary. He stretched out his legs, and Jocelyn allowed herself to admire the lean lines of him and the latent power in his limbs and body. "Will you risk further enchantments, my lord? Shall I pour you a brandy?"

He shook his head. "I'm determined to keep a clear head."

Jocelyn moved to the ornate butler's table and poured herself a small sherry to quell a new flutter of nerves. She didn't quite understand why he still had this effect on her—after all, she'd eagerly given him her virginity. Why would she be shy of him now? "You're very sensible, Lord Colwick."

"Alex," he amended gently.

"Alex." She repeated his name dutifully, enjoying the feel of it against her tongue. "You're very sensible, Alex."

"I am nothing of the kind," he said, his look intense with a heat she recognized. "Not when it comes to you. Tell me about yourself, Jocelyn. How is it that you kept yourself a virgin?"

"How?" She gave him an arched look. "I would think the method fairly universal."

"You know what I mean." He crossed his arms, unfazed. "How did you accomplish it here?"

She shrugged her shoulders, returning to her seat with her glass. "Perhaps I was too busy. It's no small feat to manage the house, make sure the ladies are safe and cared for and that our clients' needs are well met and satisfied. I'm sure I just lost track of time."

She could tell he wasn't fooled by her nonchalant answers. But she also suspected he wasn't going to allow himself to be put off the trail. At least, not without a well-crafted distraction or two . . .

"Jocelyn—"

"Why don't you ask the real question you wish to ask?"

He unfolded his arms, openly intrigued. "And what question is that?"

"You wish to know how a virgin could have managed the house in the first place."

He smiled. "Perhaps."

"I should swear you to silence before I reveal my secrets, my lord."

He slid from the chair in one fluid movement, kneeling in front of her chair and setting her glass aside to take her hands into his. "I vow to keep all your secrets, Jocelyn."

"All of them?" she teased, her breath quickening at the sudden turn of their conversation. It was a flirtation on his part, but as she looked into his eyes, a need uncoiled inside her—a need to have a true confidant, a need to trust someone else in the world and feel safe.

"All," he echoed solemnly, and kissed her hands, then turned each over to place another, more lingering kiss on the sensitive flesh of her palms.

"Well, then . . ." Jocelyn lost her train of thought at the wicked whisper of his lips anointing the soft lined valleys of her hands. "I have forgotten the question."

"Tell me how an innocent can set my blood on fire. Tell me how you could possibly know such seductive arts. How could you have tutored anyone in acts you haven't experienced?"

"It isn't . . . so much of an art as it is a science, I think." Jocelyn stood, then drew him to his feet. "I'll show you."

He said nothing, but allowed her to lead him across the room toward her study. Another wave of shyness swept through her, and Jocelyn felt her cheeks warm with telltale color. She pulled the heavy tapestry back to reveal the hidden alcove with its floor-to-ceiling shelves, overstuffed chair, and lamp. "My secret library, m'lord. I believe you'll find that an innocent can learn a great deal—with the right teachers at her fingertips."

Alex stepped past her to enter the alcove, his hands roving over the volumes of books, openly amazed at the contents of her little study. "A library? Are you saying that Rousseau, St. Augustine, and Shakespeare provide the lessons any Madame will need to master?"

She stepped inside with him, the tapestry falling closed as she tried to think of a way to explain her miniature university in the ways of love. But his nearness made a logical presentation elusive. In the confined space, he towered over her, giving the coziness of the tiny room a new aspect altogether. She pointed toward the lower two shelves. "They undoubtedly do, but I find these texts are more relevant and . . . thought provoking."

He selected one of the slim volumes at random. "*A Concubine's Tale?*"

She took the book from him, defensively setting it back into place. "Fictional, of course, but it yielded a few interesting points. The Eastern texts are more educational, but very rare. Not all the translations are accurate, but I did my best to find reliable materials. I've found them invaluable over the years."

"Indeed." His gaze captured hers, conveying his skepticism.

The challenge in his eyes was unmistakable, and Jocelyn thrilled at the game. She leaned in as slowly as she could, closing the already brief gap between them at a torturous rate that sent her own heart pounding in anticipation. Her breasts grazed his chest as she stepped forward, deliberately extending her hand slowly toward his face as if to touch him before changing direction and retrieving a book from just behind his shoulder.

Alex chuckled and she wafted the volume past him as if allowing him to catch the scent of a flower in bloom. "Shall I demonstrate how the science works, sir?"

"By all means." He bowed, only to graze her cheek with his lips and send a spiral of desire down her spine.

"You see," Jocelyn began, wondering just how far this game could go. "The instructions are . . . quite simple. According to the Kama Sutra, the act of love is one that can be learned. One just follows the steps."

"Ah, love by the book!" He nodded, shifting to lean against one of the shelves, effectively keeping her close. "Tell me the steps, then, and let us see if your science is accurate."

She knew the passages by heart. There was no need to fumble with the pages or consider what quotes might work to her advantage. Jocelyn took a slow, deep breath to steady her nerves, dropping the book onto the chair's cushion. "Whatever is done by a man for giving pleasure to a woman is called the work of a man."

He arched his eyebrows and dropped his chin to give her a comical look of protest. "Work? I'd hardly call it work, Madame."

She laughed. "We haven't even started and already you're proving to be an unruly pupil, Alex."

He cleared his throat, the ultimate image of contrite apology. "You were saying?"

She moved past him, the friction of her skirts and bottom against him ensuring his quick compliance as she took his hand and led him out of the study toward the dais across the room and her four-poster bed. "The work of a man is as follows . . ."

Jocelyn turned to face him as they reached the foot of the bed, drawing him onto it as she continued. "While the woman is lying on his bed, and is distracted by his conversation, he should loosen the knot of her undergarments."

Her unruly pupil gave her a wicked smile that promised complete obedience. Alex began to reach for the buttons at the top of her décolletage, but Jocelyn caught his wrist. "I'm hardly distracted, sir."

"Nonsense." He pressed her gently back against the feather mattress. "I was just about to dazzle you with a recounting of my boyish heroics and had planned on including a good number of self-deprecating stories to guarantee your sympathy and admiration. There's even a bit about a puppy." As he spoke, his nimble hands continued their work, and Jocelyn giggled.

"I see. How could I not be charmed?"

"Exactly." Alex hesitated, openly taking pleasure in the progress he'd made to expose the opaque silk and lace of her chemise. "I'm loosening knots, Madame. Now what?"

"According to the text, I should begin to dispute you." She sighed, shivering as the heat of his fingers penetrated the decreasing layers of cloth to her skin. Disputing him was the farthest thing from her mind, and instead, she found herself working on the removal of his snowy-white linen cravat and shirt.

"A man does love a good argument," he whispered hoarsely, his broad hands finding the small ties of ribbon beneath her breasts. "And how should I counter?"

Jocelyn closed her eyes, determined to prove the wisdom of the ancients. "You should . . . overwhelm me with kisses."

"Is there anywhere in particular the lady wishes to be overwhelmed?"

She nodded, not trusting her voice. With her fingertips she lightly traced a soft route down her throat, across the exposed skin above her breasts and over her chemise, all the while watching his reaction and the fiery heat that grew in his eyes. She drew her hand back over her collarbone and then upward to her lips, lingering there for a moment until she trembled in anticipation.

His lips lowered to kiss her skin through the sheer silk covering her breasts, the moisture of his mouth scorching the tender skin between them, trailing up to her bared shoulders and the sweet taut lines of her throat as she arched against him. At last he captured her mouth with his, savoring and claiming her kisses until Jocelyn was sure that the bed had begun to spin.

"And?" he ground out softly between ragged breaths that betrayed he was as lost as she.

"A-and?" She kissed his throat in return.

"Are you . . . overwhelmed?"

Oh, dear God, yes. "I-I'm sufficiently flummoxed. Yes."

He kissed her again, deeper and harder this time, drawing from her touch and taste a myriad of sensations that Jocelyn couldn't control and made no effort to stop. They were the kisses of a conqueror and she reveled in them, aware that there was nothing she wouldn't give him now. Nothing she wouldn't do.

"And?" he asked again.

One of her hands dropped to slip beneath the waist of his trousers, finding him already stiff and swollen. "When you are erect"—she accented the quotation with the tightening of her fingers around him, stroking the hot column of his cock and making him gasp—"you should touch me with your hands in various places and gently manipulate various parts of my body."

He shifted his weight to hold her still for a moment. "Would you . . . care to be more specific about these various places and parts?"

She laughed, another delicious coil of anticipation snaking down her spine. "The text doesn't say. But perhaps I can guess." She released the warm, firm column of his erection to stretch her hands above her head, offering herself up for the pleasures to come. "We are wearing too many clothes."

"I shall do my best to remedy the situation, Madame."

Layers of clothes were shed as he easily managed the hooks and buttons, his hands igniting trail after trail of sensual paths along her skin under the pretense of obedience to her instructions. He shed his own clothes in a similar rush, and Jocelyn gasped at the stark male beauty of his body hovering over hers.

"And?" Alex pressed one small kiss against her bare shoulder. "Your guess?"

Jocelyn licked her lips, every sensitive "place and part" of her body screaming for his attention. "It would seem . . . logical . . . to . . ."

Logic disappeared as he slowly lowered his mouth to hers with a knowing smile. "Say it, Madame."

She felt a surge of power and confidence. *He*

is playing the student. I am the teacher. I can have whatever I want—and I want this! "My breasts, my stomach, my legs, my thighs—but most of all, Alex, I want you to touch me here." She guided his hand to the slick, soft flesh between her legs, parting her thighs so that there was no part of her he couldn't feel. Swollen pink lips throbbed at the sweet friction, and she pressed his fingertips against the firm little bud that sent electric pulses through her entire body whenever he moved.

"I will . . ." His breath caught in his throat, desire choking him for a moment as she began to buck and moan against the friction of his slick fingertips. "I will do my best."

His best was a gentle and relentless campaign to discover a dozen ways to make her cry out with pleasure, until Jocelyn wondered what woman was making all that noise, only to realize she'd forgotten herself in his arms. He "manipulated" her as she'd commanded, then withdrew before she could peak—teasing her by skimming his hands lightly over each curve and indent of her body, then pressing and pinching, encircling and caressing until Jocelyn was sure she would faint.

"Alex, please!"

His fingers raked the damp curls above her slit, then finally returned to the wet, tight core to finish his "work." His cock nudged the slick heat of her thighs, but he denied her silent pleas as her hips bucked against him, begging for his body to enter hers. Instead he used only his hands and lips, following her science with a precision she knew he was using to drive her over the edge.

Her nipples pebbled as his mouth closed over them, circling one sensitive peak just as his hand slipped down over the curve of her stomach to find the soft, wet curls between her thighs. His fingers delved into hot flesh, dripping with her body's open declaration that she was ready for him—that she needed him. Jocelyn felt her inner muscles tighten against his fingers as they entered her, strong, probing caresses that her body seized and suckled in greedy spasms, eager for more of him.

When his thumb shifted back and forth over the hard little button of her clitoris, Jocelyn was sure that she might forget to breathe—her climax seemed so close . . . just seconds from—

"And?"

She screamed with frustration and bit him on the shoulder as his fingers rose from her flesh and he froze in place, awaiting her next instruction. "Alex!"

"May I remind you that this was *your* idea, Madame?" He ignored the punishment and gently kissed the curve of her ear.

Dratted man!

"You should . . ." she arched against him, involuntarily trying to guide his fingers back to their delicious labor, even as her brain scrambled for the next step. "You should do whatever is fitting for the occasion."

He chuckled, and the sensation of his breath against the shell of her ear made her shiver. "You're jesting."

"No!" Jocelyn squeezed his arm. "Alex, please!"

He kissed her, silencing her protests, the warmth of his fingers spreading the silky wet folds of her body against the swollen head of his cock. "How can I refuse such an eloquent request?"

The rhythm of his fingers increased, and the pressure of his cock at her entrance pushed her beyond restraint. Waves of pleasure that bordered on pain finally broke free from her control, and Jocelyn thought she might weep at the power of her release, a dizzying spiral of fire and ice. She hit his shoulder, rewarded by the punishment she longed for with every fiber and sinew of her being. He drove into her, without mercy, and she screamed, clinging to him, her inner muscles shuddering with renewed waves of a climax she couldn't delay. She wrapped her legs around his waist, urging him to take all that he could in seeking his own release, praying that his pleasure would somehow match hers. Each stroke was marked only with the primal sounds of their coupling, the rhythm increasing its pace until she lost track of which hands were hers and where she ended. Jocelyn cried out as her orgasm gathered in intensity and strength to become a sharp, impossible ecstasy that threatened to unravel her from her senses.

His cry mingled with hers as his crème jetted inside of her, and Jocelyn felt the sweet sting of her own tears—the moment too fleeting and too perfect not to be mourned.

After she'd fallen asleep, Alex moved as carefully as he could, silently retrieving his clothes to leave Jocelyn to her rest. He disliked the ritual of retreat, but he was unwilling to wake her. She was so beautiful while she slept, her eyes smudged with satiated exhaustion from their lovemaking, the creamy lines of her body laid out for his study, the tousled tangle of copper curls begging for his touch. She drew him even in her dreams, and Alex allowed himself just a few minutes to sit on the edge of the bed and ponder the nature of sirens before heading quietly out.

Alex tried to move as quickly as he could through the unfamiliar halls of the house to beat the dawn and nearly ran over a slight figure in a ruffled negligee coming from the other direction.

"Oh, pardon, my lord!"

"Are you all right?" He hadn't actually collided with her, but good manners dictated the question, even if he was addressing a woman wearing nothing but a sheer wrap.

"Just startled, but thank you." She stepped back, then tilted her head to one side in an innocent look of curiosity. "Are you Madame DeBourcier's friend, then?"

"Yes." He smiled, liking the way the phrase sounded.

"I'm Gilly," she offered, then leaned in with a whisper. "You may want to risk the kitchen door, m'lord. Down that hall and out the back stairs. Although it's early, I understand there are a few gentlemen in the central hall at the moment waiting for Amelia and Suzanne. They may not be acquaintances of yours, but . . . Ramis said you wanted to be discreet."

"I am in your debt, miss."

Gilly curtsied and, with a shy smile, continued a short distance before entering one of the rooms. It chilled him to think how close he'd come to potentially meeting a peer. Though it was probably inevitable, Alex preferred to delay it as long as he could.

He followed her directions and found himself in the kitchen. Unfortunately, it wasn't as deserted as he'd hoped. Around a long wooden table, several women of the house had gathered to enjoy a meal, and he was surprised to note several books spread out between them.

"I liked it better in French. I don't think everything translates into English," one of them was saying.

"Nonsense! It's the translator's fault if the prose isn't working, not the language, you goose," another replied with a confident toss of her golden curls. "Carlton's a ham-fisted old prune when it comes to—"

She was cut off abruptly when one of the women spotted him and alerted the table to his presence. They each turned to study the man who had entered their midst.

"Are you lost, sir?" one of them asked, rising from the table to saunter closer.

"No, I'm—"

"It's the Mistress's friend, Jez! Leave the man be!" An older woman with an earthy sensuality intervened and actually managed to grab hold of the sash of Jez's robe to rein her in. "Sit back down, you shameless creature," she chided gently.

Jez made a dramatic show of her disappointment. "He's too pretty anyway!"

"Would you care to join us for a drink, my lord?" a younger woman offered, closing the books in front of her. "We shall all promise to behave if you do!"

"I won't!" Jez protested soundly. "And I bet Moira won't!"

"That's not true!" another girl at the table cried out, clearly the "Moira" in question.

"Ladies, I am actually on my way out. Please don't forgo your . . . debate on my behalf. But thank you for the courtesy." He tried to bow and regain his momentum toward the back door.

"You see that, Moira? He wasn't fooled for a minute." Jez sat on the table, affording the small party a lively view of her bare legs. "One look and he knows you just can't resist a man in a tailored coat."

The older woman tried again to assert some control. "Jezebel, enough!"

"Oh, please. It's not as if the man is going to mistake any of us for good little girls. Except maybe her." Jez pointed at Moira, then tossed a piece of bread at her for good measure.

Moira blushed on cue and dodged the playful missile with the skill of long practice. "I'm not a good girl."

Jez went on relentlessly. "Moira could have been quite the respectable girl and tutored rich bratlings, if she'd wanted to."

"They're just jealous," another woman said, trying to defend the dark-haired young woman. "Moira was ward to a respectable family, before—"

"Before she fell into sin and got caught receiving riding lessons from her handsome young cousins and their school friends," Jez sighed. "Poor thing! Like every woman of the Belle, she just can't seem to keep track of her knickers!"

Alex continued on his way, nodding a farewell before heading out the door. He had no wish to interrupt their meal, and less desire to be drawn into an openly treacherous conversation at another human being's expense.

A half dozen steps down the alley, a soft tug at his sleeve turned him around. Moira's grip wasn't strong enough to hold him, but the look in her eyes kept him in place. "Don't . . . think too harshly of them, my lord. Jezebel is just trying to shock you, I think. Perhaps to test your mettle."

"I wasn't judging. And her barbs weren't aimed at me, so I'd think it was your mettle she was gauging."

Moira shook her head, smiling. "I was just the nearest target at hand—and the safest." She sobered a little before adding, "She wasn't lying. I had a good life and a chance at a respectable profession. But I have too passionate a nature to have been a governess, and I don't really regret my choices."

"It wasn't for Jezebel to share your story out of hand." Moira was far too forgiving as far as he could see.

"It's in her nature to push, but underneath it all, she really is impossibly sweet."

"I'll take your word for it, Miss Moira. Tell me"—he hesitated for a moment longer—"do you often . . . debate the validity of Carlton's translations over the dinner table?"

Moira giggled. "Only on Tuesdays. We enjoy the tutors and weekly lessons, though there are occasional complaints about how we dress for classes. Madame DeBourcier insists that we attempt a small measure of decorum, if only to keep poor Mr. Richmond from fainting. He's easily shocked."

"I see. Well, thank you again and good night." Alex bowed and left her on the steps. The brisk walk down the narrow alley cleared his head, and he wondered about the ladies of the Belle. Jez was correct in that he would hardly mistake them for innocent debutantes, but their relationships within the house and more specifically to their Mistress intrigued him. Jocelyn's library had hinted at her education, but to realize that the Belle's women enjoyed literary debates on Tuesdays and weekly tutors—it was the last thing he'd expected. Each one of the ladies held a piece of the puzzle that was Madame DeBourcier, and since Jocelyn had already proven that she was unwilling to divulge much about herself, Alex accepted that it would be up to him to discover her secrets.

I keep thinking I've gathered more information,

only to realize that she's said almost nothing of her-self. She's like a beautiful living ghost that I can't really touch.

But she'd given him complete access to the house. So perhaps the ladies of the Belle were a source of information he could use to uncover more about the elusive woman who continued to haunt his every waking and sleeping moment. The women were certainly less guarded than their Mistress.

His mood lifted as he walked on. He would solve the mystery and find a way to truly reach her.

Eight

Something in silver, sir?" The jeweler held up a delicate chain accented with pear-shaped emeralds in filigreed settings. "Very flattering to a lady's small throat."

Alex shook his head. "No, not silver. I want something in autumn tones. Gold—something in gold with a show of diamonds. Something in that style, I believe." He pointed to a far more extravagant piece that reminded him of the necklace in the photograph by Jocelyn's bed. "I want to dazzle her."

"Ah!" The man's assistant perked up at the tone, bustling to remove the offending silver bauble, and handed the jeweler a tray of more expensive pieces to entice their potential buyer. "We can create a special work for you, naturally, but these designs may suit you, my lord."

Alex took his time and finally settled on a glittering drop necklace of topaz and diamonds. He knew it would look beautiful against Jocelyn's fair skin and red hair, and he could feel a tight coil of anticipation at her surprise. She wouldn't expect the gift and he wondered if she would squeal and clap her hands or just kiss him in—

"Lord Colwick?"

Alex swallowed the ungracious curse that almost sprang to his lips before he turned around. "Mrs. Preston, what a wonderful coincidence."

"My impression exactly, my lord!" she gushed. "And especially so since Winifred is with me." She stepped aside to ensure that her daughter was included in the conversation, and once again Alex had the impression that the attractive Miss Preston was as horrified as he was at the "wonderful coincidence" that allowed her mother to push her in his direction. Her reluctance made them allies, and Alex tried to give her a reassuring look.

"Miss Preston." He managed a quick half bow. "A delight."

Her mother apparently took his gruff compliment as the best of signs. "We'd come to collect a broach I had repaired. A family heirloom, you understand, and one I look forward to giving my daughter one day . . . perhaps on a special occasion such as her wedding day if—"

The jeweler's assistant returned with Alex's selection. "Will this box suit, my lord? I took the liberty of lining it with a better velvet to show off the stones." He held the gift box open to demonstrate as Mrs. Preston sputtered shock behind him. Alex wondered if the man knew how lucky he was to be standing out of reach of Alex's frustrated fists.

"That will be fine." Alex turned back to Mrs. Preston and her daughter. Miss Preston seemed sweetly unaffected by his purchase, but her mother was openly curious and displeased. "Well, I should leave you to your errand, Mrs. Preston."

"Y-yes, of course, Lord Colwick. It is . . . always a pleasure."

He made his way back onto the street, his jaw clenched in frustration. A man with any sense knew he couldn't pray for invisibility, but Mrs. Preston was a notorious gossip and worse, an acquaintance of his sister's. His only hope was that she would mistake his purchase for a gift for Eloise.

A damned extravagant and foolish gift for a man to give his sister! Alex shook his head, dismissing the idea as ludicrous. It seemed it was only a matter of time before rumors were born, and there was nothing he could do to prevent them.

Not that it changed anything. Months ago, it might have. He'd spent a lifetime following the rules to counter his father's reputation, and the threat of scandal would have been unthinkable to him. But Jocelyn was nothing he'd expected and he was determined to savor his escape from his everyday life. She was his one sweet taste of rebellion and he had no intention of relinquishing her so easily. Even if it couldn't last . . .

A few hours later, he had reached the private sanctuary of Jocelyn's rooms, and the worries of the outside world had faded as they nested together on the settee in her sitting room. It was a domestic scene that Alex imagined was echoed in countless households across the city, as they held hands and spoke of nothing of grave importance—just sharing thoughts and savoring a few quiet moments. His desire for her was like a soft, warm haze of anticipation as he lazily caressed the tension from her fingers.

Jocelyn sighed. "I cannot think when you—"

"Mistress! Another courtesan found dead! A new darling of the Jade from all accounts and—"

"Ruthie!" Jocelyn pulled her hands away from Alex's, rattled at the interruption. "How many times have I bid you knock before entering? And where are your manners when I have a guest?"

The maid sputtered miserably, "I-I'm sorry to

burst in. Mrs. Brooks heard from one of the cartmen and I was just . . ." The rest was a mumble, as the woman retreated in a fluster of tears.

"Another? Is there some danger?"

Jocelyn returned to his side, the bloom of pink in her cheeks the only sign of her distress. "Let's speak of something else. You were in the midst of describing your friend's penchant for cards, and sharing an amusing story at his expense, I fear."

He shook his head. "Not likely. Jocelyn, you have a talent for distractions, but this doesn't seem like the best time for it."

She crossed her arms, her eyes growing bright with emotion. "I can't think of a better time."

"The authorities—"

"Will do as little as they can, and no one will blame them for it." She stood abruptly, openly attempting to evade the subject at hand. "It is illegal, this business I'm in, you realize. But these aren't common streetwalkers who are being hurt, and so it is a bit more complicated for the Yard. The authorities won't wish to draw any more attention than necessary, especially if any of those women had well-connected patrons who have no desire to be questioned."

He grasped the difficulties instantly. The ironies of the shadow world that Jocelyn and the Belle occupied weren't lost on him. Courtesans openly flaunted their beauty and hard-earned privileges in carriages and on horseback on Rotten Row, but less fortunate women were regularly arrested off the streets for the same offenses. It was wealth and connections that made the difference, but the last thing the men who provided that protection wanted was to find themselves exposed in any way to scathing public judgment.

It was an irony he knew intimately—and she knew it.

"Jocelyn," he tried again, "if you or the women of the Belle are in danger, then I want to help."

She gave him a sad smile. "You are too kind. If you wish to help, why don't you allow us to pass the last few minutes of our rare afternoon together in pleasant conversation about anything else—anything, Alex, but the girl from the Jade."

He shook his head. If he'd learned nothing else, he knew she could be impossibly stubborn when she chose to be, but there was no possibility that he would simply drop the subject. "Very well. Not the girl from the Jade. What about the other? The maid said that there had been another?"

"We can forgo conversation if you wish to—"

A knock at the door cut her off and Jocelyn rolled her eyes in frustration. "Ruthie! Are you trying to plague me to death?"

A dark, ruddy, crow-faced man came through the door and this time, they both stood in reaction. His aggressive posture made Alex instinctively pull Jocelyn behind him.

"Mr. Marsh! You are unannounced and uninvited!" She bristled like a cat, and Alex's gaze narrowed to take a better measure of the man.

"Begging pardon, my lord, but Madame DeBourcier and I have some unfinished business of an urgent nature. Fergus Marsh, at your service. I'm the owner of a similar establishment, and the lady's mentor if you don't mind my saying. You must be the gent she's taken up with. Word has it you haven't been one for the fancy birds before, but then, Madame DeBourcier has always prided herself on fulfilling even the most unique man's requests."

Jocelyn's jaw dropped before she regained her composure. "You're early for this month's dose of harassment, Mr. Marsh. I could have sworn I had you in my calendar for the week after next."

"You should go, Mr. Marsh." Alex took a slight step forward, allowing his distaste to color his tone. Just the thought of such a man knowing any of his personal business made him feel ill—the reality that Marsh was in any way part of Jocelyn's world added to his disgust. "I can naturally walk you out, if you prefer."

"Not necessary, my lord." Marsh growled. "I'll come back, girl, when your guardian angel here is off rubbing elbows with his peers."

Alex lunged for the man before Marsh could draw breath to spit out one more hateful word. The man yelped as his feet left the floor and Alex carried him backward against the wall with a bruising thud. The temptation to punish Mr. Marsh for his intrusion into the rooms that had been theirs alone was very strong, but Jocelyn's grip on Alex's arm dulled his fury just enough to spare Fergus's skull a few more bumps against the plaster. "You are not to enter this house without a formal invitation, Mr. Marsh. And if I hear of you crossing this threshold without one, you'll need a guardian angel of your own to survive the etiquette lesson I'm going to provide."

Jocelyn tugged on his coat sleeve. "Alex, please."

Alex lowered Marsh to the floor and shoved him roughly through the open doorway. "Show yourself out."

Marsh scrambled to his feet, fury twisting his features. "High and mighty now, but let's wait and see." He retreated with a limp, glancing fearfully over his shoulder as he groused his way down the hallway. "You just wait and see! There's always a price to pay!"

Alex slammed the door and turned to face her. "Who the hell was that?"

She took a deep breath and he watched as she composed her answer carefully, as if a new barrier had just been erected between them and the last remnant of their intimate afternoon was destroyed. "You shouldn't have done that, Alex. I can handle Fergus Marsh. He is a miserable acquaintance and business rival, and frankly, no one you need concern yourself with."

"I shouldn't have done that? The man is lucky I didn't throw him headfirst down the staircase." Frustration threatened to choke him. "Is there anything about you I *can* be concerned with?"

"I don't think that's what you paid for, Alex. As much as I appreciate your help—"

"Damn it, Jocelyn!" Alex ran his fingers through his hair, trying to regain his composure.

"I'm perfectly safe. Marsh will lick his wounds and—"

"How can you be perfectly safe if anyone who wants to can simply barge in this room? Where was Ramis and your footmen when you needed them?"

She stiffened her spine and crossed her arms defensively. "I will speak to Ramis about this breach in the Belle's security and I am sure it won't happen again. Marsh is all bluster, anyway, and as I said, I will see to it. The Belle is my concern."

"And you are mine." He reached for her, attempting to end the conflict.

She stepped away from him, a melancholy

look softening the gesture. "Didn't you tell me that you'd promised your sister you would escort her to a party early this evening?"

He glanced at the clock on the mantel and realized that the last precious minutes of their time together were gone. He was horribly late. But to walk away and leave in the midst of everything— it rankled him. Nothing had been settled. "You aren't getting out of this that easily, Madame."

She shrugged. "Perhaps."

"I'll come back later tonight."

She nodded, holding her ground, proud and independent, and in that instant, Alex's chest ached at the sight of her. Dangers coalesced around the Belle, and yet she stood undaunted and unwilling to yield, and Alex wondered how much more his beautiful Madame kept from him.

"As you wish, Alex. I'll be here waiting."

"You're late." Eloise yanked on a thread of her embroidery, the stiff movement betraying more of her anger than the tone of her voice.

"I'll just need a few minutes to change my clothes. Inform Adams we'll need the carriage and—"

"You needn't bother, Alex." She made another blind stab at the fabric with her needle. "I already sent word that I'm suffering from an unfortunate headache, along with your regrets."

"I'm not *that* late, Eloise." He circled the room, wary of the lecture but relieved that he didn't have to face endless hours of puerile conversation and more of his sister's heavy-handed attempts at matchmaking. "We can still attend, and Lord and Lady Chambers will be flattered at your miraculous recovery on their behalf."

She rewarded him with an icy glare. "I don't wish to make a miraculous recovery."

He took the seat opposite her. "You can't be too disappointed, Eloise. If I remember rightly, you were complaining just a few days ago about Lady Chambers's habit of drinking through her front teeth."

Eloise gasped. "I never did!"

"Oh," he conceded. "It must have been Declan."

"He has the table manners of a mongrel hound," she sniffed. "And don't change the subject, brother dear. I cannot believe you would just ignore a promise to escort me to the Chambers party. For days, you've barely set foot in this house and I'm beginning to wonder what is the cause of your distracted state."

"Eloise," he sighed. "I apologize for making you miss the Chambers gathering and, I suspect, the opportunity to shove Miss Sarah Chambers into my path, but I am not about to give you an accounting of my days."

Her needle made an indiscriminate stab at the

cloth, and Alex noticed that whatever pattern she'd intended was now completely ruined. "*If* I had hoped that the lovely Miss Chambers would make a favorable impression, you aren't making it easy, Alex."

"By my absence?"

"By your . . . behavior!" Eloise bit her lower lip, openly vexed.

"All right, let's have it then, Mrs. Wadley. Before you've destroyed that pillow cover or whatever flowery nonsense you're combating over there, and I'm gifted with the damn thing this Christmas."

"I . . . I saw Mrs. Preston earlier this afternoon and she seemed . . . convinced that you had . . . that there might be . . ." Eloise's prim ire melted away to an awkward sigh. "Not that I don't wish for you to find someone, as you know, but I've heard of no one . . . appropriate and . . . oh, Alex! I'm not sure what to say."

He stood, feeling cornered and frustrated. "Say nothing, Eloise. I hardly need my own sister fueling rumors or believing the worst. My business is my own and when I have anything to tell you, I will."

She stood as well, blushing furiously. "You are a grown man, of course. I only meant to—"

"Next time I'm late, feel free to attend without me, or drag Declan along. The poor man could use a civil outing or two." Alex kissed her on the cheek. "I'm going out for the evening, Eloise."

"But—"

"Don't wait up." He left her there, with her mangled threads and unanswered questions. He'd known when he'd run into Mrs. Preston that the woman would talk, but he hadn't anticipated the incredible speed with which her tales reached his sister. He'd thought he had days, not hours before Eloise heard whispers. It was all pure speculation on the nosy biddy's part about whatever mystery woman he was buying jewelry for, but it grated on his nerves. None of the details of his arrangement were known, but Alex's stomach knotted as he remembered Marsh. Apparently, on the Belle's side, Alex's relationship with Jocelyn was more transparent, and he had no faith in the ability of a man like Marsh to hold his tongue.

In any case, his secrets wouldn't keep for long. *Damn it!*

Did he bother to keep trying to act discreetly? Or did he boldly begin to call on Jocelyn in broad daylight and with his own carriage? Alex signaled for his coat and hat, his mood darkening. It was all well and good, he told himself, to sin boldly, but Drake didn't have to live with Eloise!

Or with the ghost of his father's drunken laughter

ringing in his ears. Like father, like son, was it true? Am I fooling myself into thinking that there is any difference between us?

The carriage was already waiting, since he'd expected to be escorting his sister, and Alex made good on a quick escape—back toward Jocelyn. *And this time, I'm locking the damn door behind me!*

Nine

He'd returned sooner than she'd expected. But Jocelyn wasn't complaining. After the wretched news of another murder, Marsh's intrusion had upset her, and Ramis's fury at discovering the lapse in the house's security hadn't helped to soothe her nerves. Ramis had blamed her current liaison with Lord Colwick, sure that the footmen were too used to turning a blind eye to a male visitor to her rooms that Marsh must have slipped past them. She'd dismissed his theories as nonsense and been too angry to speak to him any further.

When it came to Alex, her emotions were too raw and too easily bruised, and Jocelyn had lamented the fight with Ramis—and missed Alex's presence.

His arrival had come just in time, and at the sight of him, she was sure that all things would somehow right themselves. Without a word, he'd locked the door behind him and gently pulled her from her study.

"Alex, you—"

"You read too much, Jocelyn." He moved behind her, his hands feathering caresses across her shoulders.

She laughed softly. "Are you advocating that women stay out of the schoolroom?"

He shook his head. "No, never. Not after knowing you, Madame scholar."

"What are you saying, Alex?"

"You need a teacher."

His warm breath fanned the sensitive curve of her ear and Jocelyn had to close her eyes against the wave of sensation his words triggered inside her. "I thought I'd convinced you, I am well-read on this subject, sir."

His hand reached around her shoulder and gently seized upon the slim leather volume she still held in her hands. "Well-read is not a measure of experience. Even you, Jocelyn, must know the difference."

The small book would have been an easy item to relinquish. She could have escaped his hold without effort. But moving away was impossible. The masculine heat of him at her back, the gentle stir of his breath against her hair—this was an invisible snare she didn't want to escape. Still, she tried again to speak, enjoying the play. "I've seen more than . . ."

The words dried up in her throat. The proclamation was foolish, even as a thousand confusing erotic images swarmed her mind, of everything she had witnessed over long, lonely years ruling the Crimson Belle.

He shifted slightly, using his leverage on the book to pull her back toward him. There was no mistaking the press of his body against hers, the urgent solid shape of his own need. "This lesson will require you to put the books away, my dearest friend."

She opened her eyes. *This is a lesson I will take with my eyes open.* Jocelyn released the smooth leather volume and turned, savoring the friction of her body and clothing against his. "What exactly did you have in mind, Lord Colwick?"

"It's been a long, trying day for both of us, Madame DeBourcier. Tonight we forget about your books. Tonight, I want you without following steps. Tonight, I want that wonderfully clever brain of yours to forget everything else—but me."

She nodded. "I like the sound of this lesson, sir."

He smiled, a wicked, promising smile, and

then he was kissing her, with a new tenderness that sent an arc of slow fire down her spine to pool between her legs. Instead of passionate onslaught, this was sweet torture, as he reverently grazed his lips over the contours of hers—an intimate caress that drank in her sighs, his warm breath mingling with hers. There was nothing hurried in his touch. His hands cradled her face and held her close.

Jocelyn opened her mouth, her tongue darting out to taste him, desire making her impatient, but he wasn't drawn in by the forward gesture. Instead his kisses became softer, teasing the corners of her pouting lips until she thought she'd go mad unless she could taste his tongue against hers.

"Alex, please."

At last he relented, the warm heat of his mouth against hers becoming more insistent and masterful. His mouth opened to taste her and she eagerly yielded to the glorious invasion—her tongue moving against his, an intimate feast of gentle nips and touches.

His fingers dropped to the buttons of her dress, his pace still unhurried, the lazy rhythm of his hands making her groan as a coil of need tightened inside her, slick and hot and unforgiving. She tried to help him along, but he pushed her fingers away.

"I want to do this myself, Jocelyn." He slid

the fabric back to reveal her chemise and corset. "Let's see . . . where are those hooks?"

Jocelyn stepped back, amazed she wasn't ablaze by now. "Alex, exactly what lesson was it you hoped to teach me?"

"Patience." He laughed, and then suddenly, the game of slow teasing took a dizzying turn. The fastening of her skirt melted at his touch, the ties of her petticoats, the hooks of her corset, and the ribbons of her chemise—all gone, just as her hands made an equally magical conquest of the elegant layers of his clothes. It was a flurry of material and touches, warm flesh pebbling at the exposure to the cool night air, and the only sound in the room was their laughter and sighs.

She began to reach for his erection, greedy now to have all of him, but he stepped aside and bent down to sweep her, literally, off her feet and into his arms. "Alex!"

He nuzzled her neck as he carried her toward the bed, and she shivered at the play of his breath against her skin. "I like the way you keep saying my name tonight. I like the sound of it on your lips."

"Then I'll—" She gasped as he unceremoniously tossed her onto the bed. "Oh!"

"Wait there." He left her briefly to move about the room, naked and unashamed, and Jocelyn openly lay back to admire him as he strolled to turn off the gaslights and blow out the lamps. Sinew and muscle, his raw beauty was so much more powerful than she'd expected. Drawings and illustrations, ancient prints, and even photographs had yielded enough examples of male physiology during her studies, but this. This was a masculine beauty infused with heat and desire, hard and erect; he was breathtaking and entirely hers.

For tonight.

Finally there were no lights left, except for a candle by the bedside. As her eyes adjusted, the small flame's glow encompassed the bed in a soft edgeless circle, and Alex returned, his eyes dark with need.

"What are you thinking, Jocelyn?"

"I can't seem to think of anything except that you should hurry."

"Good answer." He reached out to encircle one of her ankles with his fingers. "What a delicate thing you are . . "

Delicate? I don't feel delicate. I feel like I'm about to spring from my skin and take what I want, Alex.

Before she could summon a response from her muddled brain, his hands began to trail up her calves, over her knees, and along the ripening curves of her thighs. Her legs parted instinctively, denying him nothing, but his touch barely grazed the slick pink folds of her slit, trailing over the triangle of curls and sensitive lips before whispering over her belly and ribs.

It was heaven . . . with a delicious slice of hell, she told herself as she arched back into the mattress, writhing as he knelt between her thighs and willfully explored every inch of her body, except the few most sensitive inches that screamed for his attentions. When she tried to reach for him, he eluded her with ease.

"Alex," she groaned. "I don't . . . want to be delicate. I need . . . you, now!"

"Then we shall see about hurrying this lesson along."

He lowered himself onto her, diffusing her frustration with a searing kiss and the incredible sensation of the entire length of his body pressed against hers. After the torture of feather-light caresses, the sudden heat and weight of him was like being plunged into a river of fire. His cock notched against the silken wet fire of her flesh, and Jocelyn shuddered as her body ached to feel him inside her.

The sensitive points of her breasts tingled against the rough curls on his chest, and she dropped her head to bite and then kiss his shoulder, unable to think of a single word or phrase to urge him on, to describe what she needed, or to beg him to end it.

His mouth and hands were everywhere, but

only to stoke the pressure that was building inside of her. It was as if he could read her mind, giving her just enough pleasure to push her forward but never enough to let her gather her wits to climax. He slid a finger inside her, to work it against the ripe little ridge of her clit until she was writhing beneath him, her hands tangled in his hair or clawing uselessly at his back.

Jocelyn felt the first wave, so sweet it was painful, but before she could seize it, the world turned over completely. He released her, only to turn her over onto her hands and knees, her hips held in his grip, her hands finding the sheets to clutch as she realized what was about to happen. He drove inside her in one long, merciless stroke, deep and hard, and she cried out as her body rebelled in a spasm of shock and pleasure. He bent over her, his fingers finding her again, even as he pounded into her, his cock stretching her to her limits, her inner muscles gripping him as the momentum of her orgasm at last caught hold.

Jocelyn tilted her hips back, denying him nothing, lost in the ache of this surrender as his cock worked against her innermost core. The wet friction of him, of each withdrawal, extended each taut wave of her release and Jocelyn began to pray that she would remember to breathe at some point.

She felt him grow hotter and even harder

inside her as his own climax neared, and his cry was enveloped in hers as she came in a blinding cascade as his crème filled her.

"Well?" he asked several moments later, their breathing still a rapid staccato in the dark room.

Jocelyn felt a flutter of confusion. "Well . . . what?"

"What were you reading?" his voice rumbled softly as he pulled her close.

Jocelyn smiled in the darkness and she savored the drowsy pleasure that was kindled at his question. "A treatise on flower arrangement . . ."

As he came out onto the first floor, Alex decided that it was early enough to risk leaving via the front hall, and it would be easier to find a coach along the broader thoroughfare. He'd left a note for Jocelyn this time, but wasn't sure it made much of a difference. Jocelyn never spoke of his departures or his absences, as if the world beyond her doorstep didn't exist. Stranger to him was the realization that he was beginning to view life beyond the Belle as secondary—an inconvenient requirement that kept him from Jocelyn's presence. As he walked along the hallway, a woman's voice hailed him from an open doorway.

"Lord Colwick!" The friendly greeting slowed his steps. "Come and have tea at this ridiculous hour before you head out into the dawn."

He bowed, marveling at the appearance of a lovely brunette in a dark blue wrap in the doorway, speaking of tea at five o'clock in the morning as if it were a perfectly ordinary occurrence. "I really should be going, but thank—"

"I won't bite!" She pouted, then gave him a saucy smile. "I'm not like Jezebel, my lord. Besides, Moira said you were a perfect gentleman, and I swore to her that I'd help her make up for Jez's rudeness."

"There's really no need for that."

"You must be famished! Come sit for just a moment, have a drink and eat something before you sneak off." She winked at him. "I'm not poaching! Please come sit down for two minutes and at least let me tell Moira that I concur with her assessment of your character."

He reluctantly crossed the threshold, immediately impressed at the casual elegance of her rooms, its powder-blue satins and gold-accented furniture far grander than her Mistress's. "For just a moment or two."

She left the door open and, true to her invitation, actually pulled out a tea service and began to set out the pieces for each of them.

"Miss Suzanne, do you mind if I ask how you came to the Belle?"

The look she gave him was cynical, but with a soft edge. As if she'd heard the question dozens of times but it still affected her. Suzanne cocked her head to one side. "The truth of it would shock you, my lord."

Alex's throat constricted with emotion. The thought of any woman as victim, wounded in callous trade, bothered him. Did he truly wish to hear the tale of her fall? Was Jocelyn's fall different from this woman's? It touched too close to the bone. He didn't want to imagine Jocelyn's past. He could barely tolerate thoughts of her present life. Suzanne tapped her foot, and Alex realized he'd been drifting. He gave her an apologetic smile. "It was a foolish question. Please forgive me."

Suzanne laughed, a merry, sweet sound that eased his conscience. "No wonder the Mistress favors you. You certainly aren't like any gentleman I've met."

Alex wasn't sure of the compliment. "In what way do I differ?"

"You care," she offered without hesitation. "You're worried it might be a tragic thing or worse—that Madame DeBourcier had a hand in it."

Oh, God. It was something he hadn't considered. His spine stiffened before he could stop himself from asking, "Did she?"

Suzanne's eyes darkened, but her expression was pained amusement. "Are you mad? Or blind?" She crossed her arms, a woman giving no quarter. "I'll tell you the truth of it. Sit, my lord."

He sat on the edge of the chair, wishing he'd asked her anything else in the wide world. "I'm regretting my actions to—"

"Oh, relax." She sat across from him, waving away his protests. "It's a grand story and one I honestly don't share with most. I mean, men ask where a woman is from or to hear her sad history, but it's usually just so that they can picture the sordid details for a lark."

He drew breath to assure her, but she went on quickly, unconcerned. "But when *you* ask, I know it's to do with her. You're trying to feel your way around the obstacles . . . to understand the Mistress and to see us through her eyes." She shrugged prettily. "I'm guessing you've learned we'll say nothing of her if you ask directly. But you're asking about me to learn what you can."

"And you're not angered?"

"Why should I be? If you were pursuing just any taste, you'd have taken advantage of the Belle's many offers." Suzanne leaned forward to emphasize her point, her curves arched in a brazen invitation. "But it's clear there's no beauty at the Belle but one that holds your attention. It's a bit romantic, isn't it?"

Alex's cheeks heated, but he couldn't stop a smile. "I'm honored to provide entertainment."

Suzanne relaxed her pose, diplomatically withdrawing the unspoken proposition. "It's the least you can do. And so I'll return the favor." She smoothed her gossamer skirts across her shapely thighs and settled in for the story. "I followed my nose, and it led me here."

"Followed your nose?"

"The initial facts aren't very interesting. Large family, no real money to speak of, my father died on gin-soaked sheets."

Her tone was light and airy, but Alex wasn't fooled. He held his breath.

"Ended up in my cousin's alehouse. And before you sigh at the misfortune, I should admit I loved it there. I was coming into my own, and there wasn't a man that could keep his eyes off me—including my cousin." Her eyes focused on the memories and her face suffused with happiness at the reverie. "But it was the scents that always intoxicated me. The air was heavy with whiskey and smoke and burnt oak—not to mention sweat and men. Oh, I loved that smell!" She laughed and recalled her audience of one to give him her attention. "Not that I loved the aching muscles from hauling those trays and pitchers, or even the occasional bruise from some drunk getting a hand on me."

He released the breath he'd been holding, the hiss through his teeth betraying his disapproval of the rough handling she'd endured.

Suzanne once again waved a gentle dismissal of his reaction and continued. "Nothing more serious than a pinch on my ass, Lord Colwick. My cousin John wasn't about to see me hurt. He was always quick to yell a warning if the men were too generous with their attentions."

"John demonstrated some sense."

"Oh, bother that! He had eyes like a hawk when it came to me, and I'm no pigeon. I was a strong-headed girl with a fairly good idea that there was more to life than long days in a tavern and cold nights sleeping in the cellar."

"Go on," Alex settled back, easing into place. It was clear that like any good storyteller, Suzanne desired only his attention and not his comments. He had asked for this tale and now he would hear it, no matter how difficult it might be.

She ignored the china teapot and cups and instead poured them both drinks from a crystal decanter as she continued, an image of feminine grace that belied the tawdry nature of their conversation. "I was just biding my time, making silly prayers on my lumpy, thin pallet at night for some great change to come—some great chance to have . . . more. I was barely sixteen and I didn't know what the 'more' was, but I was restless and eager to know." She laughed softly. "Eager, there's a word for you."

"No fault in being eager, I'm sure."

"No," she agreed merrily. "But then I never look for faults. It's a wasteful habit, Lord Colwick. At least I've learned that much from my experiences." She took up her glass. "Where was I? Oh, yes. I was eager."

"Yes." He retrieved his glass and waited until she'd caught the thread of her story once more.

"I'm not sure what I'd expected, but when the chance finally came, it was—more than I'd hoped. One of the boys, Rolly, normally did the service if any gentlemen took the private dining room upstairs, but he was off in the stables having a bit of play with another of the girls. So when two gentlemen arrived one night for a bit of respite on their journey, it was all too easy to take his place."

She sighed. "I stood against the wall and watched them. So fine in their clothes, their every movement and mannerism a sleek dance I had never seen in the common room below. And when I stepped in to quietly refill a glass or take a plate—oh, the sweet smell of their rich clothes and clean skin just about made me faint."

Alex shook his head, wondering at the simple seduction of a bath.

She caught the gesture and smiled, relishing the tale now. "I was a bright-eyed bird seeing the moon for the first time. But I wasn't completely hypnotized, Lord Colwick. When one of them noticed me and bid me join them, invited me to sit on his knee and poured me a glass of wine, I knew exactly what I was doing."

"You're sure of that?"

"Oh, yes. They were men, weren't they? I knew I had no more than a slim chance of being more than an evening's entertainment, but I didn't care. I was hungry for the excitement and if a girl could choose her place and time—I chose." She took another sip, her expression nostalgic. "His hands were soft and pale, so I dubbed my lap-mate Lord Hands. And the other just watched us, with eyes like liquid amber, so in my head I named him Lord Eyes.

"I drank my wine, and smiled sweetly, and flirted and basked in the surrender to come. And oh, my! It was worth waiting for."

"Perhaps I've heard enough . . ." Alex shifted uncomfortably.

Suzanne's eyes narrowed in a playful, merciless way, a siren unwilling to end the song. "But I haven't told you how Lord Hands nibbled and teased my bare neck and shoulders until I was limp against his chest and open to any game they wished to play. I haven't told you how Lord Hands bared my breasts, his smooth hands warming my round beauties, or how his fingers worked each peak until I thought I would die until a mouth took their place, or how Lord

Eyes watched him slowly slide my skirts up until—"

"Mercy! Suzanne, please." Alex held up a hand. "A bid for mercy. I thought you'd meant to omit the sordid details."

She yielded, refilling her glass. "As you wish. I shall simply say it was a ruin that left me eager to be ruined again and again. I knew I didn't want to go back."

"Back?"

"To that thin little pallet, to the men downstairs and their endless thirst and meaty, rough hands, to a future dead end of squalid couplings behind the tavern for a few coppers—or even a respectable match with some farmer or tradesman." She raised her glass and inhaled the scent of the fine wine. "I'd caught the scent of silk and perfume, of sweet powder and oils, and of sex, of course. I was not going to give it up without a fight."

"I can't imagine it."

"It isn't hard. The gentlemen were most appreciative of my maidenly enthusiasm, and I wasted no time in begging them to take me to London. Just that far! I didn't expect a place in their fine homes, but I'd heard a girl could make her own way and earn fine things. I wasn't exactly shy in my request."

"So they took you to London?"

"Lord Hands and Lord Eyes agreed that they knew just the place for a girl with my ambitions. The horses had been changed, they'd enjoyed their 'repast,' and I think the idea of spontaneously acquiring a bit of entertainment for the rest of their journey appealed to them. I snuck away without a word of good-bye to anyone. I could describe the carriage ride in delicious detail, but you've asked for mercy and I would hate to have you think me insensitive."

He bowed his head briefly in gratitude. "Thank you, Miss Suzanne."

"I will tell you that by the time we'd reached the city proper, I had been well schooled and well used." She smiled at the memory and shook her head. "I cannot imagine the impression I must have made on the Madame's back steps. Tousled and tumbled, a newly soiled little dove, I was pleasantly exhausted and admittedly befuddled. The men hadn't revealed their grand plan and I'd half expected to be just left on a street corner to navigate my own way to the infamous districts I'd heard of. So when I landed at the door of the Belle, it was like a dream."

"They just left you at the back door?" Alex was less than pleased. "They seduced you and then just dropped you off like laundry?"

"Oh, no!" she replied, unruffled. "They knew Madame DeBourcier and went to great lengths to recommend my character and beauty. Lord Eyes even made arrangements on my behalf to fund my 'debut' at the Belle."

"Jocelyn agreed—"

"Her mother, Lord Colwick. I should be clear. It was her mother who took me into the Belle, just a few months before her death. Jocelyn inherited the Belle and the title of Madame and with it, yours truly."

"You're not property to be passed from hand to hand." He meant the words, but even as he said them, Alex knew he'd crossed a line.

Suzanne seemed to enjoy his discomfort. "No, rather I am a member of an odd sort of family. And imagine my relief when the new head of the household determined to continue to be even more generous and kind and protective than her predecessor. I do as I wish, Lord Colwick. I always have. But the Belle provides a haven, a shield, and in exchange for a portion of my income, I am free to trade and sell what I wish as I will."

He wasn't sure how to respond. He wasn't sure what tragic tale he'd expected. Instead she sat before him, beautiful and almost imperial, and completely self-satisfied.

She laughed. "I wish you could see your own face. It is a priceless expression, sir!"

"I'm at a loss."

"Are you sure you don't want the sinful details?" she teased.

He finally gave in to mirth. "No, but thanks to you, I'm sure I'll have trouble sleeping, imagining them for myself."

She leaned over to pat his hand, an almost maternal gesture of comfort. "On the streets of London and in many houses in the flesh trade, there are tragedies enough to make you weep. Souls driven to degrade themselves or simply trapped in a life of pain and surrender for the profit of others, they exist without question and in great numbers, my lord. I don't deny that. This is no carefree choice. But for many of us here at the Belle, it was the choice that suited our natures and situations. We craft a future for ourselves, and when we're ready, we'll have the choice and the means to seize that future."

"And in the meantime?"

She grinned at him, a cat anticipating the taste of cream. "Silk and perfume, sweet powders and oils, and oh, yes . . . sex, dear sir."

He retreated from the interview as gracefully as he could, only to bump into Jez in the hall outside Suzanne's doorway. She arched an eyebrow at the sight of him, openly suspicious at seeing him on the first floor unaccompanied. "Lost, Lord Colwick?"

"No, miss. Thank you."

Her gaze narrowed. A dangerous beauty, Jez gave him one last icy look before continuing on her way. Without another word, he turned on his heel and headed down the hallway toward the stairs, his mind working over the revelations from Suzanne's tale.

Her mother had been Madame DeBourcier before her. Jocelyn had been born into this life. The thought sobered him. He'd guessed as much from the portrait on the vanity and what little Jocelyn had shared, but to hear it confirmed in such an offhand way made his chest ache. *Had she been a child in this house? What would a small girl see in such a place? How had it not hardened her?*

She'd inherited the Crimson Belle from her mother. Alex shook his head to clear the countless questions that crowded his thoughts. He'd forgotten to ask how many years it had been since her mother's death, or what exactly the role of the mysterious Ramis had been in all of this. As he tried to reconcile it all, it occurred to Alex that it might take more than one or two conversations with the ladies of the house to make any sense of it all. Instead of enlightening him, Suzanne's story had only added to the confusion.

If her mother was the Madame of a brothel and Jocelyn was raised here, why would the library be so invaluable? Surely her mother wouldn't have been shy in sharing the details of her craft? Or had she meant to shield Jocelyn from it all? But then, why? Was it possible that Madame DeBourcier had held greater hopes for her child—and if she had, on what basis had she founded that dream if she'd only left her a legacy of prostitution?

It was a convoluted tangle, and Alex climbed into the back of the hired hack with a sigh. At the moment, the only truth he knew was that he wasn't sure how he could give her up in just a few short weeks.

Perhaps it's time to regain my perspective before I make a complete fool of myself. Alex shook his head at the cynical laughter that seemed to echo inside his head. *Too late to worry about playing the fool now.*

He spent every free moment at the Belle, and when he was away from her, he found himself plotting how to make his next return. He fantasized about drowning her in jewels and furs—a besotted rich fool blinded by a woman's charms.

Jez had asked him if he was lost.

I'm so lost, I'm not even sure if I want to know the truth anymore.

Ten

Jocelyn awoke in a dream of bliss, then realized that once again, Alex had left her while she slept. A folded piece of vellum on his pillow came into focus and Jocelyn simply reached out to stroke the shape and feel of it. There was no need to read it, really, she told herself. In his firm and upright script, he would no doubt express his regrets and a sincere promise to return as soon as he could.

It should have softened the sting of his departure, but it didn't—not entirely.

Jocelyn pressed the note to her chest and tried to linger in bed to sort out her thoughts. The arrangement was already more than she'd anticipated—why pluck at the threads fretting over impossibilities and childish dreams? It wasn't as if he could lounge abed with her and waste his mornings—not without his long absences drawing fire from his sister.

She knew all too well that Alex wasn't ready to risk such a thing. He'd already exposed himself to a few vague questions, she suspected, though nothing too dire or he would have confessed it to her. The look on his face when Marsh had spouted his poison had been very telling.

She sighed, opened the note to absorb the expected message, and then smiled at the small satisfaction of knowing her Alex so well. *He truly is a gentleman.*

Jocelyn pushed off the covers and abandoned any thoughts of lazing. Instead, she decided with a mischievous grin that what she really needed was a shower to clear her head. Then she would dress for the day and review the next few days' appointments.

She accomplished it all quickly, reaching her desk feeling energized, if a bit languid, after a delightfully long and healthy daydream or two in the bath of an intimate interlude with Alex in soapy splendor. Jocelyn pushed away the erotic images and opened the account books, but within a few minutes her thoughts drifted again. Perhaps there was a way to keep this happiness for a time. Perhaps a private arrangement that lasted longer than a social season. A sweet understanding in which he would be hers alone for all time. They could carve out a corner of their own, apartments in London away from the Belle, a season of travel to the Continent, where no one would even look twice or—

A brisk knock at the door heralded the intrusion. "There's a woman askin' to see you, Madame. She's come to the back. Cook tried to shoo her off, but she's determined . . ." Ruthie's eyes shone with eager concern, openly distressed to be the one to interrupt the Mistress's privacy yet again.

Jocelyn closed the leather binder, making an effort not to sigh. It wasn't like Mrs. Brooks to pass along word to her unless the matter was more serious than might initially meet the eye. "I'll come down directly and see to this."

Speculation over the nature of the woman's petition was brief as she reached the kitchens. The back door was ajar, as the cook apparently stood in continued negotiations with someone on the steps. "I've sent a maid to bother her, but all this mystery won't serve you. Tell me what you're after and I'll see to—"

"I'll tell the Mistress of this house my business and none other!"

"I am here, Mrs. Brooks." Jocelyn stepped forward to relieve the cook and take her place in the doorway. Looking out, she assessed the woman who seemed unkempt and haggard. Her dress was worn and the seams frayed, though the style had once been very chic. Her bones announced that times were hard, and her age was difficult to determine, as she bore the stamped lines of hunger on her features. "I am the Mistress of this house. How may I help you?"

The woman looked down the alley behind her, as if to make sure that no one had followed her or was watching. When her gaze returned to meet Jocelyn's, her eyes were full of tears. "I would speak with you more privately. Please."

"As you wish." Jocelyn stepped aside to welcome her inside.

With just one more furtive look behind her, the woman entered as bid. Jocelyn led her over to the kitchen table and offered her a seat. "Would you like some tea? Something to eat perhaps?"

The woman nervously took a seat but shook her head. "No. Nothing."

Jocelyn sat in her chair, her curiosity growing. "Not to rush you, but your business? My maid said it seemed urgent, madam."

"Y-yes," she nodded vigorously, openly struggling to select her words. "I am not one to ask . . . favors. Especially of strangers, but I have thought long and hard . . . prayed even . . . and I can't see another way."

Mrs. Brooks gave Jocelyn an arched look from

behind the poor woman, which Jocelyn did her best to ignore. "A favor?"

"My husband's gone. All my letters to family have been returned unopened or gone unanswered. I shouldn't have married him. They never approved and I'm already dead to them." Her tone was low and almost without inflection, as if she were in a trance. But her words betrayed an education, making Jocelyn wonder just what her background might have been. Still, momentum carried the woman's speech forward. "I'm left with six children and now I am . . . at a loss. Work has been . . . difficult and I am struggling now after falling ill. My oldest died in a mill, and the littlest ones are sick. But if I can save one . . . you can see why I had to come."

Jocelyn reached for her, gently touching her arm. "I'm not sure I understand, but you have all my sympathy for your losses. Perhaps we can send some food home with you today, something for your children."

Tears welled in the woman's eyes. "I can't refuse the gift, but the favor I ask . . . it is my daughter, Edith. I-I want you to take her."

"To take her?" Jocelyn forced herself to be still, icy dread intermingling with sadness.

"I know what this house is. I know what I'm doing. You think me heartless, but she'll have a roof over her head, warm food, care, and good clothes. She won't be lost to the hell of the workhouses or forced to degrade herself on street corners."

Jocelyn bit her lower lip, but then composed herself. "There are other choices."

"No, not really." Her resignation was palpable. "Edith is pretty, with good skin. She is very clever, quick to learn, and obedient. She'll be no trouble, I swear it."

"How old is she?"

"Thirteen."

Will there ever come a day when an interview like this is easy for me? "She's young for the house. We don't use children here."

"Train her as a maid, then, until she is old enough! Please . . . I would know that she . . . she will never go hungry."

Jocelyn glanced toward Mrs. Brooks, who was looking on, wide-eyed and anxious. The cook had already been packing a basket of bread and foodstuffs after overhearing the woman's plight, but this turn held her in place by the stove. The nature of their world was not to be denied, but the tragedy of this mother's choice wasn't easy to hear. Still, Jocelyn had to push her to be sure. "And if we refuse her? Are you sure she cannot just take a position in service in a respectable residence? In the shops?"

"Without references? At her age? She is too old to start service and I've spoiled her for the work. She has no real talent with a needle and I can't afford to set her up. She's growing fast and I can see the attention she's drawing already from the local boys." Her gaze lowered to the table. "If you refuse her, then . . . I'll . . . turn her out."

It was potentially a hollow threat, but Jocelyn felt its sting. Even if this woman didn't turn her own daughter out onto the streets, it was clear that her desperation was very real.

The woman went on. "I come from a good family. Edith has some of that." Her voice was bitter. "Good bones and good manners—at least that much I could manage to give her."

"Can she read?"

"Yes!" A small flash of pride restored a bit of the woman's long-lost beauty. "She even has some Latin. I saw to that myself."

Jocelyn took a steadying breath. These requests were not unheard-of, and if she accepted every mother's pleas, the Belle could be overwhelmed into a foundling home before long. She'd turned others away, and spent nights crying at the cold reality that swirled around the thin barrier of the Belle's brick walls. But now she wasn't sure she had the heart for it. What was a haven if she became as unfeeling as everyone else who refused this girl, or worse, as those who would happily prey on a child's innocence? But what kind of sanctuary promised a child a very limited future? The Belle was hardly paradise.

Jocelyn sat back, feeling every bit the judge passing down a weighty decision. "You said you'd spoiled her for work, but you expect me to take her into service as a maid."

"Please—"

"She is too young for the house and I do not trade in children." Jocelyn swallowed hard before continuing. "Let me finish, please, madame."

The woman nodded as hope drained from her eyes.

"But, if Edith is, as you say . . . a quick learner and clever, perhaps she will understand that hard work is not a terrible thing. She can train as a housemaid or assist in the kitchen. In return, she will get a fair wage and also receive schooling with the younger women. We hire tutors on many subjects, including French and Italian, along with history and composition, and whatever else seems useful. If she studies hard enough, she may acquire enough skills to leave the house to teach, or to do something else—perhaps she can find another honest trade."

"Bless you! Bless—"

"We don't force anyone into the life." Jocelyn

stood abruptly, unwilling to accept a mother's gratitude for this "gift." "But do not fool yourself. The temptations of the Belle, the things she'll be exposed to—I cannot shield her from it all. I can keep her from the working floors and our guests for a time, but only for a time. If she is, as you say, pretty . . . then when she is older and if she is inclined . . . This isn't a boarding school. There are lessons she may learn here, that cannot be taken back."

"I understand."

Jocelyn sighed. "I'm sure you think you do. I urge you to sleep on it tonight. If you're still sure, then bring her tomorrow morning after ten."

The woman stood and with trembling hands took the heavy basket full of goods from Mrs. Brooks. "I'll bring her."

They walked to the door, and Jocelyn caught her arm. "If your situation improves, you can always come to retrieve her. I don't enslave women. If there is any other way, please take it."

The woman couldn't look her in the eye and moved to take her leave. As the door latched behind her, Jocelyn stole a moment to gather her thoughts.

"Taking in strays," Mrs. Brooks spoke softly behind her. "Just like your mother."

The comment made her smile, but also made

her feel even sadder. There was something inevitable about her life, and she hated that sensation. Still, the decision was made and she fully
expected to get a crying child delivered to her
back door in the morning. She turned back.
"Her mother may yet find a solution and perhaps we'll just have time to teach the girl a few
useful housekeeping skills for a better position
elsewhere."

Mrs. Brooks's look was pure skepticism. "As
if any respectable house would touch a girl once
she'd been in this house."

Jocelyn crossed her arms and gave the woman
a blazing glare of disapproval.

The older woman colored at the silent reproof
and attempted a more jovial tact. "Edith sounds
like a sweet thing, and I could definitely use an
extra hand feeding this crew."

Jocelyn's chin came up. "Yes." Her humor
began to return. "Now I just have to tell Ramis he
has another charge to keep an eye on."

Mrs. Brooks laughed at that and turned back
to her preparations for lunch. "Better you than
me! That tiger will growl to make the walls
shake when he hears about this."

Jocelyn ignored the gibe and returned up the
narrow back stairs to her own cozy quarters.
Ramis's reaction was the least of her worries. He
would growl, but only as a protective cat learning

she'd taken in a completely helpless kitten. But he wouldn't oppose her decision. They'd been allies for too long for her to fear his opinions. Any addition to the house had its risks, but she was fairly sure one small girl wouldn't be too great a misstep.

As if any respectable house would touch a girl once she'd been in this house.

Mrs. Brooks's words echoed in her mind and Jocelyn shivered at the ghosts of lessons learned. She was right, of course. Jocelyn could stomp her feet and glare all she liked, but the woman's words were nothing short of the truth. Her own mother had meant to protect her from the taint of the Belle and keep her from its curse.

To no avail. Once I crossed the threshold of that doorway, there was never any going back.

The fanciful thoughts of the morning and a future with Alex seemed brittle and beyond foolish now. He was an honorable man and his reputation was as important to him as any land or fortune. It was one of the things she loved about him. Jocelyn froze in her tracks.

I can love things about him without . . . loving him. She grimaced at the weak denial, but lifted her chin as if facing an invisible foe. *None of it matters and I'm too old to play the fainting miss now. He's purchased my time, my body, and my attentions—not my heart! He is an interlude, a distraction, and a means to an end. And when he returns to his respectable life, I'll have money enough to ensure the Belle's survival and my own.*

"This is the real world, Jocelyn Tolliver," she lectured herself aloud. "And when you start to forget, just ask Edith."

Eleven

Polite applause echoed throughout the theater, and Alex did his best to join in as he shifted in his chair to relieve a stiffness that had settled in his shoulders and neck. He only hoped his sister didn't quiz him regarding the plot, since his concentration during the play had entirely been taken up with thoughts of Jocelyn. He'd felt a twinge of guilt for ignoring his own household affairs these last few weeks. This outing was a small concession to Eloise, and Alex looked over to see how she was faring.

Declan was less inclined to play along. "Is it over? I swear my legs went numb ages ago!"

Eloise responded by clapping harder. "No doubt you'd have enjoyed it better if the actresses had failed to wear clothes."

Declan brightened. "Now, there's an idea! I'm sure it would have made the plot more interesting."

Alex rolled his eyes as they gathered their things and prepared to leave the box. "Enough, Forrester." The opening night's performances hadn't been spectacular, but he knew his sister wasn't in the mood for a critical debate. She'd made it clear that she was pleased to see him in "good society" once again. She'd committed him to a gathering later this evening at Lord Andrews's for cognac and gossip, two things he despised, but he knew the gesture would buy him some peace. Alex retrieved her opera glasses. "Shall we go?"

"There's a reception downstairs with the company, and I was hoping we could make an appearance." Eloise adjusted her satin wrap, patiently waiting for his response.

Declan chimed in, "I'm all for stretching the legs a bit before we climb into a carriage. Besides, these actors are bound to be more entertaining without all those lines and foolish musical numbers to hinder their natural charm from coming through."

"Declan, behave!" Alex chided, a grin giving away his sympathies. He held out his arm for his sister, and the trio made their way downstairs to one of the salons on the first floor where the party was being held.

It was a lively gathering for an opening night's celebration, and champagne was already flowing as the elite patrons mingled with the artists and performers. After a round or two of cocktails, Alex wondered how much longer he could muster a polite smile. Especially later at the notorious Andrews's home, where he'd seen more than one man go pale at Lord Andrews's sly revelations and cutting tongue. If Mrs. Preston had said anything of the necklace, it wouldn't surprise him if—

"Dead!" A loud whisper caught his attention and ended his internal speculations. Alex took a subtle step closer to a pair of dowagers to eavesdrop and catch what he could of their conversation.

"Look at the poor man! He's a gray-faced wreck and who can blame him? To have his pretty little mistress found so cruelly murdered! The scandal . . ."

"A reporter was said to have made note of the connection! His wife will have him flayed alive, but still—to have to suffer like this."

"Invested in the play to please her, I heard! And now, there he is, completely despondent with such news on opening night and not a kind word from anyone."

A gasp of shock answered the complaint. "And what would one say? Excuse me, Baron, but I'm so sorry your whore was murdered on the street? Don't be a fool!"

Alex moved off, his mind churning with the possible meaning of this exchange. It had been a few days since the last crime. Was this the same one and the news had only just reached her titled lover? Or did they refer to a new girl who had fallen into the wrong hands and lost her life?

Alex looked across the room and caught sight of the unmistakable object of their vicious whispers. He'd met Lord Ruskin only once before, retaining an impression of him as a disciplined man. But the man across the room looked lost and somehow broken. His complexion was sallow, his eyes meeting no one's as he clutched his glass and sat against the wall.

He must have just heard. My God, did someone take pleasure at telling him publicly to enjoy the scene he might make?

Worse, another idea nested with icy-cold wings inside his chest. The idea that he could just as easily be that man against the wall, that the women hadn't been specific—what if it were one of the Belle's dear birds? Or even its beautiful reclusive Madame?

He located Eloise easily and was relieved to

see Declan close at hand. He gave Declan a single look and knew that his friend would back him without question. "Eloise, something has come up. I'm afraid I shall have to ask Mr. Forrester to see you home once again."

Eloise tried to dig in, clutching at his arm, but lowering her voice for fear of drawing attention. "Alex, this is unacceptable! You cannot just abandon me on a whim! And to . . . foist me off on Mr. Forrester—again!" Her cheeks flushed with anger. "We're expected at Lord Andrews's. You promised to attend his party."

"Did I?" Alex ground out, unwilling to give in. "I don't remember making such a promise, and even if I did, I'm sure Lord Andrews will accept my sincere apology."

"Your apology?" she echoed in disbelief.

"You'll convey it to him, won't you?" He kissed her cheek and turned on his heels without waiting for her answer, then headed for the grand staircase leading down to the ground floor.

Alex refused to name the vague anxiety that hurried his steps. He had been to the Belle just two nights ago, and there had been no new signs of unrest or danger. Two endless days and nights without her in a perverse effort to prove that the life beyond her rooms could still hold him. He'd meant to regain his balance and perspective, but now he felt like a fool. He'd wasted two precious days distracted and irritable, and potentially missed being there to protect her.

He hailed a hackney and gave the man an extra coin for speed.

"I just heard."

Jocelyn looked up as he entered the room without preamble, looking a bit wild and unsettled, his gaze intense and inscrutable. She untucked her legs from beneath her and slid off the cushions to greet him. "Heard what exactly?"

The question seemed to slow him down a bit, and Jocelyn watched in fascination as his demeanor changed from a warrior braced for battle to that of a polished gentleman becoming aware of every nuance of his actions' breech in etiquette, as he realized that she wore only a turquoise silk wrap. She could almost guess at his thoughts. *Almost.*

"I heard that there'd been another murder."

Jocelyn stiffened, but shook her head. "No such word has reached us here. Where? Which bordello?"

"To be honest, I don't know. I thought . . ." He held still, his thoughts apparently taking a new abrupt turn. "It must have been the same one . . ." Alex's shoulders relaxed, a slow breath betraying his relief. "I can't imagine you would be the last to know if another girl had been found."

Jocelyn nodded. "It's true. We've been even more generous lately to our informants to keep us from being surprised with any more bad news."

She came closer, reaching up to cradle his jaw with her fingers. His concern and relief were a marvel to her. That he would care, that he would rush to be at her side—Jocelyn wasn't sure what to make of her handsome lover. He'd paid a small fortune to guarantee her attentions, but his attitude hardly reflected it. He didn't approach her as if she belonged to him, but instead as if her mood and opinions mattered. Then he'd stayed away, she suspected to simply prove that he could, and now his sudden return made her feel dizzy and deliciously unsettled.

"It's been too long, Alex," she whispered, hoping he wouldn't take it as a scold. For all her talk of science, she had avoided the library since he'd last "tutored" her, the images and texts only fueling erotic daydreams that failed to satisfy her newfound desires.

"You aren't dressed."

"I was about to take a bath before retiring." She deliberately fingered the wide embroidered sash at her waist. "Should I change my plans, my lord?"

His eyes blazed with a renewed heat at her words. She shivered at the sight, anticipating the pleasure to come. He shook his head, slowly drawing his fingers through the loose curls that had fallen over her shoulder. "A bath sounds . . . heavenly."

He took one of her hands and led her through the door to the bathroom, drawing her to the center of the room. Without speaking, he gently pushed the silk robe from her shoulders, letting it fall to the floor.

Jocelyn's breath caught in her throat as he stepped back to survey her body, his eyes openly lingering on the lush peaks and curves of her breasts and stomach, skimming over her thighs only to return to the thick, damp curls at the juncture of her legs. It was as if just by looking, he marked her as his and laid claim to every inch of her skin. The appreciation in his eyes made her bold.

He likes what he sees, and I . . . I long for him to look at me.

Sitting on the wide rim of the claw-footed tub, Alex turned on the water, adjusting the knobs and heating the water to fill the bath, even as she stood waiting, the cool evening air marbling her skin and making her nipples harden into jaunty, sensitive points. For Jocelyn, the sensation was delicious. Steam rose from the porcelain tub, and Alex trailed his fingers beneath the surface to ensure it was just the right temperature for her before he shut off the necessary valves.

He held out his hand to help her climb into the tub, then shifted so that both of his hands splayed over her hips to keep her standing in the now knee-deep water.

"Are you to wash me, then?" she asked warily, eyeing his lovely coat and crisp attire. "You'll spoil your—"

He nodded, and without taking his eyes from hers, he knelt to retrieve the soap from its dish. "It doesn't matter."

He lathered his hands, then ran them up the outer curves of her thighs, massaging up to cup the curves of her bottom before he leaned in to kiss the plump pink lips of her folds. She gasped in surprise, gripping his shoulders for balance, only to experience the whisper-sweet pass of his tongue into the tender peak of her skin before he withdrew to press his face against the soft mound of her stomach. His breath was hot against her belly, and his hands continued their trek across her skin to smooth circles of lather upward and upward. Her thighs trembled, and Alex dipped his hands into the hot water to splash the warmth up to her lower back and down in rivulets that mimicked his attentions.

Again he soaped his hands, this time ministering to her stomach and then upward to cup each breast, his slick palms teasing the orbs as they

worked the scented soap against her. His fingertips danced over the pert coral tips, the lather
making each touch more potent and teasing.
Jocelyn's breath came faster at the game. He was
touching her, but through a barrier of slippery
bubbles in a maddening pleasure that threatened
to make her knees go numb.

"Alex!"

She was coated in lather now, his thorough attention missing no curve or crevice of her body,
until she thought she would cry from the sweet
tension that began to mount within her. Dousing
her with water cupped in his hands, he sighed,
stealing quick kisses and gentle nips where she
least expected them.

"I love that you don't try to hide your body
from me. You cannot know how incredibly powerful it is to see you like that."

"Powerful?" Jocelyn savored the word. "What
a world of temptation comes with that word! It
makes me think of being a tyrant and commanding you to do my bidding."

"Try it." The challenge hung in the air between them, and Jocelyn assessed her opponent.
There was nothing submissive or weak about
Alex Randall. But he'd invited her to attempt to
wield her newborn power, and the very thought
of conquering him made her thighs slick with
hunger. He stood before her, his elegant evening

clothes impeccably tailored to accent his broad shoulders and long, lean lines. Every detail of his dress bespoke his station, a confidence emanating from him that made her want to see his reserve stripped away.

She deliberately slid down to sit in the water, lounging back like a sultana in the long claw-footed tub, the water clouding from the soap on her body and giving him only elusive glimpses of all he desired.

"Undress." The command came easily to her lips. "I would see your body as well. Unless you wish to hide it from me . . ."

He smiled as she used his words against him, but complied easily enough.

He began to undress, slowly, lingering over each button until she thought she would jump from her skin. To hide her impatience, she knelt into the bath, stretching her legs like a tigress to make a show of pretended indifference. "You're a tease, sir."

His clothes were shed at last to join her wrap on the carpeted floor, and Jocelyn was finally free to look her fill. She was sure it was a novelty to have a man submit to such a study. Her eyes eagerly roamed over him, admiring the strong lines of sinew and muscle, openly pleased at the sight of his huge erect cock defiantly jutting toward her as if to demand her attention. Her lips parted in excitement as his erection seemed to jerk and bob toward her—as if this part of him had no intention of being ignored.

"And?" Alex demanded, desire making his voice rougher and sending a delicious thrill down her spine.

She stretched out one foot, caressing his thigh and grazing his manhood before pressing her toes against his right hip bone. "You missed a spot."

He arched an eyebrow in surprise, but moved to do her bidding. Again, he soaped his hands so that he could attend to the errant foot she proffered. His strong fingers worked the sinews and muscles of her foot, pushing against the places that ached from a long day and finding each point that would make her gasp and sigh. Every toe received attention, and he gently labored up her calf and then back down to encircle her ankle until she was sure she would melt from the glory of his touch. The exercise seemed all the more decadent, as she was the only one who could receive pleasure from it. But his arousal never wavered, and Jocelyn realized that this act of service was making his blood even hotter.

He bent down to retrieve her other foot, and Jocelyn gripped the sides of the tub so that she could comply without sliding too far into the water. Alex continued his ministrations, balancing each stroke of his hands to make sure that neither slender foot felt slighted by the other. Jocelyn leaned her head back against the porcelain, marveling that such sensations existed in the world as the hot water and silky lather swirled around her and his hands worked their magic.

"Is the tyrant pleased?"

"Impossibly so," she conceded. "I shall have to give you the ultimate reward."

"And what reward would that be?"

"To do what you will." She gave him a wicked smile and leaned further back into the water, lifting her own breasts to touch them as he had earlier.

"What sort of tyrant are you?" he asked softly, releasing her feet from against his abdomen as he stepped into the tub, straddling her with his thighs.

"The kind who knows when to delegate," she jested, giggling at the beauty of her scheme as every bit of him was now well within reach. Jocelyn tried to repay him in kind with soapy hands across his muscled abdomen and back, but Alex moaned and caught her hands to bring them both to cradle his taut shaft. She stroked him, instinctively playing off of each intake of his breath and sound he made as she worked the magic of her eager fingers against his thick cock.

"Damn it," he muttered, and Jocelyn realized

she had pushed him too hard for any more delays. Without tender preamble, she was lifted from the water only to find him positioned behind her as she braced herself against the wall, gripping the pipes for balance as his hands held her hips to align his swollen head against her tight, saturated opening. A single heartbeat counted the time it took him to achieve her. She cried out as her body took in every inch of his invasion, welcoming the fiery length of him into her innermost core.

She moved against him as he plunged into her in a primal rhythm that made her blood sing. A familiar coil of tension began to mount inside her and Jocelyn welcomed the release to come. But before she could achieve it, one of his hands moved across the round halves of her bottom, then shocked her by slipping inside the valley of her flesh, circling her tiny pucker with one soapy finger before pressing into her, slick and firm, to touch her as she had never thought to be touched. She would have protested but for the mindless wave of ecstasy that robbed her of speech and logic.

It was a surrender like no other.

Her orgasm was so intense, she had a fleeting thought that when the French called it the "little death," they apparently didn't mean it in the poetic sense. With her orgasm, her knees gave out, and she was sure she would have fallen if Alex's grip hadn't been so sure and strong. She lost track of everything, only vaguely aware that he was carrying her out of the tub to lay her out on the carpeted floor, her silk robe beneath her, and Jocelyn sighed as the room spun around her. But Alex was there, a solid fragment of heated flesh she clung to, even as he spread her thighs to press his shaft against her overripe, sensitive folds. Wet, silken flesh gave way to the rock-hard pulse of his need, and Jocelyn arched against him as he drove into her body in one slow, merciless stroke.

And then there was nothing she could do but give in to the relentless slippery friction of his cock buried to the hilt inside her, urging him to do it again and again, harder and harder, deeper and deeper, until she couldn't feel where he ended and she began. Her muscles seized him, tightening with spasms of another climax that sent her spiraling over the edge of control. The world shrank into nothingness and Jocelyn welcomed it with a cry of triumph, with Alex's shouted release echoing in her ears.

Long moments later, they lay together wrapped in quilts and Jocelyn savored the hypnotic weight of her own satiated limbs, beginning to drift into blissful sleep.

"I have something for you."

Alex's pronouncement brought her back from the brink of sleep, and Jocelyn glanced up at him through her lashes. A wicked curl of anticipation worked through her, even as another part of her protested at an additional wanton excursion. Jocelyn playfully pushed against him. "You are tireless, sir."

He caught her hand and pressed it to his chest, spreading her fingers gently against the steady pulse of his heart. "I'll accept the compliment, but that's not what I meant."

"No?" She tried to keep any hint of disappointment from her voice. Truly she was exhausted, but the simple contact of her palm against the strong, steady beat of his heart seemed to work a magic of its own on her senses, dismissing the aches and fatigue. "What did you intend?"

"A gift." He leaned back, extending his free hand to retrieve a small leather case from his waistcoat on the floor. "A trifle, but I wanted you to have it."

"A trifle," she echoed, tentatively taking the case with fingers that felt strangely numb. "With the fortune you've paid me, I hardly think—"

He silenced her with a kiss, drawing on the swollen, tender flesh of her lower lip to tease it gently, grazing her with his teeth. "You're welcome. Now open the box, Jocelyn."

Jocelyn let out a slow sigh of pleasure, her mouth tingling at his touch. He was entitled to buy her gifts and it was foolish to protest the sweet gesture. She forced herself to look away from his gaze and open the case.

"Oh!" Her eyes widened at the glittering contents, shocked at the extravagance and impossibly thrilled in the same moment. "It's . . . oh, my!"

"You like it, then?"

"I . . ." Jocelyn found herself momentarily speechless, as Alex openly enjoyed her befuddled state.

"A man might be easily motivated to spend a thousand fortunes just to see the priceless look on your face right now, Jocelyn." Alex reached over to lift the necklace from the box and began to drape it around her neck. "It suits you."

She blushed, her fingers tracing the shape of the delicate stones against her skin. "It's beautiful, Alex. Thank you!" Eager to see for herself, she pushed off the bed to catch her reflection in the vanity mirror. It had been years since she'd received a gift of any kind, and Jocelyn felt as giddy as a child at Christmas at his generosity. She was naked but for the glittering display at her throat dangling down between her breasts and her breath caught in her throat at the raw power of the sight. "This necklace would make a charwoman look like a queen, Alex."

He laughed, openly leaning back against the pillows to admire her. "I'm not sure I want to test that."

She returned to the bed, playfully threatening to toss the empty case at him before she curled up against him. Her fingers crept back up to the necklace. It was a token to keep her close, a romantic exchange that put a lump in her throat. It would be easy to mistake these intimate gestures for something else, she reminded herself. Easy to mistake generosity for something more, out of a naïve wish for the impossible. How many times had she lectured the girls, or held them in her arms while they cried after lamenting the mistake?

"Who was your father?"

"W-what?" The question caught her off guard, and Jocelyn wondered if he'd deliberately brought up an impossible subject to ward off the tender intimacy between them. Perhaps he wanted to remind himself of her unsuitability.

"Did you know him?" he asked softly, his eyes warm and kind, unaware of the discomfort his idle curiosity was causing her.

"We're not comparing family trees, Lord Colwick." She pulled her hand from his. "Choose another game to play and I will happily oblige you."

"Is it a game, Jocelyn? I was just curious if—"

"If I have a father you can call on?" She lay next to him, trying to distract him. "Now, there's an odd fantasy!"

"If your mother was . . . in this profession, then it's all you've ever known. I was simply curious if—" He cleared his throat and tried another tactic. "I wish to know more about you. It's only natural, isn't it?"

"Ask me anything, Alex. But I . . . I don't want to talk about myself or my mother. It's really not a topic worth discussing."

"Tell me about the Belle, then." He pulled her against his side, raising himself on one elbow to study her face.

"The Belle is . . . as you see." She wriggled to gain a more comfortable position or to escape his questions, he wasn't sure which. The movement accented her beautiful breasts as the sheet slipped to reveal the sweet coral peaks that hardened at the cooler air, but Alex was determined to have his answers.

"And what do I not see?"

She became very still, and he could see her eyes turn a solemn emerald color as she considered her answer before speaking. "The numbers of the ladies are deliberately small, less than twenty, to maintain a peaceful house and give a better return. Those with their own rooms earn the right to have a personal maid if they wish. The maids are . . . apprenticed to each girl, and if any client chooses, he may elevate that maid in the house to a room of her own and invest in her 'debut.'

None of the other servants are available for appointments, with strict banishment to any man who harasses the house's regular staff." She took a deep breath. "Enough?"

"Go on. I'm fascinated."

She gave him a sexy look of skepticism, but obediently continued. "The women all have their own unique talents and specialties, and while they are free to accept or decline contracts, they cannot refuse a client of the Belle any reasonable request during an appointment. It ensures our male guests a certain 'guarantee of success' and maintains the house's reputation for supreme hospitality."

"Any reasonable request," he echoed. "What would be an unreasonable request?"

She shrugged. "There are so few, honestly. We don't offer children here and I once had to intervene when a client attempted to include one of the women's beloved cats in his fantasies." Jocelyn blushed. "It was an interesting evening for everyone involved."

He shook his head. "To say the least!"

"Naturally, any special inquiries usually are directed to me in advance. Any additional expenses incurred for a guest's pleasure are added with interest against his bill." Jocelyn smiled at some private jest. "It has made for some odd shopping lists. But as I told you, there are certain tastes we do not meet and they are generally referred somewhere else."

Alex tried to absorb it all, the intricacies of servitude and mastery when it came to the flesh trade. "Is it difficult to find so many willing beauties?"

She shrugged. "Hardly. London abounds with willing beauties, but I discriminate when making any new additions. The Crimson Belle is known for its generosity toward the ladies of the house. For example, three times a year, a couture designer of the first water arrives at the house to make sure the women of the Belle outmatch any rival. Patrons have been known to contribute to their wardrobes, but we don't rely on them. And weekly, I have tutors on various mornings come in to instruct the women on a variety of subjects and skills."

"Tutors?"

"Didn't Zeus decree something to Deucalion about his daughters?"

"About getting them tutors?" Alex's brow furrowed as he tried to recall his long-forgotten lessons in dusty Greek legends.

" 'Put roses in their hair, put precious stones on their breasts, see that they are clothed in purple and scarlet, with other delights—but that they also learn to read the gilded heraldry of the sky, and upon the earth be taught not only the labors of it but the loveliness.'" Her expression took on a dreamy, faraway look as she recited, before she recovered with a blush. "Perhaps I insist my ladies read too much, but even the ancient Greeks saw the benefits of a good education."

"Did they?" Alex was awash in astonishment. Her translation was from a Latin text he recognized, and he wondered how a woman in such a place would know these things. She must have been schooled outside the Crimson Belle—or had her mother also hired tutors for the ladies of the house?

She stretched out, a copper-colored cat beginning to relax and warm to the topic. "Occasionally, a man will hire away one of the ladies to be his mistress, and they are free to contract as they wish, providing the Belle is paid a handsome fee for its investment. It is all extremely democratic and fair—and profitable."

A faint knock at the door interrupted them, and Jocelyn called out, "Yes, who is it?"

"Edith, Madame. I brought fresh linens."

"Wait." Jocelyn stood, wrapping herself in a silk robe as she crossed to the door. Opening it, she took the pile from Edith's hands. "Thank you, my dear. Now be careful on the stairs and get to bed! It's far too late for these chores and you need your rest."

Edith bobbed a graceful curtsy, but Jocelyn

noted the curious glance she cast into the room to catch a glimpse of her Mistress's guest.

"Off with you now," she added again gently, and closed the door behind her. She gave Alex an apologetic look. "There's no clean place to set them in the hall and I didn't wish to see her making an unnecessary trip up three flights as a result of my laziness."

"She is . . . very young."

Jocelyn bristled defensively. "I told you. I don't sell children here. She is a housemaid at present and Mrs. Brooks has her under her wing."

"I was just surprised at her age. It wasn't an accusation, Jocelyn."

"Wasn't it?" She retied the sash of her silk robe and arched her back to stave off the fatigue that threatened to overtake her after she set the linens down on a sideboard. "Of course it wasn't. I'm the one who hates that she is here. I'm the one who hates the lessons she'll inevitably learn in this house, even if she is consigned to the regular staff. I'm the one who hates that there is always another girl waiting on my doorstep to take her place and that no matter what I do . . . I can't save any of them. Not really."

He came up behind her and drew her back against his chest, molding her against him and running his hands along the lines of her shoulders and arms. "You do what you can, and I'm sure that no one would expect you to do more."

She retreated from his touch and leaned back against the bedpost. "I'm afraid I disappoint you, my lord."

"In what way?"

"It's as if you have some illusion about the house—about me. I'm not the pure, generous benefactress of some sort of illicit boarding school that harbors lost little lambs, Alex." Jocelyn fought against a ball of icy pain at the wretched admission. "They'll tell you how kind I am—to hire tutors, to insist on a physician attending them monthly, to give them a sense of autonomy. But they won't tell you . . ."

"What?"

"They won't tell you that I hire tutors for the women to educate and refine them, but that it's for profit more than their benefit. Our clients prefer pretty accents to go with pretty faces, and if the customers perceive quality, they'll pay more for the privilege. I insist on the physician because we have to run a healthy house, and if a woman is infected with venereal disease, she can't trade. It gives the authorities an excuse to arrest her and to close down the house. What kind of benefactress am I now?"

He came forward to hold her shoulders, and her eyes filled with tears, unable to look at him. "There, now."

"I want to be . . ." She lifted her head. "I want to be better for them. I want them to have a good life here. But I can't change the way of the world. They sell themselves—no, even that isn't accurate, is it? I sell them, just as I've sold myself to y—"

He kissed her, stopping her from saying it. He'd purchased her body without a moment's hesitation, but now he couldn't bear to think of the coin that had passed between them. Now there was only Jocelyn in his arms and the smell of jasmine on her skin, and the salty-sweet taste of her tears on his lips. He kissed her until she sighed and yielded to his touch, and there was no more talk of the world beyond her door.

As he left, the conversation and the hurt in her eyes haunted him. *So many secrets.* But her bearing, her delicate features and flawless manners—her very character and essence give every impression of good breeding. She must be the natural daughter of a gentleman, his every instinct proclaimed it. He doubted she knew the identity of her father. If she knew, why not tell him? But if he could prove his theory . . .

If he could prove it, it would be a gift to her, to clear some of the pain that haunted her. The knowledge would comfort her, and more—demonstrate his sincerity and interest better than any bauble. He would hire that Bow Street runner that Drake had once recommended, and who knew what possibilities could be uncovered? If nothing else, he would have the truth behind the beauty who kept losing her slippers and seemed incapable of sitting properly in her chair, but could quote from the Greek myth of Deucalion.

"Roses in their hair," he echoed to himself as he took the stairs and made his way from the Belle, cheered by thoughts of Jocelyn with garlands of scented blossoms in her hair.

Twelve

❧

The next day, Amelia was gone. Just as she'd wished, there had been no formal farewells and no fuss made before she'd slipped out with her baggage to make her way into the world. Within a fortnight, she would be sailing to America and her life at the Belle would be completely behind her. Jocelyn had instructed Ramis to break the news to the girls only after Amelia had left to avoid any tearful fits. Not that she truly expected any. The breakfast table was quieter than usual, and most of the girls were doing their best to smile and pretend that nothing had changed. Their company was never constant, but it wasn't easy to dismiss the awkward ache of Amelia's empty place at the gathering.

"Well, I, for one, intend to stay safely under

this roof! It seems they only find those girls out-side the bordellos," Moira said.

"Not this dove!" countered Jez with a toss of her blond curls. "No one is caging me. I shall come and go as I please. I'm off with Lord Russell this afternoon, thank you very much, and you dowdy gits can hide here and wait for your fur to mold."

"Ha! No one's molding at the Belle, and no one's asked you to stay locked inside," Suzanne countered.

A lively debate began around the table as Jezebel made a grand exit to prepare for her afternoon. Jocelyn kept her eyes on her own plate for the time being. As more details of the last murder at the Jade filtered through the grapevine, she couldn't blame them for speculating on the dangers. The press had made small note of it at last, although not to link the tragedies. So far, the respectable world continued to keep a safe distance from their troubles. Amidst the women of the Belle, she knew discouraging the conversation would only make it worse. At least she'd ensured that Amelia was safely away. Although none of the violence had yet directly threatened the Belle, Jocelyn had a sinking feeling that this miraculous omission wouldn't last forever.

Beneath the high collar of her morning dress,

Jocelyn felt the topaz pendant against her heartbeat. She'd shown it to no one, feeling protective about the tenuous happiness that it represented. Memories of the previous night muted the voices in the room, and Jocelyn indulged in the mental retreat, letting her thoughts drift to Alex.

His reserved demeanor fell away when he touched her, and she loved the raw, unbridled way he possessed her. But he was ultimately a titled gentleman, and she knew that no one would ever guess that the polished and polite Lord Colwick would indulge himself in an illicit arrangement with the notorious Madame.

She'd once thought to use their alliance for political gain, but Jocelyn knew it was the worst kind of self-deception. She'd never before parlayed any client's patronage to the Belle for advantage—not for bribery or blackmail. Never before and certainly not now. She had no intention of betraying Alex's trust or exposing him to scandal for any reason.

She experienced a natural ease in his presence that made her feel fearless and safe. Alex treated her with such care. He'd even made her forget the ten thousand pounds. At least until . . .

His question about the identity of her father had hurt.

Why? Why does a simple question about my pedigree sting so much?

Jocelyn's appetite evaporated in an instant as the answer sank in with an inescapable sensation of despair. It mattered because it highlighted the impossible differences in their worlds. It mattered because she wanted to be able to answer him. Her mother's vows to never marry again were no guarantee that Jocelyn was the product of a marriage. She was more likely the illegitimate daughter of one of her mother's patrons—an inconvenient by-product of the Belle's trade in business. It had never bothered her before. But now it mattered because Alex looked at her with sincere concern in his incredibly beautiful brown eyes and she didn't want to admit that there was no chance that they were on equal footing. It hurt because . . .

Because I love him.

She stood abruptly, conversations at the table ending in surprise as she left without a single word of explanation. Jocelyn ignored the astonished gasps and whispers behind her and fled to her rooms.

Let them think I'm upset about Amelia leaving—or the girl from the Jade. Jocelyn shook her head. *Better that than the truth. After everything I've taught them, after all the wisdom I've dispensed like so many headache powders—how could I be so stupid?*

There was no answer to counter the chaotic

swirl of her thoughts, and Jocelyn could only pray that by the time Alex arrived, she'd absorb the revelation of her feelings and be able to master herself enough to hide them.

"What do you think?"

Alex eyed the stallion, noting the animal's unmistakable lines and strength. The market square was crowded with animals of every class, but Declan had certainly selected one of the most striking to be auctioned that afternoon. At seventeen hands, the thoroughbred was a powerful and beautiful beast, but Alex wasn't sure if Declan's sanity was intact. "I think we should have gone to the club for drinks."

"Come on, Lex! You told me to think of investing more."

"I don't think buying a racehorse is what I meant when I gave you that advice." Alex took a few steps back to study the animal again. "I'm certain I said something about bonds."

Declan crossed his arms impatiently. "I'm going to make a fortune and have a bit of fun along the way."

"Am I jealous of the fortune or the fun?"

"Both, old man!" Declan countered merrily.

"It's your money to lose," Alex conceded, sighing before he continued. "I should apologize for last night. I have no doubt Eloise vented her fury in your direction when I left the theater. I meant to thank you for stepping in."

"What are friends for, if not for handling hissing cobras and getting their ears boxed?" Declan reached out to stroke the horse's neck. "Though admittedly the sacrifices would be easier to bear if you'd share a few details, Randall. What was so urgent that you had to flee the theater?"

Alex shrugged. "A previous obligation."

"You are the most obliging man I know, Lex." Declan gave him a knowing look. "I like it that you're ignoring the fact that I generously share all my bawdy tales with you, sir! Did I mention that I heard there are some lovely new doves at the Swan?"

"If I had such tales, I'm sure I would do the same—and I'm not interested in the Swan."

Declan leaned over in a show of conspiracy. "It must be some lovely commitment to make you so remarkably scarce these days."

"I'm sure I have no idea what you're talking about, Forrester."

"Come now, friend. A man can't help but speculate when your 'urgent matters' keep you out all night."

Alex held his ground. "I'm not in the mood for confidences."

"You mean you don't trust me," Declan corrected him with a grin.

Alex found himself smiling back before he could help himself. The Irishman was unflappable. "Not even as far as I am able to carry you."

"And here I was, planning on sharing all my newfound fortune with you after this lively beast brings me glory!"

Alex laughed. "More likely you'll end up begging for a loan to cover that animal's boarding."

Declan's laughter rang out as well, until the man's attention was caught by something across the small clearing. "Now, there's a lively creature I'd prefer to bid on."

Alex looked to see what steed had captured his friend's eye and had the jolting surprise of seeing a familiar beauty in a sumptuous peach dress on the arm of a distant acquaintance. Before he could redirect Declan, Jez's eyes met his and Alex knew that she had no idea of showing mercy.

"Lord Colwick!" Jezebel released her escort's arm and made her way toward them, drawing additional male attention from passersby as she wove through the small crowd near the enclosures. "What a thrill to see you again so soon!"

Declan's eyes widened in amusement, openly enjoying the change in Alex's complexion. "A thrill," he echoed. "You must introduce me, Lord Colwick."

"If the lady wishes," he proffered, silently commanding her with his eyes to refuse the introduction.

"Of course she does," Jez said, ignoring Alex and rewarding Declan with a wicked smile.

"Mr. Declan Forrester," Alex ground out the words. "Miss Jezebel . . ."

Jez laughed as she offered her hand. "What a naughty man! I don't think he even knows my last name, Mr. Forrester. Can you imagine?"

"Your beauty must have pushed it from his feeble mind." Declan bent over her fingers. "Is that a jasmine scent you are wearing, my dear?"

"Why, yes, it is," she purred, touching the column of her ivory throat with one gloved hand. "Do you like it?"

"Oh, yes!" Declan grinned, then turned to his friend. "It's quite distinct, isn't it, old friend?"

Damn it. It was a collision of worlds Alex would have preferred to avoid.

She leaned closer, her voice dropping to offer a sultry confidence. "Lord Russell likes a bit of excitement in public places. I only hope we don't scare the horses."

Declan coughed, a sputter of merry shock drawing attention to the trio from the other patrons. "H-how delightful!"

"Have you ever been to the Crimson Belle, Mr. Forrester?" Jez purred, a kitten not bothering to hide her claws. "You should ask your friend to bring you next time."

So much for Declan mistaking her profession. Alex began to scan the square, casting about for any excuse to drag Declan away from the indiscreet wench before his friend had more details of Alex's private commitments than he ever could have wanted. But before he could move, the nightmare took on an unbelievable turn. Miss Winifred Preston stood less than twenty paces away, and as always, her sour-faced mother was at her elbow. For Alex, it was as if everything had slowed to stretch out the wretched torture of the moment.

Mrs. Preston spotted him, and his last hope of escape withered and died as the insufferable woman prodded her offspring in their direction. Clearly, the sight of another beauty vying for Alex's attention was something Mrs. Preston viewed as a challenge. "Lord Colwick?"

Alex glared at Declan, and for once, his friend seemed to sober up and perceive the danger. Declan shifted to stand a bit closer to Jez, shielding her from Mrs. Preston's open study.

"Ah, Mrs. Preston." Alex stepped forward to halt her progress. "An unexpected . . . surprise to see you both out today."

"Yes. Though I am starting to believe it is simply fate that you and Winifred become better acquainted, for everywhere we go—there you are." Mrs. Preston's smile faltered as Jez moved past Declan to join their small circle. "Winifred was just saying that she hoped to see you again."

"Mother!" The young Miss Preston's embarrassment was palpable, and Alex wondered which of them was more miserable. If fate had anything in mind for the two of them, it apparently involved public humiliation.

Then everything seemed to spin out of control. Civility demanded that he reassure Miss Preston that her mother's comments hadn't caused any harm, but as he spoke his apologies, Mrs. Preston leaned in to say something to Jezebel that Alex couldn't quite hear. And before he could assess the damage or even directly ask what had passed between them to make Jezebel beam in triumph, Declan unfortunately chose that moment to intervene and escort Jezebel back to Lord Russell.

The man's timing is as impeccable as ever. Damn it!

Left alone with Mrs. Preston and Winifred, Alex did his best to maintain his composure. "Will you be bidding on any of the livestock today, Mrs. Preston?"

"Winifred needs a good mount," the woman answered blithely, "but I think we'll wait. You have to be patient, Lord Colwick, if you want to rein in a winner."

Alex sent up a silent prayer of his own for patience, refusing to waste any more time on the woman's poorly disguised wit. "The lovely Miss Preston seems capable of making her own choices. I wish her all the best luck in her search for happiness. Now, I'm afraid I have to be going and will ask your pardon. Good day, ladies."

He bowed and turned on his heel to seek out Declan. It took only moments to find him again at the temporary paddock of another overpriced thoroughbred. "Declan, I trust you can find your own way back to the house?"

"You're leaving?" Declan almost managed to look innocent. "Don't you want to stay for the auction?"

"I've had enough for one day."

Declan shook his head, lowering his voice to counsel his friend. "There's no need to be embarrassed, Lex. What matter if you find your sport where you wish? It never occurred to me that that's where you've been disappearing to in the night. But you must know I'm the last man who would ever think to cast a stone."

"Declan—if our friendship means anything to you, please abandon this subject."

Declan sighed. "Very well. Even though I am dying to ask if you've seen the mysterious Madame of that house. Especially since I heard that almost no one has ever seen her face."

"Forrester." Alex ground out his name as a final warning, and Declan at last conceded the point.

"The subject is hereby abandoned." Declan held out his hand. "You have my word on it."

The men shook hands, and Alex left his friend to his pursuit of a fast fortune and, if the gods were kind, an even faster horse. For now, he was off to the Belle, for if ever a man deserved the solace of his mistress's arms, it was he.

By the time he arrived, Jocelyn felt completely prepared and strangely calm. The revelations of her feelings had been pushed aside after an afternoon of practice. She didn't want to fall into the trap of tender embraces or lower her guard when he teased and flattered her. Tonight she would love him as only a courtesan could—and if it shocked him into leaving her . . . then it might be a small mercy. At the very least, she would try to satisfy him and guard her heart—if she could.

"You're here." She abandoned her chair in the corner and took his hat and coat before drawing him toward the bed's dais.

"I would have sent a message, but Declan forced me to attend a—"

Alex's train of thought was halted abruptly as she dropped to her knees, her fingers tracing the hardening outline of him through the expensive cloth of his trousers.

"Jocelyn . . ."

"Shhh . . . ," she soothed, as she began to release the buttons that strained against the pressure of his flesh. "I've been thinking of this all day."

It wasn't a lie. She'd spent the entire afternoon reading the Kama Sutra in regard to mouth congress. *Auparishtaka.* It was a lesson she'd recited for others a hundred times, but for once, it was now her turn to apply the knowledge and seek a man's ultimate release.

He reached down to stop her, and might have if her fingers hadn't found his shaft to draw it out against her lips. Instead of lifting her to her feet, Alex entwined his fingers in her hair and Jocelyn closed her eyes to savor her task.

Even now, she marveled at the weight and power of his body as his cock moved against her hands. She cupped her fingers over the swollen head of him, pressing it like a ripened plum, the scalding heat of his velvet-soft skin telegraphing his desire. Jocelyn parted her lips as she slid her mouth along the sides of him, until her teeth grazed his sensitive ridges and gently bit into the apex of his cock.

His fingers fisted in her hair and he moaned in reaction, and Jocelyn continued to move against him.

"My God, woman . . . you shouldn't . . ."

Shouldn't fall in love. Jocelyn was determined

not to relent. She squeezed him with her palms, drawing his thick cock out so that she could kiss the tip of him. She pressed her lips together, savoring the soft friction and the salty-sweet single drop of crème that coated her lips from his arousal.

His hips bucked against her and Jocelyn knew he was ready for more than simple kisses. She ever so slowly opened her mouth to pull in the head of his cock to work her tongue against it as she suckled him. Alex groaned, and Jocelyn teased him by almost releasing him before pulling him back into her mouth, each time a little faster and harder, as her hands held him in place.

"Damn it, Jocelyn," Alex managed through gritted teeth. "You're killing me."

"Am I?" she purred, before abandoning the engorged tip of him to trail sensual openmouthed kisses up and down the length of him. It was a worship of his very essence, and Jocelyn lingered over every touch to ensure that she held the reins. Her own body throbbed, her slit becoming saturated at the exercise, but Jocelyn refused to lose her focus.

She took more of him into her mouth, testing the sensation and discovering how best to please him. She suckled and tasted him, trailing her fingernails lightly through the thick, manly curls around his cock until she could feel him growing even hotter inside her mouth. His climax was close, and it spurred her on to push him—to somehow control the uncontrollable. To take all of him and absorb him into herself.

At last, she had what she wanted. His climax came in short, sweet bursts and Jocelyn basked in the power she wielded, hungrily drinking his crème as if he alone could sustain her.

She released him with a wicked smile, and he fell back onto the bed with a moan.

"I'd . . . meant to see if you were hungry for dinner," he sighed, a slow smile betraying his mirth.

Jocelyn giggled and fell across his chest to lie on top of him. "But I have already had dessert!"

They both burst into laughter, and Alex held her tightly against him, dropping kisses onto her face and hair. Jocelyn closed her eyes. *I have to stick to my plan. I have to remember that no matter what I feel, he is only here for his money's worth. My heart is only truly forfeit if I'm foolish enough to let him know he has it.*

"Jocelyn?"

"Yes?"

"I wish to have dessert as well."

Her eyes opened in surprise, and before she could think of a clever answer, the dratted man made it impossible for her to think at all.

Thirteen

~

Gilly brushed out her long brown hair, keeping a subtle watch on the young girl setting out her dinner tray and straightening her bedclothes. Edith was making a clumsy attempt at spying in return that made Gilly smile. *Curiosity is a powerful thing.*

"Go on," Gilly coaxed her, turning on her vanity chair to face the young maid. "Ask."

Edith worried her bottom lip with her teeth, nervously mustering her courage. "Mrs. Brooks said I was not to bother anyone with questions."

Gilly nodded. "Mrs. Brooks is very kind and would rather you learn about pastries and how to make gravy."

Edith's eyes reflected her disappointment. "Yes, I suppose so."

"But you can ask whatever it is that's kept you staring at me for the last five minutes, if you wish."

"I didn't mean to stare!" Edith squeaked.

"I don't mind." Gilly laughed and set her brush aside. "It's just that you looked a little sad and I thought . . . perhaps if you ask it, then you'll feel better."

"I wondered—I wondered if . . ."

Oh, dear. Gilly tilted her head to one side, hoping she wouldn't have to say too much. They were under strict orders not to shock the poor child.

"Were you . . . left here too?"

The question lodged a painful lump in Gilly's throat. *Poor thing.* "No. I found my way to the Belle on my own. I was lucky, I think. Luckier than most."

"Lucky?" Edith asked, a world of unspoken hurt welling up in her eyes.

Gilly left her seat to take Edith's hands into hers. "We all land somewhere. Some people jump blindly, or are pushed, or think they know where they're going even when they have no idea. Some people choose their own path and surprise even themselves. But ultimately, everyone finds their place in the world. For me, the Belle is home."

"And for me?" Edith whispered tearfully.

Gilly shook her head. "I think this is just a

wonderful place to catch your breath. Just let Mrs. Brooks fatten you up. Learn to speak French and let Ramis keep you safe."

"He's frightening, Miss Gilliam," she confided.

"Ramis?" Gilly asked in shock. "Why?"

"He never smiles."

Gilly's brow furrowed as she considered it. "I'm sure you're wrong. He is so kind, and so . . ." She caught herself drifting into a reverie on the topic of the handsome and mysterious Ramis, and gave a firm shake to return to the important matters at hand. "You're safe here, Edith. You must listen to Mrs. Brooks and follow all her rules."

Edith risked a small smile. "Even the rule about not asking questions?"

Gilly laughed. "Especially that rule! Now out with you and back to the kitchens!"

Edith retreated with a lighter step, and Gilly returned to her preparations for the evening. As she brushed her hair, she threw up a silent prayer that of all the lessons Edith might learn, she was done with loss.

"Another?" Alex asked after watching her face read the note that had just arrived from the Swan. They'd been indulging in a languorous morning, half dressed in smallclothes with a breakfast tray between them on the bed. But the world had intruded yet again, and now she had retreated to the end of the bed to gather her wits.

Jocelyn tore the note in two and discarded it. She couldn't believe the news, but there was no denying its impact. This time the murder had occurred just a few streets away and it was simply too close for comfort. "Just like the others."

"What can I do?"

She looked at him, awed at his reaction. "Do?"

"To protect you." His gaze never wavered, and Jocelyn accepted that it was his very nature to see everything in a straightforward manner. Where she saw a labyrinth of entanglements and danger, he was ready to fearlessly forge ahead if it meant securing her safety.

A wave of doubt washed over her. "You should stay out of this."

"Let me help." He pulled her close, his lips grazing her forehead. "Please."

"We've already talked about this." She reached up to lightly trace the concerned furrows in his brow. "There is little you can do."

"I am not a man without means, Jocelyn. I may not be all-powerful, but I am *not* entirely incompetent. I can contact the authorities and pressure them to move faster."

"I never said that you were anything less than heroic," she soothed. "It's just . . . I don't want you to be disappointed when you accomplish nothing. Besides, what will you tell the police when they inquire as to why you are interested in this murdered prostitute? They'll want to know why you're concerned."

His brown eyes darkened as he appeared to weigh the implications. "True, but easily solved. I'll just note that this nonsense is too close to respectable neighborhoods to be ignored. As a man with acquaintances living nearby, I cannot help but express concern that certain unsavory elements are beginning to attract the wrong people and threaten good people." He folded his arms, a bit proud of his improvisation. "What do you think?"

"I think you're standing in the house of the 'unsavory elements' they'll assume you're referring to," Jocelyn answered defensively. Everything in his answer was logical and reasonable, but she felt her hackles rise. "I think I was right to advise you to leave it for now."

"I think you're too proud to accept my help."

She dropped her head, burrowing against him and pressing against the solid strength of his body. "I want to protect all of them, Alex. I have no pride when it comes to it. I need you, Alex. More than I can say."

He enfolded her in his arms, a shield and haven against the horrors of the world. "Then let me do what I can."

She wriggled against him, savoring the masculine scent and feel of him and marveling at how impossibly safe she felt in his presence. *So stupid. I've fallen in love and now I'm coming to need him. What will I do when he leaves? When he decides he's had enough for his money—enough of this messy, dangerous business of prostitutes and murder? When he stops rushing to my side when I need him most?*

She pushed the thoughts away, unwilling to waste the present moments in a foolish trade for the imaginary or real heartaches that awaited her in the future. He would leave when he wished. But it wouldn't be today. She moved her lips over his chest, reveling in the strong beat beneath her mouth's caresses. He groaned at the distraction, and she tipped her head back to smile up at him. "You can help me by taking my mind off these things, my lord. Or perhaps you can make it impossible for me to think of anything at all . . ."

His brown eyes warmed, his body hardening in response to the wicked request, and he shifted her against him to ensure that she was unable to escape. "This was not entirely the 'help' I had in mind, Jocelyn."

"No?" she asked with a flirtatious flutter of her lashes. "Are you sure, my lord?"

Whatever arguments he'd intended, they evaporated as he began to nibble on her neck and remove the last of her undergarments. Jocelyn closed her eyes with contentment and accepted the gift of his touch and his time.

Alex closed the door behind him, leaning against the frame for a moment to gather his thoughts. It was harder and harder to creep away from her rooms, like an illicit thief. *Perhaps I should try again to talk her into meeting somewhere else away from—*

"We don't need you," Ramis said quietly, and Alex reeled around to find the giant had once again managed to appear behind him without a single sound of warning.

"We?" Alex wanted to make sure he'd understood the man.

Ramis's expression remained neutral as he repeated the words. "We don't need you. I am afraid the Mistress is mistaken in trusting you."

"That is for your Mistress to decide." Alex wasn't intimidated in the slightest.

"I can protect the Belle as I always have."

Alex gave him a cynical look of disbelief. "Was that your protection, then, that allowed a man like Marsh into her rooms unchecked? You'll forgive me if I don't take comfort in your efforts to keep her safe."

Ramis's eyes flashed with fury, but his expression never changed.

"I am not here for you." Alex straightened his coat and squared his shoulders. "If you'll excuse me."

Alex made his way down the narrow staircase, aware now that Ramis followed him. At the first floor, Ramis remained in the hallway like a dark and forbidding guardian watching to ensure that Alex made his way out. The gesture angered Alex and he glanced back at the manservant. "You're not going to frighten me away."

Ramis simply stared back. "I won't need to, Lord Colwick. You shall go."

"You're wrong." Alex tasted fury as he left the stubborn servant, determined not to gratify the man's claims with pointless argument. His surly protectiveness of his Mistress might have been commendable on a different day, but Alex was in no mood to debate with the man. He left the Belle without looking back and ignored the burning coal of jealousy that fired in the pit of his stomach every time he considered the bond between Jocelyn and Ramis. "We, indeed . . ."

Ramis waited until the sound of Lord Colwick's footsteps had long faded before he moved from the doorway. It was not his place to interfere. But Ramis's life and love were here, and this man was just like all the others. *He comes and goes with no thought to anything but himself.*

Ramis wanted him gone before it went too far. Already the Mistress was in danger of a broken heart. He had seen her light up when this man arrived, and grow quieter and fragile each time he left. The life of the Belle could crush a Mistress left vulnerable . . . and Ramis wasn't sure anything could protect them if it happened. *No, the Mistress must be strong for all of them. The women look to her as a sailor to the stars.* But this man . . . he endangered everything they had fought to build here.

"Ramis?"

It was his turn to experience surprise, as, lost in his thoughts, he hadn't heard Gilliam approach. "Miss Gilliam. I had not seen you there."

"Is it true a girl was found . . . murdered?" Her eyes were bright and anxious in the lamp-lit corridor, and she put her hand on his arm. "Is it true, sir?"

"One of the Swan's." He glanced down at the small white hand that rested on his coat sleeve. These women did not touch him, and he marveled that she would do so. The warmth of her fingers managed to reach him even through the layers that separated her from his skin, and the gift of it calmed him. "Don't fear, Miss Gilliam. This evil will not come to the Belle. The Mistress and I will take extra precautions to see that you are safe. Already I have doubled the men at the doors to make sure that all will be well."

Her expression cleared, a childlike faith shining up at him. "Of course, and I am not afraid—not really. It's just that . . ."

"Tell me." He held still and waited.

"It's Edith. I promised her that she would be safe here. She's so young and homesick for her mother. She's bound to be frightened if she hears about all this." Gilly tilted her head. "Perhaps you could tell her one of your stories and then she'll feel better."

He smiled. Only the sparrow would think of such a thing. Only Gilliam would think of a little girl in the scullery instead of herself. Without hesitation, he tore two brass buttons from his embroidered waistcoat. "A talisman to ward away evil spirits, Miss Gilliam." He lifted her hand from his arm and pressed them gently into her palm. "One for each of you."

"Oh," she exclaimed softly, her fingers trembling against his. "You ruined your coat, sir."

"Tell her . . ." He took a deep breath before he released her hand. "Tell her to keep it close and no harm will come."

"It's perfect." Gilliam cupped her hands to her chest as if she guarded treasure. "Not that I was afraid, mind you. But she'll feel better if she knows I have one too."

"Yes. It is so."

She retreated to her rooms in a graceful dance of white lace and silks, and he indulged himself to watch her go until her door was shut firmly behind her.

No demon shall harm you, sparrow. God willing.

Fourteen

A lex stared out the window at the walled garden, frustrated beyond words. Fear for Jocelyn and her beloved charges edged into his every waking thought, but as Madame DeBourcier, she was determined to keep him out of it and rely entirely on Ramis. The contradictions of his beautiful and stubborn lover made him crazed. She needed him, but then ordered him to stay out of things. She distracted and unraveled him with kisses, and made him feel as if he could conquer the world, only to pronounce him too tender to be involved in such grim matters. Their "business arrangement" was not what he'd expected.

His butler cleared his throat from the doorway to politely signal his presence. "A Mr. Peers to see you, m'lord."

"Thank you, Adams. Send him right in."

Alex's mood lifted instantly. Drake had recommended the Bow Street runner, but had warned his friend that the man's style was roughly as polished as a warthog's. Drake's assessment wasn't too far off, but he hadn't hired the man for his manners.

"I'm still diggin' when it comes to the Madame's history, m'lord. Mind ye, she's a ghosty thing and it ain't as if her peers are free with their information. They seem to resent her success over there if ye ask me." Peers shifted his weight, warming to the topic. "Mind, she kept a lot of her mother's staff, so the history's there for the having and for a few coins. The women will close ranks, but the footmen are a sure bet. It's just a matter of asking about to see who enjoys sharin' nostalgic tales over a pint or two. I'll know her father's name before a fortnight's passed, m'lord."

Alex held up a hand to stem the flow of the conversation. "I know you will. But in the meantime, I'm also sure you're aware of the recent violence against the soiled doves in the city. The killer may threaten the Crimson Belle as well, so I want you to do what you can to discover if there is a link between the women who have met such terrible ends. The authorities—"

"Have only just started to scratch at it, from

what I know of the thing." Peers took out a soiled handkerchief to mop his brow. "Mind, these are highfliers and not just street doxies, so it may be the uniforms ain't wanting to make a show of it in case things get political an' all."

"Uncover what you can, and report to me." Alex held out an additional sum of money. "Let this motivate you to be thorough, Peers, and quick to your business."

Peers accepted the payment with an awkward bow and shuffled from the room. Alex turned back to the window with a new sense of resolve. He'd conceded to Jocelyn's arguments against contacting the authorities directly, but Peers was the perfect compromise. That he'd already had the man in motion to uncover her parentage was irrelevant as far as Alex was concerned. If Peers uncovered a link, they could take the necessary steps to guarantee the safety of the Belle, and for once, he would demonstrate to his dear Madame that not all of his "missions" were doomed to failure.

"More porridge, miss?" Edith asked timidly at Moira's elbow.

"Oh, yes, please," Moira replied, before Jez threw a small bit of toast across the table.

"You'll get fat at this rate, lovely!" Jezebel

cooed. "But then some gents like a bit of meat on their girls. A bit of bounce to keep their hands full, eh, ladies?"

"Jezebel!" Jocelyn chided, all too aware of the young Edith circling the table to serve them breakfast under Mrs. Brooks's watchful eyes. She couldn't really censure any of them, but Jez's barbed wit was hard to ignore. "Leave Moira to her meal. She is as thin as a rail, and should try a bit of the sausage mash."

Moira blushed. "Thank you, Mistress."

The chatter around the table picked up again, and Jocelyn began to hope that the peace of the house might hold for a time. Despite the troubles, their appointments had increased nicely the last week. The bishop had sent word that he approved of his new hostess for afternoon teas, one of her richest clients had expressed a wish to contract exclusively with one of the girls, and two of the Belle's "personal maids" seemed ready to debut and begin earning for the house. Now, if only—

"What a delight to run into Lord Colwick at the horse markets near the racetrack the other day!" Jez's voice easily carried over the merry din at the table to capture Jocelyn's complete attention. "His fiancée is the prettiest little thing."

Silverware clattered against china and the room became still. It took a moment or two for

Jocelyn to realize that it was her fork that had fallen—her numb fingers that had lost control. Before she could absorb all the implications, Jez went on. "Miss Winifred Preston has apparently landed the man and made her mother quite happy at the bargain. A dowry well spent, she told me, to see her daughter so well matched."

No one answered her. Wary faces around the table all watched in mute horror as Jocelyn slowly stood up from her chair. Without a word, she left the room and ignored the petty look of victory on Jez's beautiful face.

His fiancée. Miss Winifred Preston. She sounds perfectly respectable . . . "the prettiest little thing." Jocelyn marveled at the pain as she climbed the staircase to escape the others and their pity or scorn. Never before had she been in such a position. The entire house knew of her arrangement with Alex. They'd have thought nothing of it, but her feelings were transparent to them and now . . .

Instinctively, she knew the source of Jez's venom. For years, Jocelyn had kept herself apart from the women of the house. Overseeing them, advising and providing for them, and speaking as if they were family, but she'd never actually been one of them. So perhaps secretly, Jocelyn accepted that she might have taken solace in her choice to stay just slightly above the tawdry business of the Belle—and Jezebel had resented her for it. Jocelyn had played the lady all along—until Alex had arrived.

She made it to her room before she let the tears come. It had been one thing to admit that she'd lost her heart in the sweet tangle she'd created. But to know that there was another woman . . .

It was a blow she hadn't expected.

I'm so blind. Of course he would marry. I'm not some naïve thing off the first mail coach, am I? Did I imagine he was really mine because he shares my bed? He'd paid her for the privilege and in an ironic twist, it seemed Miss Preston would pay him for the privilege of being his wife. It was all a matter of contracts and arrangements. Every woman in the house knew it all too well. It was a wretched dance of deception and desire, and she was the teacher who had simply forgotten the steps.

She'd ignored every bit of advice she'd ever given, and played the ultimate fool. Somewhere in the quiet hours of the night, she'd allowed herself to indulge in fantasies of a future with Alex by her side, of a legitimate life where she was free to love him and be with him openly, where he would marry her and give her children and—

A knock at the door jarred her from the brutal lectures rattling around in her head. "Mistress?"

Ramis's voice carried through the closed portal. "Are you well?"

Jocelyn wiped her face, aware that it was a useless gesture. Ramis would miss nothing. "Come in, if you must."

"Are you well?" He repeated the question as he entered with a tray holding the breakfast she'd abandoned.

"I am, but if you think I'm in any mood for porridge, you are off the mark, old friend." She took a deep, ragged breath, to steady her nerves and moved to the side table to pour herself a glass of port.

"Jezebel spoke out of turn. It was cruel, Mistress, and unwarranted."

Jocelyn held up a trembling hand. "She had reason enough. Leave it, Ramis."

"Do you believe Miss Jezebel speaks the truth of it?"

"I think yes. And it is . . . a relief."

"A relief?" he asked, openly skeptical. "You don't care that he has another?"

"I care deeply," she admitted, her head high despite the threat of fresh tears, determined to brazen it out. "I care more than . . . more than I wish to say. But I'm relieved that I—that I can still feel. I've seen the women retreat from their hearts and forget what it's like to care. At least I haven't lost my ability to love, Ramis."

"He wounds you."

"Because I let him." She set down the glass without touching its contents. "It is my choice to let him and my choice to never let him know it. Lord Colwick has always been honest with me, and I will not transform into an idealistic idiot simply because I momentarily forgot my place in the world."

Ramis answered her with silence, his eyes steady with open sympathy.

She did her best to smile, ignoring the icy churning in her stomach at the lies her pride forced her to tell. "He pleases me, and the arrangement we have is . . . perfect. So yes, I am well enough, thank you, Ramis. This changes nothing."

Ramis sighed. "I dread to mention this, Mistress, but I had come up with an additional bit of bad news."

Jocelyn stiffened. "Let's have it."

"Marsh is below stairs in the gold salon. I had not realized you were in a state, but Edith found me and relayed the worst of the events in the kitchen. Clearly, he can be dismissed to trouble you another day." Ramis bowed and began to retreat. "I will see to it."

"No." Jocelyn shook herself. "I'm not going to hide in my room all day. And it seems Lord Colwick's insistence that he follow the rules has sunk in a bit."

"I am not sure this is wise. You are well enough, but there is no need to—"

She cut him off with a wave of her hand. "Of course there is. He may have word of the killer."

"I will tell him you are coming." Ramis bowed again, touching his forehead before leaving to carry out her orders.

She checked her reflection in the vanity mirror to ensure that the evidence of her heartache was gone. She pulled her hair up in a simple twist and then added a touch of rouge to her cheeks to give her complexion a livelier look. "Do your worst, Fergus Marsh," she challenged the mirror, and headed downstairs to the gold salon.

Fergus Marsh was dressed in his usual macabre imitation of a blackbird, his overly abused hat an unrecognizable lump in his nervous hands as he paced the room. "You'd think you'd learn not to keep me waiting after all these years, Madame."

"I was sure you'd come to expect to be kept waiting, Mr. Marsh, after your last visit. I didn't wish to disappoint you." Jocelyn moved to take a seat on the sofa, determined that if nothing else transpired, she would at least enjoy the miserable distraction of his company from her own heartache at Alex's engagement.

"Damn cheeky creature." He stopped his pacing to address her, refusing to sit. "It's dangerous times like these when you may wish to reconsider keeping the Belle. A woman with sense might take a good price and see herself safely away from this mess."

"Thank you, Mr. Marsh. But as you have never considered me a woman with sense, I marvel that you would think to offer that bit of advice. I'm flattered, actually."

He sputtered in frustration before he tried another tactic. "If you continue in your foolishness, you won't see a farthing for the property, Madame! Make no mistake."

"Ah"—Jocelyn made a show at relaxing, tucking her feet up into her skirts—"and to think I was worried that you'd come with news of the murders! And instead here you are to advise me in regard to my business practices again . . ."

"What news could I share? If it is one man, we have no proof. It seems clear that whoever this animal is, he is not going for the common strolling dollies—but most think that he isn't crossing into our parlors. None of the women have come to harm under a brothel's roof. Jenner doesn't agree and thinks the killer must be a paying customer. He suspects he comes to the houses and picks his next bird before doing the deed outside so that he won't be caught."

"It's possible," Jocelyn noted.

Marsh shook his head. "We've been comparing

our lists, but few names overlap and none with all the women who've been killed. Of course, we can't assist you with the names we have, as you stubbornly refuse to keep records—much less share them with your betters."

Jocelyn sighed. "Discretion rules here, sir."

"Death will rule here soon enough." Marsh looked as if he was tempted to spit on the floor. "The Swan is a stone's throw from your doorstep, and if things track, then one of the Belle's pigeons is next to fall."

"You are a veritable seer, Mr. Marsh." Jocelyn dropped any pretense of a game. "So the news is that you don't know anything but to come here and spew dire hints of impending doom."

"I came as an old friend who is willing to offer you some of my muscle for added protection."

"Out of the dear generosity of your nature, I take it?"

"For a price and one you'll pay without complaint if you wish to keep every overpaid whore in this house alive until they discover the killer."

Jocelyn smoothed out her skirts and stood slowly, as regal as a queen. "No."

"Think about what you're refusing, Jocelyn."

"I'm sure I've asked you never to use my Christian name, Mr. Marsh. You can show yourself out, can't you?"

"Don't be a fool." Marsh rose to his feet, his

eyes blazing contempt. "Your lover, for all his talk, won't be able to stop this. There will be blood on your doorstep before the week is out, and you'll want to remember this conversation! It's on your head, Madame!"

Jocelyn said nothing, glaring at him with equal disregard until Marsh's color deepened to a mottled purple in his rage. At last he stormed out, slamming the door hard enough to rattle the fixtures and paintings on the walls.

It was long seconds before she realized that she'd held her breath. Alone, she made her way up to her rooms, where she could sit down, and rested her forehead against her palms to wait for the wave of loathing and terror to pass.

They look to me for protection, but if Marsh is right . . . oh, God.

She heard the door open and close gently but didn't even look up. "Not now, Ramis! Go away!"

"Even if I'm not Ramis?" Alex asked, locking the door behind him to guarantee them a temporary sanctuary.

She looked up with a startled cry to see his handsome frame leaning against the door, a vision of male beauty that stole her breath and in a single moment made her heart ache with joy and pain.

Alex crossed the room to kneel at her feet. "Jocelyn, has something happened?"

Had something happened? She'd learned he was engaged, but had it truly changed anything? The nature of their arrangement? The way his touch affected her? Her love for this man?

"No," she answered, drinking in the welcome sight of him. "It was . . . a headache."

His eyes blazed with concern, and he reached out to caress her cheek. "Perhaps you should rest."

She covered his fingers with hers, turning his hand so that her lips could graze the sensitive well inside his palm. "It's a miracle, Alex. The pain is gone."

She pushed away thoughts of Winifred Preston and horrible men who preyed on women outside their houses. Jocelyn seized the moment, refusing to surrender a single second of happiness to the disasters that waited outside the door. He'd come to her. She was his lover, and for now, there was nothing else she wanted to be.

"Do you remember the first time you came to the Belle?"

Alex smiled. "We met downstairs and I remember thinking you had lovely taste in art-work—and lovelier eyes. I couldn't forget you and so I returned to call with my card only to have Ramis force me to cool my heels."

"You said you wanted me." Jocelyn placed her hand against his chest to cover his heart.

"I still do." He leaned in slowly to claim her with a searing kiss that threatened to undo her. He suckled her lower lip, before his tongue explored every taste and texture of her mouth against his.

Jocelyn responded, matching each move he made and allowing him to set a gentle, sweet pace that made every inch of her come back to life. She wrapped her legs around him and laid claim to the only things she could—to his touch, to her own feelings, and to the memories that no one could wrest from her.

None of the texts she'd studied came to mind. Not a single image or design, and Jocelyn accepted that this was exactly as it should be. Her fingertips fluttered over his face, engraving every handsome line and feature onto her senses. "Make love to me, Alex."

He complied without another word between them. Alex trailed sweet fire from her lips down the pulse of her neck and the soft exposed skin of her throat. Unhurried, he tackled the small bone buttons of her dress and unhooked the corset beneath it to bare her breasts. He teased each pert mound, encircling the coral tips with his tongue only to exhale against her to bathe her in sensation. She writhed and sighed, arching against the sofa to yield to him any part of her body he desired.

Alex worshiped her in a way she'd never dreamt of, reverently touching her feet and making her squirm at the sorcery of the touch of his lips against her toes. She felt like a feast, spread out on an altar for him to taste and sample, and in between courses, his eyes sought hers—the raw yearning in his caramel-brown eyes underscoring her own need.

"Alex, I—"

He grabbed her hips and unhooked the waistband of her skirts to slide them slowly down over her knees. She anticipated him spreading her legs to sample her damp folds, but he surprised her again by drawing her completely off the furniture as he leaned back to lie prone on the rug.

Jocelyn froze a bit in confusion, until she realized his intent. He guided her forward until she was literally astride his face, her knees parted so that his mouth was just beneath her clit. Before she could think, his tongue flicked over the tiny nub in an intense miniature lathing that left no room for modesty or reserve.

Her body took over, her thighs moving to lift and lower her hips against his mouth, until she found her own rhythm, a sweet gallop of a ride that made her throw back her head and arch her back as her climax began to build. His tongue was relentless, and Jocelyn shuddered as the first wave broke over her. His hands reached up to steady her as his mouth coaxed another wave, and another from her core before she sagged back, unable to hold herself upright as spasm after spasm exploded through her small frame.

He lifted her back onto the sofa, kneeling again between her thighs, but this time, to grip her hips and bury himself inside of her. The solid heat of him filled the void, and her wet lips held him tight with every stroke. He withdrew to press against her clit before moving into her again with a deliberate and powerful thrust.

Jocelyn clung to his neck and tasted her own crème on his tongue before the next coil overtook her. For a fleeting moment, she couldn't remember why it was wrong to love him . . . why it was impossible to have him . . .

"I wish you knew." He whispered against the shell of her ear.

"Knew what?"

"Knew what an oasis this is for me, Jocelyn. I can forget the world, and when I look at you, nothing exists unless we desire to say it does."

Oh, God. I want to forget too. Jocelyn soothed his brow with her fingertips and kissed him before he could read the pain in her eyes—for whatever sanctuary the Belle had once offered was forever lost now that she knew he would truly belong to another woman.

"There is no world beyond this, Alex. Just make love to me," she begged him quietly, and once again, her beloved Lord Colwick complied.

Fifteen

Pale early-morning light through the one small garret window finally crossed into his sleep, and Alex relinquished his hold on the elusive illogical thread of his dreams. Last night they had ultimately abandoned the silk rug and gone to her bed. Before he made love to her again, he'd even made a great show of propping her desk chair under the door handle as an additional measure to keep out any more interruptions.

Stretching out, he wondered what it would be like to wake each morning with Jocelyn in his arms—not to gather his things and quietly return to his own house, sneaking past the servants to diffuse his sister's disapproving looks. Instead he imagined her in his master suite, an exotic jewel in his stately quarters, sprawled across his bed, naked underneath the family crest carved into the headboard.

Alex sighed as his body tightened with the fantasy, a pleasant warmth flooding his senses until his cock was rock-hard against her. He closed his eyes and let his thoughts drift, enjoying the turn of his thoughts and the taut friction they triggered.

She awoke slowly from the unmistakable sensation of his erection prodding her hip and nudging up against her bottom. She smiled in anticipation of a morning well spent. She stretched slowly, arching her back to deliberately press against him until he moaned from the sensation.

"Jocelyn . . ."

"Yes?"

"You are a beautiful, wicked creature to torment a man like this." Alex's hand gently seized her waist, holding her firmly in place against his body.

She laughed, lazily shifting her hips to savor the coil of desire that had begun to grow each time the silken firm head of his cock moved against her. "Wicked?"

"Most definitely." He began to kiss her bare shoulder as his fingers slowly slid into the soft wet tangle of curls between her legs. "I think you should stay in bed until you've mended your ways."

Jocelyn laughed again. "Hardly a punishment, but you'll have to release me before too long, Alex. After all, yesterday was a bit trying and there is so much to do—"

"Let Ramis earn his keep." Before she could think of a witty response, he moved with cat-like reflexes and instantly shifted her so that she was beneath him. Alex captured her wrists in his hands to pin them easily against the mattress and rewarded her with a devilish grin. "The Belle can do without its Mistress this morning. Whereas I . . ." Alex lowered himself, letting her feel the urgent taut weight of his cock between her thighs. "I cannot."

"Alex!" she squealed in surprise, instantly aware of his strength and the delicious sensation of being completely helpless and at his mercy. "What are you doing?"

"I am seeking retribution." He nuzzled the sensitive curve of her throat, his warm breath and tongue sending waves of luscious heat down her spine.

"Retribution?" She tipped her head back into the pillows, yielding to the attentions of his mouth and the sweet havoc he was creating inside her.

"You've held me captive for weeks. My every thought and action draws me here—to you.

Every time I tried to stay away, it only made it worse, my sweet. And so now I shall see if I cannot take the reins and . . ."

His words trailed off, the desire between them unraveling the thread of his thoughts. He released her hands only to cradle her face, lowering his lips to hers in a slow searing kiss that commanded her surrender and obedience. His tongue met hers, an unhurried invasion that belied the insistent nudging of his cock between her legs.

Her thighs parted to welcome him, and Jocelyn gasped as the head of his cock lodged against her slit, her body stretching to accommodate him once again. He held himself back for just a moment, his hips poised to drive into her and Jocelyn shivered at Alex's gift of this delicious power.

She rocked her hips upward to urge him on, to communicate her compliance and was rewarded within the space of a single heartbeat as he plunged into her slick passage, pressing against her deepest core hard enough to make her moan. Jocelyn clung to him, lost to the storm of pleasure and pain that each stroke evoked until he shuddered in her arms and she felt the flood of his crème inside her.

"Alex. That was—"

He placed two fingers over her lips, his breath

ragged and uneven as he regained his composure. "Wait."

He kissed her again as he withdrew, distracting her from the ache of her own lack of satisfaction, before his fingers trailed down to soothe the flesh he had plundered.

"Alex, you don't have to—"

"Wait, woman," he growled playfully, ignoring her feeble attempts at escape.

His fingers began an indolent exploration of the slick folds between her thighs until he'd uncovered the swollen taut bud he sought, tracing the sensitive ridge with his fingers. Each movement sent a small shock wave through her frame until Jocelyn was sure he truly meant to torment her with ecstasy. She bucked her hips uselessly against his hand, wordlessly begging him to help her achieve the release she now desperately needed. At last, the slow rhythm broke away into a gallop, his fingers working a magic she couldn't name as they flew back and forth over her clit. Faster and faster, until his touch drove her past any semblance of control, beyond any connection to rational thought. She climaxed in a shattering wave of heat that made her see nothing but white lights, so intense was her orgasm.

Jocelyn recovered slowly, marveling at the way her fractured senses happily blended back together gradually returning her to an awareness of Alex and the world. "Oh, my!"

Alex chuckled. "I'd meant to just wish you a good morning, but I'd say that went well."

She smiled, reaching up to push his hair back off his brow. "Extremely well. I'm surprised I haven't insisted on you waking me up every morning."

"I wonder. The ladies of the Belle certainly expend a great deal of effort to fulfill the fantasies of their male clients. I glanced at a shopping list you left on your desk, and it was definitely educational."

"Was it?" Jocelyn closed her eyes at his admission. *Oh, dear. If he asks about the talcum powder, riding crop, and silk ropes, I'm not sure I can keep from laughing.*

"It made me wonder . . ."

"Yes?"

"I wonder what your fantasy would be?" His fingers traced the soft outline of her shoulders and arms as he spoke, sending gentle ripples of pleasure across her bare skin.

It was the last thing in the world she'd expected him to say. "M-my fantasy?"

"Something beyond what can be found in your library, I suspect," he coaxed her gently. "What would you dream of doing, Jocelyn?"

"You'll think it foolish, Alex." She was more

tempted than she wanted to admit, but any real fantasies she harbored had little to do with erotic positions or forbidden sins of the flesh. She hated to disappoint him. But in the cocoon of the gray light between night and day, the illusion of their isolation fueled her sense of trust.

"I won't." His fingers continued their paths, a whisper of touches that made her sigh in submission.

"I've never . . . been asked to dance."

"Really?"

She pushed against him playfully. "I should have lied and said something about swimming naked in public."

"A lovely prevarication, but I liked the truth." He kissed her forehead, calming her nerves to draw her closer against him. "It seems a simple thing to remedy."

Jocelyn laughed, shaking her head. "Hardly. It's not as if Madame DeBourcier's name appears on any invitation lists, nor would I want it to!" She shifted to face him, bravely going ahead with a full confession. "I know men often make fun of those poor nervous young ladies making that dreaded debut—but there was always something elusive and magical to the ritual of dance cards and orchestras. I would have liked to have gone to a grand ball and been asked to dance."

"You'd have been faced with a stampede of eager partners, Jocelyn."

"You're sweet to say it." She put her head down on his shoulder, content with the compliment.

He reached out to entwine one of his fingers in the lengths of copper curls that draped across his chest. "One day, I will ask you to d—"

Jocelyn placed her fingers gently over his lips, cutting off the promise he was about to make. "At a grand ball? With everyone watching? Alex . . . I think I lost my dance card over nine years ago. Please, don't say it. It's an idle fantasy."

"It's more than that."

She kissed him, a slow, sweet taste that made her light-headed with longing. "I'd rather hear you promise to take me moon bathing, Alex."

A scream shattered the peace. From downstairs, a keening that made the hair on the back of her neck stand on end cut through the morning quiet and propelled them both to their feet. Within seconds they were half dressed, and she was racing down the stairs toward the commotion below, with Alex on her heels.

"The kitchens!" Jocelyn burst through the wide doors to find Suzanne sitting forlornly at the table, quietly sobbing over and over, "It should have been me! It should have been me!" Before she could ask her any questions, the keening repeated and led them out of the kitchen onto the back steps.

It took only a fraction of a breath for Jocelyn to realize what they were seeing. Edith was in tears, clinging to Mrs. Brooks as they knelt at the foot of the steps.

A few steps beyond, Ramis held a lifeless Gilliam to his chest. Beyond grief, he keened an unholy melody that Jocelyn knew she would never in a thousand lifetimes forget. The sight of them—Gilly, so small and unnaturally still in his arms, still pale and beautiful, but her head at an angle that betrayed how she had been horribly broken. In death, her sweet brown eyes now looked through them all into a void of agony and nothingness.

"Ramis . . ." Jocelyn could only speak his name, before her breath gave out when his eyes met hers—the void in his eyes matching Gilly's.

He began rocking Gilliam like a child, crooning and crying in a language Jocelyn had never heard, what could be only a heartfelt entreaty to the gods to restore something forever lost. She hardly recognized him, his face was so twisted in pain. He moved Gilly protectively, and the dead girl's hand slipped from her chest; and from her fingers a single brass button clattered onto the brick street.

At the sight of it, Ramis's head fell back, a cry of such strength overtaking him that his throat corded with the strain of it, even as no sound escaped his tortured lips. He lay Gilly down, collapsing for a moment on the ground and covering her petite frame with his. Jocelyn slipped from Alex's grasp to reach him, desperate to offer what comfort she could, but Ramis's pain wouldn't allow it.

"No!" He launched to his feet to face them all, a fierce warrior, suddenly frightening as he looked at them with eyes they didn't recognize. Gilly's body lay on the ground behind him, and for a moment, Jocelyn was sure he meant to kill anyone who tried to touch her remains.

"Ramis," she whispered. "Ramis, my dearest friend. Please . . ."

"It was Marsh!" He spat the words, his eyes wild now with hate.

Alex stepped forward to try to pull Jocelyn back, but she refused to believe that Ramis could ever hurt her. Even now. "Ramis, we must call the police."

"I heard him! He promised blood on the steps! He told you he would do this thing, and now . . . it is done." His voice broke, but rage drove him on. "I will see to him. I will see to him and this will all be done!"

"Ramis, no." Jocelyn tried to break away from

Alex's hold, but before she could manage it, Ramis had turned and fled down the alley to disappear from view. "Alex, let me go!"

"He could hurt you, Jocelyn, and not even realize it. What if he . . . did this thing?"

"No, Alex!"

"It wasn't Ramis, sir!" Mrs. Brooks protested. "Edith found the body, poor thing, and Ramis came running when the yelling started."

"It wasn't Ramis and now he's gone after Marsh!" Jocelyn pulled free, a tigress defending her own. "But it can't have been Fergus, Alex! Ramis will commit murder in a blind act of vengeance and I'll lose him forever! You have to stop him, Alex. Please!"

"But if Fergus threatened—"

"No! Not the Belle directly! Not . . . Fergus is bluster and ignorance, Alex. Ramis is mistaken, and if he harms Marsh there'll be no going back! Please, Alex. Ramis is more than family to me! I cannot lose him now."

"No, and you won't." He kissed her quickly and left her on the steps with Mrs. Brooks and her frightened charge.

Alex stole another man's clothes out of the laundry before sprinting to the stables to steal the mount he needed. Ramis was on foot, but Alex was taking no chances. The sound of Jocelyn's blurted pleas for the black man's safety rang in his ears, but he ignored it. Whatever their differences, he meant to stem the tide of bloodshed and save the man.

He rode with reckless speed, narrowly avoiding a collision with more than one hackneyed coach before he reached Marsh's brothel, the Crescent. The house seemed as quiet as a tomb and that gave Alex pause.

Where are the footmen? Even at this early hour, guests could be leaving.

It wasn't a good sign. He took the steps to the front doors two at a time and burst inside just in time to discover Fergus on his knees in his nightclothes, pleading for his life as Ramis held a knife to his throat. A staircase to the left was lined with women in various stages of undress, all quietly watching the drama unfold beneath them with eyes as big as saucers.

"I-I don't know what y-you're saying . . . R-Ramis . . . I never . . ." Marsh's charms were having no effect, and Ramis's arm tensed as he prepared to slice Fergus's throat open.

"Ramis, don't. He is hardly worth your own life." Alex held still, hardly daring to breathe.

"He is not worth hers!" Ramis tightened his grip into Fergus's hair to stretch his head back farther. "But mine . . . I will gladly give mine to see him leave this world. I will join him in hell for it and smile for the chance to witness his suffering throughout eternity. Demons will weep for my laughing."

"He's mad!" Fergus looked to Alex, desperate for an ally. "I've killed no one! W-why would I kill one of your birds? I've been here since I saw your mistress last night! I-I'm still in my nightgown, for God's sake! Ask anyone! Ask anyone you want, Ramis!"

They all nodded, a terrified chorus. "H-he was with Polly! Weren't he, Polly?"

"It's true, sir! I . . ." She looked less than happy with the admission. "He kept me all night and been yellin' fer breakfast when you came in!"

"They lie for you."

Fergus held up both hands. "Why would I damage the goods I'm after? Y-you've heard me say I wanted the Belle for myself! You heard me!"

Alex wasn't sure if the man was helping his cause or making it worse.

Ramis shook his head. "I have heard you threaten the Belle, you vile garbage!"

"I didn't mean it! Not . . . not Marie's girl! Not ever when she's . . ."

Ramis's eyes grew even colder. "You . . ."

"Ramis, wait!" Alex stepped closer. "If you kill him, you lose her forever."

Ramis looked up, confused. "What are you talking about?"

"If you believe in hell as you said, then think of heaven. For she is there, is she not?"

Tears filled Ramis's eyes. "As God wills . . . she will shine like a star there . . . my sparrow."

"Your sparrow waits for you there, Ramis. Murder Fergus and she will wait in vain. You would torture her for an eternity knowing that you'd done this thing in her name. Gilliam would not have wanted this. You have to know that in your heart."

Ramis looked back at Fergus, his resolve wavering.

Alex went on. "You don't honor her by committing this foul deed. Gilliam doesn't deserve to have a wretch like Marsh for her memorial. Surely you loved her too much for that."

The moment hung on the most tenuous silken threads, Fergus's ragged breathing the only sound metering out the seconds. Until at last Ramis released him and Fergus stumbled away to collapse at Alex's feet.

Fergus growled, his hand massaging his throat as if to ensure he wasn't cut. "Black bastard! I'll see you ha—"

Alex's fist struck him with the force of a hammer and drove Marsh to the floor. "You'll see that you mind your manners and keep this incident to yourself, or I'll destroy you myself. Do you hear me?"

Marsh looked up at him, nodding, his lower lip trembling as his face grayed in pain. "H-he would have killed me."

"He might have," Alex agreed, then he grabbed the front of Fergus's nightshirt and pulled him closer, lowering his voice so that only Marsh would benefit from his words. "But if you ever bother Madame DeBourcier again or so much as set a single foot across the threshold of the Crimson Belle, you most definitely will wish that he had."

At Marsh's nod, Alex released him without warning and stepped over his prostrate form to follow Ramis back out of the Crescent. They caught their breath on the steps and Alex signaled for a carriage to take them both back to the Belle.

The short ride passed in a dreamlike fog. Ramis remained silent and unresponsive, and Alex felt as if he had retrieved a dead man. He'd saved him from killing Marsh, but looking at Ramis, he saw little mercy in the act.

If it had been Jocelyn in that alley, could I have stayed my hand? Could I think or even draw breath? Would I want to be saved from any hell that would bring an end to that kind of pain? It was unthinkable.

It was easier to think of Fergus. Jocelyn's instincts were accurate enough. He was such an openly hateful man, it made no sense for him to stalk his own women along with others. The woman, Polly, had been believable enough, and from the way Fergus treated them, they owed him no loyalty to lie. Hell, this would have been their chance to rid themselves of the wretched man if they'd been quicker to think on their feet!

But if not Fergus . . .

Then who?

He tallied the victims in his head, tracing the killer's path from the Crescent to the Jade, then to the Swan, and now the Crimson Belle and poor Gilly. The strangest thought coalesced and he suddenly couldn't shake it.

Hadn't Declan mentioned all those brothels? Almost in that order . . . He shook his head. *No, not almost in that order—exactly in that order.* But it was too fantastic an idea. He'd known Declan forever and the only thing the man was guilty of was a lack of discipline. But still . . .

It was impossible!

No, a small, dark voice corrected inside his head. *Not impossible.* He'd patronized all those houses and expressed great interest in the murders. Like a man wanting to relive them in the telling?

It was wrong! Declan wouldn't hurt a fly.

Still, as the carriage pulled up to the Belle, he realized he wasn't getting out. "See to him, Mrs. Brooks." The cook and footmen helped Ramis out of the carriage and up the steps as if he were infirm or made of glass.

"Won't you be coming in, m'lord?" she stopped to ask, dark circles of concern under her eyes. "Madame was most terribly anxious that—"

"No," he cut her off. "There is . . . something I must attend to." He tapped the roof. "Driver, home with all speed!"

And with that, the carriage pulled away, leaving an astonished Mrs. Brooks to tend to Ramis and direct the rest of the servants into the house.

Sixteen

～∞～

Alex didn't even wait for the carriage to come to a halt before leaping down to race up the steps and into the house. "Declan!" His voice echoed off the polished marble surfaces and Alex tore off his coat in frustration to throw it on the floor, just as the butler rounded the corner.

"Adams, where is Mr. Forrester?" he asked curtly.

The normally unflappable butler managed only to point upstairs before muttering, "I-I believe he's still abed, but—"

Alex didn't wait for the rest of it.

He took the stairs two at a time toward the first floor, then down the hall to Declan's room. Without knocking, he threw open the door. After all, if the man had just committed foul murder, he might betray some sign of it, although he still couldn't quite believe that jovial old Declan was—

A scream cut off his thoughts, and Alex faced a completely different scene than the one he'd dreaded.

Eloise jumped from the bed, and Declan scrambled to get her behind him, for modesty's sake and also to shield her from her brother's rage. "Now, Randall . . . this isn't how it looks!" Declan grimaced. "Well, it *is,* but not entirely. If you'll allow me to . . . dress." Eloise pinched him from behind to protest, but made no sound.

"Damn it, woman. The man can tell I've lost my clothes. It's not as if mentioning it suddenly gives him ideas!" Declan's color deepened as he readjusted the sheet around his waist.

Alex struggled between pure relief, shock, and the unsettling urge to laugh. It was pure scandal to find his married sister abed with his best friend, and fury would have been the natural reaction, but he just couldn't muster it. Declan was no villain, and Alex felt like a dunce for entertaining the notion. "By all means, dress. I'll be . . . leaving."

He turned and closed the door behind him. There would be time later to hear what the lovers planned—if anything—and play the role of disgruntled brother.

With a sigh, he retreated quickly and demanded the carriage again. He cursed the delay in retrieving the coat he'd thoughtlessly discarded, a string of expletives echoing in the hall. A great solver of mysteries he was not. Whoever had done these terrible deeds still walked freely and there was nothing to be done. Nothing except return to do whatever he could for Jocelyn.

She needed him now, and instead of standing by her, he'd run off on a fool's errand.

Returning to the Belle, he rushed into the foyer and began to hand over his hat and coat, asking one of the footmen, "How is Ramis? Has there been any news?"

"And you are?" a deep male voice interjected from the doorway to the private salon. As the man stepped forward, Alex realized that he must be an inspector sent regarding the murder. Notepad in hand, he was a square bulldog of a man with eyes that never seemed to stop moving. The man's flint cold gaze raked him up and down and Alex had no doubt the man never missed anything.

Alex hated the smothering chill that crept up his spine. "A friend."

"Won't you step in, friend?" The man stepped to one side of the door frame, and Alex caught sight of Jocelyn in the room beyond with a sheer gray veil across her face. Even with the thin barrier, he could see that she was pale and shaken, though composed.

"Have you no name, sir? Or a card?" The man went on, "I ask only because no one beyond the house seems to know of this girl's death yet . . . so I'd have to hazard the guess that you were here when things occurred. Yes?"

Oh, God. It was a simple thing to admit. But if his name was reported in connection to these murders . . . Drake's fate echoed inside his skull and Alex's heart began pounding at the nightmare of it all. What would his nickname be when the press determined that his mistress ran a brothel and that he'd raced to protect another pimp from her vengeance-crazed manservant? Would the reporters then insinuate that he was involved in the murders of all these fallen women? The Deadly Duke would seem like an angel in comparison and his father's follies would be all but forgotten.

"Sir?" the inspector prompted again.

"I'm not sure it's—"

"He is a friend to the Belle, Inspector Taggert. Surely you can understand when a man is reluctant to admit to such a thing," Jocelyn interjected smoothly, drawing the policeman's focus back to her. "He is a gentleman and a respected Peer of the Realm, and too polite to tell you that he'd prefer not to sully his name by having it appear in your meticulous notes."

"Even so . . ." The man's words trailed as he

measured the situation, eyeing Alex's expensive coat and aristocratic demeanor before looking back to Jocelyn. "If he has any information—"

"If he did, he would not have come in the door with questions of his own," Jocelyn countered. "Inspector, no one wants this killer found more than I. G-Gilliam . . ." Emotion choked her briefly before she went on. "Gilliam was like a younger sister to me. But please let us send this poor man on his way, so that we can focus on the business at hand. If he does reveal anything later, I assure you, I will let you know." She drew closer to the inspector and whispered something in his ear that Alex didn't hear.

"Very well." The inspector nodded, straightening up to close the small leather notepad and tuck it away into his coat pocket.

Jocelyn stepped around the man to face Alex. "You should go."

"No, this is . . . Jocelyn, I—"

She shook her head, cutting him off, a fiery flash of anger in her eyes. He'd used her Christian name in front of the inspector. He'd overstepped and worse. He was no help to her now. "As Madame of the house, I'm asking you to leave, sir. I'll send word when this mess has cleared, but until then, please don't return."

Seventeen

In the ground-floor foyer of the Crimson Belle, his worst fears were strengthened as the footmen moved to bar him from entering. Days had passed and still there'd been no word from her. He took a small measure of comfort from the appearance of the house's new burlier footmen and security measures, but since they prevented him from seeing her as he wished, it didn't do much to ease his mind. He'd sent messages, and hated every syllable that humbled him as he begged to see her. She'd said she would send for him when the mess had cleared, but Alex wasn't sure that anything could be resolved while he was away from her. At last his patience had reached its end. He was desperate to know how she fared, and the silence of her replies was deafening. Finally, he'd decided that he would just have to take matters into his own hands. This thing started at her summons, but it wouldn't end with them. *I've been a fool.* He'd told himself in the carriage that fateful day that he couldn't live without her, and then he'd walked away.

"Madame DeBourcier isn't receiving, m'lord. I'm afraid you will have to leave."

"She'll 'receive' me! Inform her that I have no intentions of—"

"Lord Colwick!" Jez greeted him, the façade of sweetness in her smile fooling neither of them, but confusing the servants into at least loosening their grip on his coat sleeve. "You're naughty to keep me waiting."

"The Mistress said she doesn't wish to—"

"Don't be a dolt, Martin. He's a paying customer and you didn't even ask him if he might prefer another lady since Madame DeBourcier isn't available!" Jez reached the bottom of the stairs and snaked her arm into Alex's. "Come with me, then. Let's see if we can't take care of your troubles."

The footmen stood aside, but not without protesting. "I'll speak with Ramis to make sure, Jez."

She pouted and gave them a flippant look, even as she began pushing Alex up the staircase. "Makes no matter to me, boys. Though I think it's cruel of you to pester the poor man when he's suffering so! Out of his mind with grief, and you're going to speak with him about such a little thing as a regular client coming in for a bit of comfort and solace. If he beats you senseless, don't come moaning near my door."

Once they were safe on the landing and out of earshot of the servants, she purred in his ear, "Come, my lord. I know you won't be talked out of seeing her, but . . . are you sure I can't tempt you?"

"Thank you, Jezebel." He gently removed her hand from his arm. "I am in your debt."

"Hardly." Her gaze narrowed, the last vestige of "sweetness" falling away from her eyes. "You are quite the puzzle, aren't you, Lord Colwick."

The kitten had claws, but she continued to escort him through the house toward his goal. "You don't like me, do you?"

She shrugged. "I don't like any men, Lord Colwick. But you are harder to dislike than most, if that comforts you."

As they walked along the second-story hallway, Alex heard a woman weeping and his steps slowed.

Jez tapped her foot impatiently, trying to wave him on. "Don't trouble yourself, my lord. It's just Suzanne. She hasn't stopped wailing since they found Gilly. Useless thing, she'll ruin her beauty and end up brushing out another woman's petticoats if she's not careful."

"Was she terribly close to Miss Gilliam?"

"No," she replied airily. "Which makes all these tears more annoying if you ask me. But who can guess what's going on inside that head of hers?"

"Indeed."

"Oh, as if *you* are enlightened!" she scoffed, and stopped in front of the servants' staircase to the top floor. "I don't care what you think of me, m'lord. I make no pretense of who and what I am. I hold no fairy-tale disguise up to the hard realities of this life I've chosen. But you—you'd hold a tankard and try and convince yourself it was a teacup! You'd drink piss out of a goblet if someone told you it was fine crystal! I won't apologize for throwing a few rocks at your windows. You've dodged them well enough." She turned back down the hallway with a graceful swoosh of her skirts, and over her shoulder she sneered, "Leave now, Colwick. While you still think you're smarter than the rest of us!"

He took three slow breaths to ease the anger her impertinence had fueled. Long, frustrating days had done nothing to weaken his resolve, but Jez's attack was something he hadn't anticipated. Still, he'd wasted too much time already obediently waiting for Jocelyn to send for him, and he wasn't about to waste any more of it arguing with Jezebel about crockery.

He raced up the stairs to reach Jocelyn, pushing Jez's nonsense from his mind.

He knocked at the door and waited for the invitation to enter.

"Come," her voice came, muffled and soft.

The sight of the room made him feel relieved, as if just reaching this sanctuary was enough to assure him of success. But there was no sign of Jocelyn, so he took a few steps around the corner to discover her in her tiny alcove study with the tapestry tied back for air.

She glanced up in surprise from her chair, and his chest hurt at the paleness in her face and signs of recent tears. "L-Lord Colwick."

Her use of his formal title didn't go unnoticed, but Alex decided that she had every right to withdraw slightly as she grieved for her friend. He knelt before the chair, preventing her escape. "Jocelyn, I couldn't wait any longer to see you. I had to . . . know that you're all right."

"As you see," she answered carefully, "I am perfectly fine. I'm drafting a letter to Edith's mother to reassure her of her daughter's progress."

Alex shook his head. "You sent no word. I confess I lost my mind worrying. I am not suited to waiting, Jocelyn. Not when it comes to you."

"There was no news." She stood and pushed past him out of the alcove. "And I thought it best to leave things as they were between us."

"As they were?" He followed her into the larger room. "Jocelyn, I owe you an apology. I shouldn't have let you dismiss me that day. I should have shouted my name and—"

"I used to tell a certain friend of yours that a woman can suffocate in a sea of shoulds. I'm sure that wisdom holds for a man as well, Alex. There is nothing to apologize for. You did what you had to do. Giving your name or declaring your connection with the Crimson Belle wouldn't have accomplished anything to the good. Gilly is still dead and you only would have added your reputation's demise to the mess."

"No." He moved closer, aching to hold her and heal the breach that stood between them. Watching her, he realized how skilled she could be at hiding her true self. In the role of Madame DeBourcier, she'd dismissed him to protect his reputation and accepted the blame for the violence that had shattered her world. But it was Jocelyn he'd hurt by allowing it. He knew her as no one else ever had and the sad chill in her eyes made it so much worse now. "You needed me, and I . . . I failed you, Jocelyn. I've wasted too many moments of my life trying to make up for another man's sins, and ended up cutting myself off from the world. Let me make it up to you. Let me prove that there is nothing I won't do for you."

She held up her hand to wave away his words, and he captured her cool, slim fingers with his and pressed them against his heart. "I love you."

She pulled her hand away, the look on her face a mixture of shock and pain, before she mastered her expression into cold disregard. "You mistake lust for love, Lord Colwick. It is a common enough error within these walls, and I would be the worst kind of villain to take advantage of your confused state."

"Damn it, woman! I love you and I am definitely not confused!"

Jocelyn crossed her arms, openly unconvinced. "A resident of bedlam doesn't exist who agrees that he's insane. Trust me, Lord Colwick. You are mistaken."

"This is no mistake." He deliberately kept his voice level. "I love you and I want you to leave this place. Jocelyn, come away with me. Let me care for you."

At last the icy wall she'd put up around her began to give way, and her eyes filled with tears. "As your mistress? Will you set up a house for me and buy me a carriage?"

"As the woman I love, and I will buy you a dozen carriages if you desire them."

"And what will your wife say to this?"

"My wife?" Alex was sure he'd not heard her correctly. "I have no wife, Jocelyn."

"You will. I heard of your engagement to Miss Preston, Lord Colwick. I suppose congratulations are in order."

"Winifred Preston? Are you mad? I've no such intentions and whoever repeated that gossip was terribly misinformed."

She shrugged, her expression growing even sadder. "It doesn't make any difference. You're an honorable man, Alex, and one day it will finally strike you that you need more than a bedmate. You need a respectable wife who can give you the legitimate sons you'll need to carry on your line."

"Jocelyn . . ."

"I refuse to see you hurt and humiliated by an unthinkable match between nobility and a reputed whore." She held her ground, lifting her chin as the tears spilled down her cheeks, and silently challenged him to deny the truth.

"Don't say that. I've never thought of you as . . ." He couldn't even say the word, and something in him choked on it as the untruth knifed through him. Of course he'd thought of her that way. He'd paid her readily enough and never corrected her when she mentioned their "business." "It's not who you are, Jocelyn."

She smiled, defiant and beautiful. "I never thought it was, Lord Colwick. But it doesn't matter what I think. You fear scandal more than anything else, and as the Madame of the Crimson Belle, scandal is all I'll ever bring you."

"Leave the Belle!"

"I won't abandon the women of the Belle. They need me now more than ever. I vowed to keep them safe, and . . . while I may have failed Gilly, I can't stop trying. My place is here and I believe you've had your money's worth."

He seized her by the shoulders, wanting to kiss away her stubborn denials. "Damn it! I love you, Jocelyn. There has to be a way!"

She began to shake her head and he lost control. He seized her face to stop her refusals, cradling her head in his hands to take the kisses his soul craved.

He tasted the salt of her tears on her skin, and then kissed her with all the longing of a lifetime of searching. He claimed her as his love with every searing touch, drawing from the soft, sweet heat of her until she clung to him with an equally desperate strength.

"Don't—" A sob escaped and she pushed away from him, putting her fingers over her lips as if to cage her grief.

"Jocelyn, I'll marry you! Scandal be damned! I could survive cannon fire if I knew you were mine."

"Scandal be damned? You wouldn't even tell

that inspector your name when he asked! What will you say when someone asks you why you kept company in a whorehouse? Or why your wife looks strangely familiar?"

"I-I would say . . ."

She broke from his grasp and rushed to tug on the bell pull to summon a servant. "Get out, Lord Colwick."

She refused to meet his gaze and clung to the fabric. "Just get out, Alex."

"Jocelyn, did you hear me? I want to marry you."

She closed her eyes, her hands still holding the pull. "I swore to my mother on her deathbed—on her deathbed, do you hear me? I made an oath." She slowly opened her eyes, and Alex's breath caught in his throat at the implacable sorrow he saw there. "The Belle is my fate, not yours."

"You are my fate, Jocelyn."

"The Season is over, Lord Colwick. You've had your money's worth and I . . . I had more than I bargained for. Please." Tears choked her before she could go on. "Just leave."

"You can't mean this! This was more than business between us, Jocelyn." He seized her by the shoulders, desperate to force her to see the truth. "I love you!"

She refused to answer him, to look him in the eyes, and before he could compose another argument to win her, the footmen arrived like a wall of uniformed muscle.

"Mistress?" asked one of the men he recognized from downstairs, eyeing Alex uncomfortably.

"Please show Lord Colwick out, Martin. He won't be returning to the Belle. Ever!"

"Jocelyn, this is ridiculous! Damn it, don't do this!" Fury and frustration made him fight the hands on his shoulders, but ultimately he had no choice. They would carry him out, and he wasn't about to start a brawl in the very rooms she'd made sacred for him.

Once more, Alex found himself on the wrong side of the ornately carved doors of the Crimson Belle.

And this time, there was no way in.

Eighteen

⁂

The summer rain matched his mood, and Alex didn't bother making any pretense of looking at the letters on the desk in front of him. Adams just dutifully brought new posts as they arrived and made no mention of his lack of responses.

Good man, Alex thought as he watched the rain race down the windows. *When I feel human again I should try to remember to tell him so.*

"Alex."

Alex sighed, turning back toward the dim interior of his study and the apparition of his sister, who had apparently garnered the courage to brave his presence. "If you've come to defend Declan, I'm in no mood, Eloise."

"Why should Declan need defending?" She

stood her ground. "I'm just as guilty. More so, I think, since it was I who set out to seduce him."

Alex grimaced, running a hand through his hair. "I find that hard to believe, and truly, I'm not sure if I wish to picture the affair in any sort of detail."

She crossed her arms, expelling a huff of frustration. "Men! If he were expounding the virtues of some courtesan, you'd want to hear every nuance, but as I am your sister—"

"Exactly! As you are my sister, I feel partially compelled to kill the man!"

A small smile ghosted across her lips. "Partially? I'll take that as a good sign."

Alex glanced up at the ceiling and offered up a small prayer to save a tiny bit of his sanity when it came to his sister and a certain Irishman. "All right, Eloise. I surrender. You aren't here to defend yourself or the lying bastard. Was there a purpose to the conversation? I have work to do."

She arched her eyebrows, her gaze sweeping over the piles of untouched correspondence. "Yes, I can . . . see that you're busy."

"Well?"

"We're in love, Alex." She held her head high, and the flash of triumph in her eyes was like a sharp kick to his stomach. "We're going to be together for the rest of our lives."

"Does your husband know this?"

"Mr. Wadley has been in Italy 'on business' for two years. Before that, he may as well have been on another continent, for all that it mattered to me."

"How is that possible?" he asked quietly, his voice edged in concern.

"I was young and stupid, and I thought that if I married an undemanding and uncomplicated man that I would be blissfully happy. I deliberately chose a man very different from our father, a man who didn't have a single vice or blemish on his character. Mr. Wadley was safe and I knew he would let me hold the reins and direct him as I wished." Eloise's gaze dropped to the carpet. "It just didn't occur to me that within weeks of our wedding I would loathe the sight and sound of him eating toast so much that I would direct him to sleep in another county."

"Eloise . . ."

"I am a selfish creature, Alex. I don't think poor Mr. Wadley stood a chance."

Alex shook his head and came toward her, softening a degree at her painful confession. "I take it you think Declan has better table manners."

Eloise chuckled, her eyes lighting up with mirth. "Among his other lovely qualities."

"He is a good friend, Eloise, but you must know that since I know him better than most, I can tell you truthfully that he is the worst sort of man." Alex cleared his throat, wondering how to phrase things for his sister's delicate nature, while ignoring the burning weight in his stomach at the hypocrisy of criticizing Declan when his own behavior was so beyond the pale. "There are worse things than a man who slurps his soup. His character is nothing short of depraved. His evenings spent gambling and . . . in the company of loose women."

Eloise held up her hand in denial. "You're wrong, Alex."

"Eloise, he was constantly inviting me to—"

"To places he knew you would have absolutely no inclination to go," she finished for him. "He knows you better than most, too. Declan deliberately played the rogue knowing full well you would steer clear."

"And why would he do that?"

"So that we would be guaranteed of our privacy." She touched his face. "You never made it easy when you were so antisocial, and Declan knew he couldn't keep refusing your invitations to the club or to the coffeehouses. So he—"

"Misled me like a champion." Alex was amazed. "I avoided him like crazy and you . . ."

"You avoided me since I made a point of pestering you about finding a wife. Not that I wasn't truly hoping you'd meet your match and find happiness . . ." She bit her lip. "We were miserable company on purpose, but only so that we would have the time we desired. I . . . never meant to hurt your feelings. We were as discreet as we could be, because we knew that after everything that had happened with Father that you hated gossip and scandal above all things. I would have done anything in my power to spare you the whispers, but—"

"Go, Eloise. Be happy and don't ever look back. I don't care what people will say. I never should have. Hell, if we are honest, you and I, the story will hardly mark more than a moment or two of public attention. Your husband has been little more than a ghost for years and no one can have missed that you've lived separate lives all this time."

"But a divorce!"

He shrugged. "Bother with one if you wish, but I don't see that it makes any difference. Declan loves you, doesn't he?"

She nodded, speechless.

"Then be happy, Eloise."

She embraced him, kissing his cheek and laughing in relief, years falling away from her face. "You are so dear to me, brother." She leaned back to study his face, her eyes clouding with concern. "And you? Will you be happy, Alex?"

He kissed her cheek and released her, the

tender levity of the moment evaporating. Happiness was a hard stretch from his current vantage point, but admitting his own defeat would only make her departure bittersweet. "Yes." He swallowed afterward, praying she wouldn't press the issue.

She beamed at him. "Good! You deserve to be." She smoothed her hair. "Well, I should go speak with Mr. Forrester. He'll be very relieved you've decided against pistols at dawn."

"Only because he knows I'm the better shot."

Eloise giggled. "Perhaps I'll let him stew a bit longer. He has been a romantic fool with his own mortality nipping at his heels."

"You're a wicked thing, Eloise, and, I suspect, exactly the woman to keep Declan on his toes for the rest of his life."

"Thank you, Alex!" She embraced him again and then practically skipped from the room to go torture poor Forrester before ultimately sharing her good news.

The last trace of warmth left the room with her. Alex returned to his post at the window, hating the depression that pressed in from the corners of the room and threatened to crush his spirit. There had to be an argument to make her see reason! He'd gone to the Belle again and again, only to be turned forcefully away. *Damn it, there has to be a way to right things between us and put the world on its axis again.*

"My lord," Adams intoned from the doorway. "There is a Mr. Peers to see you."

The investigation. I'd forgotten it.

"Afternoon, m'lord." Peers shuffled in, a dripping mess from the weather. "I swear it would drown fish out there today."

"Didn't Adams offer to take your coat, Peers?"

The Bow Street runner shrugged. "Didn't see that this would take too long, and frankly, I didn't see the need for all that fuss."

Alex marveled that a man could be oblivious enough to stand in a puddle he was creating in the midst of his study, and then astute enough to ferret out the most private facts and secrets in other people's lives. "As you wish. Did you make any progress on the murders?"

Peers blinked before answering. "The police have gotten a bit keener since the last girl. I'd say they've almost got a hand on him now. All brunettes, all a similar look, I heard. But I actually came with my report on the lady, sir. Not that it was easy, mind you." Peers visibly puffed with pride at his accomplishment. "I made note of it all in here, m'lord." He pulled a thick brown envelope from inside his coat pocket.

Alex eyed it for a moment, hesitating.

"It's all there, sir. Bits of her history and a copy of her grade cards from one of the fancy schools her mother shipped her off to—I also found the truth of her mother's money and how she came into that brownstone." He paused for dramatic effect, clearly pleased with his finale. "I even found out who her father is . . . a tasty nugget of information, m' lord, if you don't mind my saying! A bit of a surprise when I got his name, since he's—"

"Thank you, Peers!" Alex cut him off, wrenching the large envelope from his grasp in a sudden lunge. "That will be all."

"W-well, yes . . ." Peers managed an awkward bob before starting to retreat. "If there's anything else you need . . ."

"You're the man I'll contact." Alex ushered him out without any attempt to hide his urgency to have him gone. He put coins into the man's hands and closed the door behind him, leaning against it as if he intended to keep out a horde of bloodthirsty invaders.

The envelope in his hands was heavier than he'd expected.

My God, it's Jocelyn's past at my fingertips. The proof I thought I needed . . .

He groaned. *The proof I thought I needed to rationalize my feelings for her. I wanted to discover some lofty connection, a rich blood relation and a fairy-tale story of tragedy and mistaken identities. I wanted it so that I could love her without fear.*

But the fear had left him the instant he'd thought she was in danger. Every misstep since then had been out of sheer blind habit. It sickened him to think that weeks ago, this report would have meant something to him. He would have been relieved to know about her parentage, as if confirming her worth. Or if a more humble background had been revealed, would he have felt bolstered in his generosity?

He walked to the window and focused on nothing but the burning twists and turns of his thoughts. He'd been so sure that hiring Peers and uncovering her past would be like a gift.

Alex scoffed at the idiocy of it. How in the world does a man gift someone with her own past? With her own secrets? It was the worst miscalculation of all. He'd done nothing for her. He'd only selfishly acted to satisfy his own curiosity—and desires.

He'd worried about hiding his tracks and completely lost his heart. She'd said he was honorable, but she'd been the one to hold to her promises and trust him so completely. She'd been the one to insist that the past only hindered a person who refused to embrace his future.

Her entire history. Her mother. Her father.

Alex walked over to the fireplace and set about starting a blaze. Once the flames danced vigorously, he dropped the packet of papers on the coals.

Jocelyn.

I've lost you.

Nineteen

an I have it?"

"W-what? I'm sorry, Moira. I seem to have drifted." Jocelyn forced herself to focus on the matter at hand. She had too much on her mind. "I didn't sleep well last night, so please ask me again."

"You look as though you've not slept for several nights! Poor thing!" Moira bit her lower lip. "You should ask Mrs. Brooks to make one of her infamous toddies. When I first came here, I had trouble sleeping and she put me right as rain."

Jocelyn put her head in her hands and made a quick silent prayer to the gods to save her from cheerful, sympathetic girls and Mrs. Brooks's tonics. "Just ask again, Moira."

"Can I have Amelia's old room? Jezebel said

she didn't want it, but I just love the colors in there. May I . . . move my things?"

Jocelyn looked up. "As you wish."

"Oh, thank you, thank you!" She clapped like a child and retreated to happily begin her packing and inform the others of her trade.

Jocelyn wilted once the door closed behind Moira. She was struggling to uncover the energy to contend with the smallest decisions and would have agreed to almost anything to get Moira to withdraw and leave her alone.

It had taken an entire day to restore her rooms after Alex had left. She'd thrown a royal temper tantrum, frustrated by grief and driven into a frenzy of anger at the cruelty of her heart's betrayal. A library of wisdom about keeping one's wits about them during the most intimate acts a human being could contemplate—and she'd known nothing of love.

And now the Belle she had sacrificed everything for was a hell she despised with every fiber of her being. To face a lifetime of it—it was more than she could bear. There had been endless hours of tears, but they had finally passed.

Now she was just numb after almost ten days of wretched and relentless time.

This was my choice. To have this life. To taste him and know what it feels like to surrender body and soul to a man. To let him go.

"Mistress?"

Ramis entered, his tread soft and tentative. His countenance was ravaged by grief from days of isolation, and Jocelyn watched the tangible fog of his pain recede from his eyes, if only to allow for simple conversation. It frightened her to see him so broken and lost.

"You should be resting, Ramis." She came toward him, holding out her hands to offer what comfort she could. "The doctor said that you must try to sleep if you can."

He shook his head and ignored her hands, only to kneel on the carpet in front of her desk. The sudden movement startled her before she realized that he hadn't collapsed when his head dipped to rest against the floor, but was prostrating himself.

"Ramis!" She knelt next to him, mortified, gripping his shoulders to try to push him back upright. "You must stop this! What are you— what is the meaning of this?"

He raised himself for a moment, then dropped back in a controlled ritual of humiliation. "I cannot apologize, Mistress. Never as I would wish, for there is little a man can do to make things right."

Tears welled in her eyes, and Jocelyn fought to be strong. There had just been too much these last few days for her to break when Ramis needed her most. "Hush now, my friend. Please look at me and know that there is nothing for you to apologize for . . . nothing for you to make right. Please."

He lifted his head, and his dark eyes spilled their unshed tears. But his voice was steady. "There is much you do not know, Mistress. And now it is time to set the scales to balance if I can."

"As you wish," Jocelyn whispered, a new sense of disconnected dread entering her awareness. "Is it . . . Gilly?"

He shook his head. "Only in that her soul demands that I become a better man to deserve her in the afterlife."

Her eyes widened in alarm. "If you mean to do yourself harm, Ramis, then —"

He held up his hand, gently cutting off her lecture. "No, Mistress. I speak of many years before I am free to go to her."

Jocelyn's relief was short-lived. "Ramis, speak plainly. What balances are you talking about? What are you trying to set right?"

"I should have seen that it was in my power to free you after your mother died. I had the strength but I didn't know it."

"I don't understand." Jocelyn sat back on her heels. "My mother . . ."

"It is easier to want nothing to change. Now that I have lost Gilliam, I see the suffering now.

I see the damage and the unnecessary pain that I stood by and allowed you to endure by taking on too much at too young an age."

A dozen questions sprang to life in her head, but Jocelyn waited patiently for him to continue—unwilling to upset him any further.

"I should have seen it. But your mother made me swear an oath, to help you to take her place and . . . to keep her secret from you."

"Her secret? About owning the Belle?"

He shook his head slowly. "About your father. She never wanted you to know because she was ashamed and wished to protect you. He had become so cruel and twisted and she insisted that you be kept from him at all costs."

Silence spun out between them as she knelt across from him, staring into his infinitely sad eyes, and at last the truth came to her. "Marsh."

She didn't even need to see him nod and confirm it.

Marsh. Her father. A man she'd hated for nine years. A man who'd monthly insisted on odd visits to spit venom at her no matter how often she invited him to stop calling. He'd cursed her and kicked her chairs, and then come again and again . . . to bluntly brag about where she was vulnerable to attacks . . . to warn her of the other owners' threats . . . to hint at hidden dangers she needed to watch for. Fergus Marsh. Her father.

He was looking out for me in an odd way. He was . . . protecting me.

Ramis bowed his head. "He suspected but your mother would never confirm it. To this day, I don't think he is sure. They became enemies and I cannot say what is in his heart. But it makes my . . . sin all the more."

"Your sin?" she asked breathlessly.

"I meant to kill him, Mistress."

"B-but you didn't. They will uncover who did these things and—"

"Mistress." The quiet address captured her attention immediately.

"Yes." She held still, not sure she could survive any more revelations. She reached over to touch his hand. "Go on."

"It was in my power all along to free you, and I do not know if I will ever be able to atone." He pulled his hand away before she could protest. "You are a recluse truly. The masks have served a purpose you did not intend. To the elite, you are almost invisible. To those in the trade, a shadow, and even if there are a small handful who know you by sight, I will pay handsomely for their silence."

"Ramis, what are you saying?"

"Men see what they expect to see. No one in the respectable houses of London will recognize you. Because they aren't looking for you there."

"I wouldn't be looking for me there either, Ramis."

"And if they did see a resemblance to a woman they once saw, they will hold their tongues to protect their own reputations. It is all too simple."

"Too simple, Ramis. What are you saying?"

"I will take the Belle. It was I who demonstrated how your mother ran the house. It was I who had that knowledge, but insisted that you be burdened with it instead of sparing you this life. I will uphold your mother's legacy of benevolence and see that no more are lost. I will protect them all as no one else can."

Her lips parted to argue, but awe kept her silent as his words sank in. *He'd been there all along. He'd been the authority I relied on those first months and years. Ramis had been the hand that had guided. He didn't need my grip to keep him steady. He could take the Belle and downstairs, they would barely note my absence. Nothing would change.*

"Take the young one, Edith, with you as a lady's maid. There is no reason for her to remain here," Ramis's instructions broke into the sweeping storm of her thoughts.

"Ramis, I'm not sure I can just—"

"Go. Leave this place as you tell the others to whenever they ask. Take the great fortune you have earned and make the life you desire." He bowed his head. "The life that was stolen from you."

"You never stole anything from me!" Jocelyn threw her arms around his neck, ignoring him as he stiffened, shocked and unready for the gesture. She burrowed her face into his shoulder as the tears came, burning her cheeks in scalding, salty tracks. "Y-you've given me so much . . . I . . . don't know what to say."

"Say that you will go."

Too simple. It's too simple. Oh, God . . .

"I'll go," she whispered, then gave in to the sobs that wracked her body. She grieved in his arms for the oaths they had taken, the vows kept and broken, and the loves they had lost.

He pushed her away, holding her at arm's length. "Enough of this! You are free. You have much to do, Mistress." He released her to stand and then held out his hand to help her to her feet.

"Much to do?"

"You have a name to bury and one to resurrect, Madame."

Jocelyn felt a small smile tug at her lips; an alien sensation came over her, and it was only later that she recognized it.

Hope.

Twenty

"You look like hell, Randall."

"You're too kind," Alex replied with a wry smile.

Drake continued, undaunted and openly enjoying a chance to speak his mind. "It's a Christmas ball, Alex. Shouldn't you ask one of these women to dance?"

"Shouldn't you be mingling with your other guests?"

"Servants' gossip is starting to place wagers regarding your health, Alex. If it's a woman, I highly recommend you resolve the situation—or make it a point to eat more."

"My health is extremely good"—Alex shifted in his chair—"and I am *not* pining!"

"You should practice saying that in a mirror

if you wish to be more convincing, Saint Alex." Drake sipped his brandy. "Now confess."

"What is there to confess?" He stared into the flames and wished himself a hundred leagues away. "That I learned my lessons too late? There is no reward for a man who sacrifices love to avoid the threat of a scandal."

"Not a bad bit of wisdom to acquire," Drake sighed. "I'd say you're a better man for it."

"Better to burn at the stake, old friend."

"A fitting end for a saint, Alex," Drake noted drily.

Alex rolled his eyes. "I think I've had enough of your brand of commiseration for one evening." He straightened his back and shoulders, preparing to rise and make his escape. "Thank you for the invitation, Your Grace. Please tell your lovely wife that it was a delight to see her again."

"So she's not worth it?"

"Pardon?" Alex froze in his chair.

"Not worth risking scandal—the mystery woman you've been sulking about for the last few months. Is that what you meant?"

"No." Alex stood indignantly. "She is decidedly worth it, and if the choice were mine to make, nothing would stand in my way to proving it." He tugged down on his waistcoat to smooth its lines and to give his hands something to do besides striking his best friend.

Drake stood as well, his stance far more relaxed and unaffected. "Don't be so quick to take offense, Randall. It seemed a fair question."

Alex took a slow steadying breath. It was foolish to lash out at Sotherton. "It's not the question. And I'd rather not talk about it, if only to protect the last shreds of my dignity."

"Ah." Drake shook his head, lifting a glass of brandy. "No man's dignity ever survives a true and earnest pursuit of love. You should mourn its passing and focus only on the delights to be had when you win."

Alex laughed, the last of the tension leaving his frame. "My friend has become a philosopher. Marriage has softened you, Drake."

"Perhaps."

"Leaving so soon, Lord Colwick?"

Alex turned to realize that Drake's lovely duchess had come up behind them. "I'm afraid so."

"But there was a young lady I wanted to introduce you to. She once did a great favor for me." Merriam caught his arm. "She's only recently returned to England for the winter season with a very nice income. A good family, I'd heard, though the details are a bit vague. Born abroad, but sadly her parents have passed. I was sure you'd like her."

"Forgive me, Your Grace, but if you've turned matchmaker, then I must definitely take my leave." He bowed, kissing her hand before straightening. "Drake is a terrible influence on you, Merriam. I should warn you to—"

A merry laugh from across the room froze him midsentence, and Alex wondered if everyone else shared his impression of time coming to a sudden and glorious stop. He marveled at the melody of this woman's laughter like muted bells—before turning around to confirm the impossible.

Drake's voice rumbled behind him, "Now, *this* should be interesting."

Alex ignored him. "Introduce me, Your Grace."

Merriam gave him an arched look, humor lighting up her eyes. "You're sure? I mean, if you have to leave . . ."

Alex firmly took her arm and began escorting her toward the vision across the room. In a rich green velvet dress of modest drape that accented her gorgeous curves, she was a Christmas confection with her copper curls gleaming in the salon's lamplight. Across her bared shoulders and throat, the familiar glitter of gold- and autumn-colored gemstones drew his eyes, and Alex was sure that something in his chest began to tear away. Flushed and lovely, she smiled as he drew closer, as if she'd expected him all along.

"Lord Colwick, may I introduce you to Miss Jocelyn Tolliver," Merriam managed with only a hint of a knowing smile. "Miss Tolliver, Lord Colwick has expressed a keen interest in meeting you."

"Thank you, I am genuinely flattered." Jocelyn curtsied, then turned to include the mulish-looking woman to her right. "May I also introduce my chaperone, Mrs. Clark?"

"Of course." Alex managed the rest of the ritual in a haze. "Miss Tolliver, may I request the next dance?"

She nodded, and before Mrs. Clark could fuss, he was leading her toward the doors of the ballroom. Without a word, he pulled her into his arms and out onto the dance floor. There was nothing and no one else in the world but this petite beauty in his arms. The strains of the waltz came to him as if muffled by panes of glass, but he did his best to keep some semblance of the rhythm as they spun around the floor. As he moved with her, each sweeping turn made his head swim with the desire to lift her against him and carry her from Sotherton's house. Or just carry her upstairs to the first empty room he could find.

Finally they spoke.

"Where?"

"France," she answered softly, her eyes never stopping their study of his. "I needed a trousseau."

"Did you?" He leaned close, his breath caressing the shell of her ear and making her shiver.

"You look thin, Alex."

He smiled. "You look the same, but even more beautiful, Jocelyn."

"I was surprised you'd stayed in London for the winter."

"Declan and my sister wanted to remain in the country, and I was terrible company for the lovebirds."

"Mr. Forrester and your sister? Really?"

"It barely even made the papers, since Wadley meekly agreed to an annulment. Not that they were concerned if he had made a fuss. But I decided it was better to be banished to the city, where I could continue to harass Ramis into telling me where you'd gone."

"He would never have told you."

"He never did," Alex confirmed with a pained smile. "I'll do my best to hate him a little less for your sake, now that I've found you again."

"If he hadn't offered to take the Belle . . ."

"As I said, I shall strive to hate him a little less," he conceded, his hand gently squeezing hers as he guided them amidst the other couples.

She sighed in contentment, then turned more serious. "Did you hear that they caught Gilly's murderer?"

"Yes." He finished a turn to ensure they were

away from prying ears. "Suzanne's cousin. The instant I saw it, I knew it was true. She'd screamed that it should have been her when they found Gilliam. And her tears—even Jezebel noted how odd it all seemed. She must have seen him and put it all together. I can't imagine what a horror this has been for her!"

"He'd been obsessed with her all along, I suppose. And when she left his tavern to come to London, it only became worse. He said she was kidnapped and corrupted. The papers said that he believed that by finding her and killing her, he would have her back in some odd way. Suzanne had no idea until the very end, when . . . when he mistook Gilliam for her."

"All those innocent women . . ."

"All brunette and tall. All in fine houses he could never get inside. So he attacked them whenever they were outside—because they were all . . ."

"Like Suzanne," he finished her thought.

"She decided to stay at the Belle." Jocelyn closed her eyes for a moment. "She said she couldn't imagine a different life."

"I couldn't imagine any life without you, Jocelyn. Tell me you love me." It was a gentle command, but it was as if his world hung in the balance, awaiting her response.

"I have always loved you. When you were a

saint, but especially when you were a sinner, my lord."

He drew her even closer, the room melting away as he marveled at the spectacular jade green of her eyes when she looked up at him. The urge to kiss her was a powerful need he had no wish to fight. His steps slowed and he leaned over to brush his lips over the wild pulse at her temple before moving across her cheek toward her mouth.

At the last second, she pulled back a fraction of an inch. "Mrs. Clark is deadly with that fan of hers, Lord Colwick. And you . . . realize you are about to kiss a complete stranger in the middle of a ballroom . . . yes?"

"Deadly, you say?" he teased, holding his place but refusing to retreat.

"I hired her with it in mind, my lord." She gifted him with a flirtatious glance through her lashes. "I am, after all, an innocent woman of great wealth without any living relatives. A girl cannot be too careful, Lord Colwick."

"Can she not?" Alex framed her face with his hands, determined to seize his happiness before she could disappear again or before—a sharp *snick* of a fan caught him on the back of the neck. Jocelyn gave him an arched and silent look of "I told you so" before Alex halted to face his attacker.

"Mrs. Clark." He kept one of Jocelyn's gloved hands in his. "I'm not sure that is the proper method for cutting in."

"You, sir"—the woman drew back to threaten another smart blow—"aren't going to lecture me about what is proper. You are acting far too familiar and—"

"I apologize, Mrs. Clark." Alex forced himself to give her a sober look. "But as I intend to marry her, perhaps you could forgive a man's enthusiasm."

"Y-you—you were just introduced!" she squeaked, and Jocelyn had to cover her mouth to keep from laughing.

"So we were." He gently put his fingers under Jocelyn's chin to tilt her face up toward his. "But I know what I want when I see it."

He kissed her, and then bent over to lift her off her feet, cradling her against his chest and turning about the floor, until she squealed from the giddy joy of it.

Jocelyn put her head against his chest and sighed, "We're causing a scandal, Alex."

He nuzzled her ear, laughing softly, and whispered, "At last!"

Acknowledgments

What a wonderful year! I don't think I'd have survived it, though, without the graceful and powerful presence of Ruthie Blair, who took my infant daughter in hand and gave me the time I needed to remember how to write again. (Apparently motherhood is a little bit more of an adjustment than they let on . . .)

To Maggie Crawford, my incredible editor, I wanted to say thank you, not just for the work on the books, but also for being such a wonderful and supportive friend. I am grateful for you every single day. And of course to Meredith Bernstein, my agent, who has never complained about all the baby pictures I send and laughs with me and makes sure I'm on the right path—you are invaluable to me in so many ways.

Thanks to Robin Schone, to Judi McCoy, to Cindy Cruciger, to all the Butterscotch Martini Girls and all the talented writers I seem to bump up against every day. Thank you for inspiring me to do a little better with each book.

And I have to thank Geoffrey, for loving me and putting up with me and gracefully ignoring me when I talk to myself.

I have no use for whey-faced widows or limp-boned virgins.

She recalled the biting words with acidic clarity. Moments after she'd met a man who had made her heart come alive with desire, and made her wonder if all the years of longing had ended, that very same man, Julian Clay, the Earl of Westleigh, had quietly spoken those words to a nearby companion. Unaware of the devastating blast he'd delivered to the trembling soul on the other side of the column, he had chuckled at his friend's mumbled reply and set the wheels of Fate in motion.

That the words referenced her own slight impact on the notorious rake was not in doubt. Or at least that was what Merriam told herself with the cruel precision of long years of practice.

Merriam the Mouse. It was a nickname her father had given her that had lingered throughout her youth, and even into the lonely nightmare of her marriage to an older and indifferent man. Her husband had teased her with the pet name, using it when he wanted to dismiss his quiet wife and return to more important and pressing matters: matters that included his business interests, endless correspondences, and sleeping with her maidservants.

But the mouse had survived him. And tonight Merriam was determined to taste the forbidden pleasures whey-faced widows and limp-boned virgins only dreamt of—lust and vengeance. Julian Clay would be hers, and she would show him just what a mouse was made of, then leave him wanting and aching—the satisfaction hers alone to savor. She would bring London's most notorious rake to his knees, and then . . . she would walk away.

Lord Milbank's Grand Costume and Masked Ball was notorious for its decadent and outrageous delights. No self-respecting member of London's high society would ever admit to attending it, which of course meant no one who received an invitation would dream of missing it. It was the most coveted invitation of the Season.

Merriam handed over her own gilt envelope tied with red ribbons, amazed at the steadiness of her fingers. For her, weeks of preparation would culminate in this one night. After days of careful study and nights of restless need, the mouse was transformed. Tonight, she would be the cat.

"Has Merlin arrived?" she asked.

"Yes, m'lady," the butler responded.

"Could you have one of the servers find him and tell him that his familiar is here?" She ignored the twist of the heated knot in her stomach at her brazen request.

He nodded. "As you wish, m'lady."

Merriam smiled. *Oh, yes, the lady wishes to teach the sorcerer a new kind of magic.*

In black silk and draped velvet, she entered the crowded room. Amidst costumes of blinding color and opulent flashes of jewelry, Merriam knew she would stand out. Her costume made a mockery of modesty, a widow's darkest weeds turned into a sensual invitation. Her black velvet mask and cat's ears were simple, but the black ties that held them on and laced through her hair were deliberately too long, draping over her collarbone, accenting her bare shoulders and the curved flesh above her bodice. Her figure of bold curves was displayed in simple lines, finished with a shocking glimpse of red satin beneath the black velvet, drawing the eye down to the flash of color that hinted at the shape of her legs and slim ankles through the strategically placed slits in her skirt.

She had even gone so far as to dye her brown hair to jet-black with one crimson streak to match her costume.

Madame DeBourcier's last bit of advice echoed in her mind: *You must feel sexual, invincible. It will emanate from you like heat, the scent of a woman who is ready, accessible, and willing. You must feel this power, then draw him to you.*

She circled the room, avoiding small talk and ignoring the subtle bids for her attention from some of the bolder male guests. With every silky step, she felt a well of electricity start to pool between her legs and along the column of her spine. But several anxious minutes passed, and her confidence began to falter. She'd confirmed the layout of the house and even where the tryst would take place but. . . . *What if her information about his costume had been incorrect? What if he wasn't even there? What if—*

"You should be more careful." His voice came from behind her, the deep, masculine growl sending a delicious chill across her skin. "I thought familiars were supposed to stay close to their masters."

She turned to face him. "Ah, but then I am close, am I not?" He was taller than she remembered, but fear could color one's perception, and even as a cat, she knew this game could take many turns. He was masked, with his hair pulled back and powdered silver to match the gray silks of his beaded overcoat, embroidered with symbols of ancient magic and power. He was a strikingly handsome Merlin, and she made no effort to hide her appraisal, measuring him from head to toe as if Julian Clay were already hers.

At last, her eyes met the glittering heat of his through the barriers of mask and costume, and she felt the first hint of victory. *Mine.*

He watched her, fascinated by the open challenge in her eyes. Who was this woman who presented herself, a sensual offering from gods he couldn't remember praying to? "You could not be close enough for complaint, my dear familiar," he countered softly, trying to recall that, no matter who she was, the rules of "polite engagement" would still apply.

She took a slow step closer, her face tilting up to look at him, and he felt his breath catch in his throat. She was like a magnificent panther, and his hands itched to stroke every sleek line of her body.

"No? Let us see then, Sorcerer, how close a woman can get before you . . . complain." With a subtle shift, she moved past him, then glanced back over her shoulder, daring him to follow, as she sauntered toward a private corridor, away from the lights of the party.

He followed without hesitation, dismissing any rational thought to caution or care. The truth of the rumors of courtesans and whores mingling amidst the Ton at Milbank's infamous affair appeared all too possible. He watched the hypnotic sway of her hips as this "cat" led him into the shadows of his host's hallway. He anticipated being led into one of the house's bedrooms, but she held out her hand and drew him into an alcove hidden by heavy velvet drapes. Moonlight through the window cast them both in shades from purest white through the gray of shadows to deep darkness, and he noted their small, secret space appeared to have a conveniently cushioned window seat wide enough to accommodate a tryst.

He drew the drapes and turned, reassessing this creature in velvet and silk, her skin like cream inviting him to drink and her chin angled with pure bravado. But instinct whispered that here was no courtesan, no jaded prostitute. In the light of the moon, he reveled in the details of his "seductress" as she bit her lower lip and seemed to struggle over what to do with trembling hands that conveyed inexperience. Her eyes caught the direction of his gaze, and she began to try to hide her hands in her skirts. But he caught them effortlessly, intent on uncovering the mystery that pulsed with raw need behind her mask.

Her hands were soft—her fingers long and tapered, her nails buffed smooth. They were the hands of a lady fluttering for escape, betraying her nervousness. No, this was no practiced whore, or even, he suspected, a wanton creature who had lost track of the lovers' beds she had visited. She was something else entirely. But exactly what, he could not yet say.

"How shall I please you, then, Master?" she purred, drawing his attention from her hands, forcing herself to face him in the cool and confined world of velvet and stone they would share for as long as the game lasted.

"Shall I tell you how?"

"Yes."

"And show you how?"

She swallowed, her heart skipping at the unbidden images the question evoked. After hours in Madame DeBourcier's parlor discussing the finer points of seducing a rogue, the time for talk was gone. Merriam wondered how she could ever have come to this place, could ever have conceived of anything so foolish, so laughable. But then he pulled her into his arms, and his mouth was on hers, tasting, teasing, consuming. She clung to the rugged heat of his chest and arms, feasting on the sensual fire of his kisses, devouring the raw pleasure, and gasping in shock to find, in just this first taste, that she may have underestimated her own need. Her own hunger.

He stroked the velvet of her dress with one hand. Finding the top of her bodice, his fingers dipped beneath the material to catch the peak of one nipple and free her breast from its confines. Merriam threw her head back, surprised at the streak of electricity that flowed from the touch of his hand on her breast, arching down to a sharp ache between her legs. God, she wanted his mouth there . . . everywhere.

"Who are you, Cat?"

She shook her head, fighting her need and the impulse to tell him anything . . . everything and anything he asked if only he would put his mouth against the sensitive coral tip of her breast. "Please . . ." The ragged whisper tore past her lips.

His mouth traced down the line of her jaw, guided by her desire. He gently took advantage of her exposed throat and followed her pulse to her collarbone, and to her breast to capture with his lips the impertinent peak that jutted into his fingers. He rolled his tongue around the flushed, taut flesh, mirroring the movement with his hand on her other breast, and grazed her with his teeth, nipping at the sensitive tip. She arched her back, her breath coming faster as he tried to teach his familiar about pleasure. Her own and his.

He tasted her breast, suckling her, drawing from her as if she were life and pleasure embodied. Her soft sighs and whimpers spun the heat and tension within him beyond his control—beyond recall or reckoning. He reached down to draw a hand along the outer line of her thigh, lifting one of her legs up around his waist and shifting back to press through the layers of her skirts. He worked his arousal against the damp core between her thighs. She bucked against him, and his lips released her breast as the eager, unpracticed message of her movements nearly undid him.

He took one of her hands, which were clutching

the lapels of his coat, and slowly loosened her grip. His tongue flicked along each fingertip just as it had lingered on her breast, teasing each sensitive pad and suckling each indent between fingers until he felt a small measure of control return.

"I . . . I want to touch you." Her whisper ended his strategy in one swift intake of breath. The cat's eyes glittered in the moonlight, and he accepted a new definition for the word *surrender*.

"Then touch me."

He offered no assistance, beyond freeing the hand he had just worshiped with his mouth. A hand that now memorized the landscape of muscle and bone beneath the smooth folds of his shirt as she relentlessly sought her prize.

She prayed he wouldn't notice her trembling fingertips but forgot that concern when her touch encountered the unmistakable length of him, the straining power of his need against the buttons of his trousers. Merriam dropped her eyes from his, captivated by the sight of her hands shamelessly caressing and stroking him through the cloth.

Whose hands are so bold? Is this me doing this? Aching to touch more of him? To have all of him? Who is this woman?

The power of the questions made her giddy, and without the need for any more urging, she freed him from his pants. The buttons gave way easily. The stark light and shadows revealed his erection in all its beauty. Merriam smiled at the sight. She was surprised at the length and girth, for he was much larger than her late husband.

She ran her fingers along the silken skin, teasing then gripping, stroking his flesh, making his breathing change. The heat of him burned her as she reveled in the hardness and the way his flesh jerked against her palms, swelling and beckoning for more of her touch, more of her attention. Suddenly, she wanted more too. Madame DeBourcier had said there was one way to enslave a man, to drive him wild, but Merriam had privately dismissed that portion of the lecture as completely beyond the pale. Now, though—now, all she wanted was to taste him, to drink in the power of his flesh and to know what it would be to have the swollen, ripe head of him against her tongue and in her mouth. Merriam knelt down, her skirts fanning out around her.

"It's so beautiful," she murmured, and then she kissed him, slowly drawing one ivory pearl of moisture from the swollen tip and drinking in the sweet musk and salt before her mouth opened to enclose him.

He bit back a groan at the sensation, the sight of her on her knees, the unexpected brush of her breath against his erection, her whispered exclamation at his beauty. God, he wasn't sure how much longer he could keep from exploding. Her lips, her mouth, her tongue, so inexperienced, but God, she wrapped her fingers around him, the pressure exquisite, and the enthusiasm of her kisses made his thighs quiver. She closed her mouth over him again and pulled him slowly into its heat, the tip of her tongue flicking back and forth across the sensitive juncture at the tip of his shaft. His fingers tangled in her hair, his jaw clenched, determined to make it last.

Turnabout is fair play, kitten, he thought as he lifted her to her feet. Kissing her deeply, he used his tongue and teeth to seize control—her breath mingling with his until she sagged against him with a sigh. He held her upright while he reached down to cup the soft curve of her bottom, stepping forward until the backs of her knees met the window seat. Gently he set her down on the cushions, holding her so that she was balanced on the edge of the bench, and knelt facing her. His hands spread her thighs and reached to her ankles to push up the sensual barrier of her petticoats. The material trailed over her knees and brushed along black stockings secured by saucy red ribbons, revealing that his cat was a bold creature after all. For above her stockings, the receding line of black and crimson cloth showed that she wore nothing at all. Moist and glistening curls above her lush and ripe succulent lips beckoned to him.

"W-what are you d-doing?"

He grinned. Her naïve and breathless question made him wonder again at the mystery of a woman who would dress so provocatively, no undergarments but silk stockings and ribbons, yet tremble like an untried virgin at the prospect of his most intimate kisses. "I thought we were going to find out how close a sorcerer could get to a woman before he 'complained'?"

"Oh."

There was almost no sound behind her response as he deliberately held his mouth above her, the air from his words the first feather touch against the wet satin of her skin. "But if you're shy," he intoned softly, "let us see what we can do."

His hand caught at one of the layers of her red silk petticoat and trailed the light material back over her, covering her with the thin illusion of a barrier against his touch. And then he lowered his mouth against the cloth and demonstrated how a sorcerer uses an illusion to achieve his desired ends.

His tongue traced the outline of her moist folds, the red silk wet within seconds from his mouth, from the liquid of her need, her body so slick, so ready to take him. But for now, there was only the tantalizing pressure of his tongue through her petticoat; heat and pressure, even the alternate cold and heat of his breath, all played against the silk. Merriam gripped the pillows, fighting and reveling in it all at once. To be touched there and not entirely touched. It was maddening.

"Are you shy?" he whispered against her, his tongue flicking over the tight bud of her clitoris.

Merriam had to bite the palm of her hand to keep from crying out at the sensation.

The mouse was shy . . . the mouse would never spread her legs . . . would never pull them open so far that her muscles ached to give a man the access he wanted . . . she would never beg for him to penetrate her . . . to remove the damn silk . . . Ah, but tonight was different . . .

"I-I'm not shy," she managed to say through clenched teeth, her hips riding up to maintain the contact, cursing the existence of silk in the world.

The reward for the admission came quickly, as the wet cloth was dragged back across her skin, making her gasp when air struck the exposed and tender flesh. He blew a cool breath at the trailing edge of the silk as he removed it. And then his touch ignited her, the reality of his mouth, his tongue, his teeth against her—with nothing to keep him from tasting her fully, from exploring the contours and textures of her sex.

Merriam writhed against the cushions as she felt one of his fingers penetrate even as his tongue began to dance over her clitoris, a gentle and feathery flickering that contrasted with the increasing pressure and strength of his moving finger. A delicious tension, a red-hot coil, began to mount, and she gripped his head, her hands pulled at his hair, instinctively seeking more. More of the pressure. More of the teasing.

He added a second finger, stretching her. Pain and pleasure made her eyes fly open as the relentless dance of his tongue continued. Finally, the coil exploded. She bucked at the wave of ecstasy, shuddering as her muscles clenched against the fingers still pushing into her. Merriam cried out as the wave seemed to gather momentum. She arched her back with the ebb and flow, and he pulled his mouth away and drew himself up to kiss her—his fingers still penetrating and withdrawing—as she came. She could taste herself on his tongue, and the thought tugged at the coil of her release, the start of another cascade of explosions.

He pulled his hand away, and Merriam groaned at the searing heat of his erection against her still shuddering flesh. She was still coming as he spread her legs wider and positioned himself to drive into her. Merriam felt a small lash of fear at the reality of his daunting size against her. She had a fleeting thought that her body couldn't possibly accommodate him. "W-wait . . ." She tried to catch her breath, to wriggle away but his hand held her hip, trapping her. He took his other hand and caressed her with his own swollen tip, and her body reacted, another tremor jerking her hips up and around him, and Merriam knew she wanted it. She suddenly wanted to claw him for more. Even if he rent her in two, she would have it all.

"Say yes," he commanded, pressing into her.

"Yes." His eyes held hers, her body tightening around the head of him, aching at the new presence, the first hint of the invasion that would come, writhing to escape even while a deeper drive made her hips quiver, tilting upward to try to take in all of him. He stopped, just barely inside her, and she could feel him trembling with the effort to hold still.

"Say yes," he commanded her again.

"Yes." And she was rewarded with just another inch, just one more thick, glorious inch of him, and he watched the realization come to her: that there was a great deal more of him and that the power was hers. Even as his body was held in a position to conquer, he yielded control to her to surrender completely and take him, or even then, she had the power to refuse him. So he asked, his voice rough and unsteady, "Yes?"

"Yes! Oh, dear, yes, yes, yes!"

He plunged into her, driving himself in completely, swallowing her small cry of shock and pleasure with his mouth. Then slowly he began to move, his jaw clenching at the molten heat and friction of her body, so tight—the slick passage of a virgin, but no . . . She wrapped her legs around his waist, her ankles urging him to take her—deeper, faster, harder. His cat was no virgin. She countered his every move, drawing against him, pulling him in, crying for him to pound the innermost core of her body, and he wanted it to last. He wanted to make the magic last, the enchantment of her scent and the feel of her beneath him, her hips rocking him, her muscles contracting and milking him, draining him.

"Oh! Oh, my!" Her fingernails dug into his shoulders, "I-It's happening . . . a-again!" Her innocent shock at her ability to climax again stripped away his last illusion of control. By God, he wanted her to scream with it. He wanted to be the one to teach her that she could come again and again— until the lines between pleasure and pain were no more. He would take her until there were no illusions between them, nothing but the sustenance of need. And then he couldn't hold it back any longer, a scalding orgasm tearing from him, jetting into her as he ground against her sensitive clit and felt the unmistakable grip and spasms of her answering climax.

The game had definitely taken a turn, but even so, Merriam's return to reality was slowed by the sweet ripples of her climax, the ache and burning between her legs setting off another wave of desire when he shifted slightly, withdrawing his still firm length a fraction of an inch to take his full weight off her. A whimper of protest escaped her throat, her legs tightening to hold him captive. He kissed her throat and nuzzled her, apparently unwilling to beg for mercy. "Are you keeping me, then?" he teased, and she tensed, all too aware that he was not hers to keep, that it was time for the cat to free her prey.

She pushed against him, shuddering at the sensation of loss, the ache between her legs, her flesh throbbing with hunger even now. She turned her face away, seeking composure, repeating silently over and over that victory is in the having, and that, at the very least, she would have the memory of the cat to keep her warm on the cold nights to come. Merriam the Mouse straightened her dress and re-adjusted her bodice, standing to shake the wrinkles out of her skirts, refusing to meet his curious gaze. The trembling in her hands was the only sign of her turmoil.

"Tell me who you are," he said softly.

She stepped back with an odd smile and shook her head. "I should thank you. I didn't know it could be so . . . wonderful."

"This isn't amusing," he said more loudly. "I must know your name. I have to see you again."

Her chin came up defiantly; behind the velvet mask, her eyes shone with unshed tears. "You will, but you won't look twice. Let's just say that the next time you cut me in public, I'll have the pleasure of recalling this night and knowing that this is one whey-faced widow who is grateful to have had the honor of your attentions." Taking a deep, unsteady breath and squaring her shoulders, she transformed herself into a woman he could not touch, a woman who would never allow a man liberties such as moonlit trysts and forbidden caresses. "Good evening, sir, and good-bye."

Before he could protest, she slipped through the curtains and was gone. *Whey-faced widow?* he asked himself. *What the hell was she talking about?*

The next time he cut her? After eight years of self-imposed exile, he'd returned to England only two weeks ago. Drake Sotherton, the Duke of Sussex, found himself alone in the alcove, the scent of her clinging to his skin and clothes. He pulled a hand through his hair and tried to absorb the meaning of her parting words. He was a man who was used to getting what he wanted—and he'd be damned if he knew what had just happened, but she'd not escape him that easily.

The past is heating up...
Don't miss these bestselling historical romances from Pocket Books!

A Malory Novel! **Captive of My Desires** ❧ Johanna Lindsey
On the high seas, love takes no prisoners...

A Wicked Gentleman ❧ Jane Feather
Someone wicked this way comes...

How to Abduct a Highland Lord ❧ Karen Hawkins
She took his freedom...He'll steal her heart...
How can two wrongs feel so *right*?

Indiscretion ❧ Jillian Hunter
A steamy reunion on the Scottish Highlands results in
desire, in delight, and indiscretion.

Caroline and the Raider ❧ Linda Lael Miller
She plotted a daring rescue—but never planned on a
dangerous passion.

The Perils of Pursuing a Prince ❧ Julia London
Some passions are worth the risk.

If You Desire ❧ Kresley Cole
How much desire can a Highlander resist?

Lose yourself in the passion...
Lose yourself in the past...
Lose yourself in a Pocket Book!

The School for Heiresses ❧ Sabrina Jeffries

Experience unforgettable lessons in love for
daring young ladies in this anthology featuring
sizzling stories by Sabrina Jeffries, Liz Carlyle, Julia
London, and Renee Bernard.

Emma and the Outlaw ❧ Linda Lael Miller

Loving a man with a mysterious past can force you
to risk your heart…and your future.

His Boots Under Her Bed ❧ Ana Leigh

Will he be hers forever…or just for one night?